SHADOW LANDS

Also by K.F. Breene

Skyline Series (Contemporary Romance)
Building Trouble, Book 1
Uneven Foundation, Book 2
Solid Ground, Book 3

Jessica Brodie Diaries (Contemporary Romance)
Back in the Saddle, Book 1 – FREE
Hanging On, Book 2
A Wild Ride, Book 3

Growing Pains (Contemporary Romance)
Lost and Found, Book 1 – FREE
Overcoming Fear, Book 2
Butterflies in Honey, Book 3
Love and Chaos, Cassie's Story

Darkness Series (Paranormal Romance)
Into the Darkness, Novella 1 – FREE
Braving the Elements, Novella 2
On a Razor's Edge, Novella 3
Demons, Novella 4
The Council, Novella 5
Shadow Watcher, Novella 6
Jonas, Novella 7
Charles, Novella 8

Warrior Chronicles (Fantasy)
Chosen, Book 1
Hunted, Book 2
Shadow Lands, Book 3

SHADOW LANDS

BY K.F. BREENE

Contact info:
www.kfbreene.com
Facebook: www.facebook.com/authorKF
Twitter: @KFBreene

Acknowledgement

There are a select group of people that are interracial to getting one of my books published. Without them, my work would be lackluster, at best.

First, the beta readers. Keri Frey, Heather Spencer, Heather Kuebler and Cassandra Jean helped me shape this series, filling in the holes as needed. Their honesty and disregard for my ego was horrible and awesome at the same time. They are each greatly needed and treasured.

Then my editor. Oh the poor man. Steve Lockley is a master with a ton of patience. He reworded, reworked, and applied elbow grease to polish up this grammar nightmare. I bow at his feet.

My proof-reader, John Adriaan, is always so sweet and laid back. He is constantly encouraging. Being that I give him no notice of when I need him, and expect a quick turna-round, I think this means he was a saint in a past life!

My fan proof-readers are the step before the plunge. Donna Hokanson and Fiona Wilson find all the little issues that everyone else missed. And if a few squeak by, it's not for lack of their effort!

Finally, where would I be without the reviewers and readers? In my basement without pants, probably. Thank you to all of you who have supported me, left reviews for me, and poked me in the eye when I got down on myself. I couldn't do all this without you!

CHAPTER 1

"CAPTAIN, IT'S TIME." SANDERS STEPPED back to allow Cayan to climb the stairs onto the deck of the ship.

They'd spent nearly a week stuffed into the various passenger areas and holds of Jooston's ship, the captain that everyone called SeaFarer, while the vessel pitched and rolled on the early winter sea. His men weren't sailors, and as such, many spent much of their time retching over guardrails or into buckets. Now that they had finally reached their destination, though, he wondered if they wouldn't rather stay aboard the craft, sickness and all.

"Are the men ready?" Cayan asked, emerging onto the sun-faded and weather-beaten deck.

"Ready and eager, sir," Sanders answered.

"That right?" Cayan asked with the doubt plain in his voice.

Sanders smirked. "As eager as can be expected when showing up at a place inhabited by a bunch of savages that eat people. Or so we've always been told…"

"Myths. Apparently, people coming to the island

and presenting themselves as Chosen isn't unique. SeaFarer said that it's a regular occurrence."

Sanders snorted. "Some hothead realizes he has a little of that mind-power and comes here looking for glory, huh? Idiots."

"How would they know they didn't have a full dose of power unless someone more experienced told them?" It wasn't the first time Cayan wondered about his own power. He had more than Shanti—that was undisputed. But how did they know that this Inkna proclaiming himself Chosen didn't have more than Cayan?

"Regardless," Cayan said, pushing his doubt to the side. "The trials are only the first step. If we *do* secure the allegiance of the Shadow people, we'll then have Xandre's army lining up to nab Shanti. This is still a bad situation."

"Always was, sir. Luckily, we specialize in bad situations…"

Cayan put on a stern face as he neared the bow of the ship, staying out of the way of scurrying deck hands preparing to dock. SeaFarer turned from his position to survey the island as he heard Cayan approach. His hard gaze hit Cayan for a moment before turning back. In an accent as rolling and surging as the ship, he asked, "She is proclaimed, yes?" He nodded at Shanti.

She stood at the rail, looking out across the water. Her brother, Rohnan, stood next to her, rigid and still.

Beyond them rose great ragged cliffs, stretching out to the sides barring the way to land except for one tiny opening into a harbor.

The ship drifted slowly closer, aiming for the maw within the rock.

Cayan glanced at the tops of the cliffs for an idea of what this island might have to offer. Green reached down over boulders and between the densely packed trees, peeking out over the ocean. A light drizzle sifted down from the sky, chilly and wet against his face. Shanti would not only have to combat whatever awaited her within the trials, but also the elements. Exposure to the cold and wet for long periods could result in sickness and even death.

Cayan looked at Shanti, a surge of hope infusing him. She'd grown up in those conditions. She'd often said her village was nestled in a thick wood, and that she and her people trained among the trees. They hunted and gathered, gone for days at a time, living off the land. Cayan didn't know if it was also wet, but the western coast had a colder climate. She'd be used to surviving in this and already had an advantage.

"She will be proclaiming herself Chosen, yes." Cayan could just barely see the empty harbor with the lone dock reaching out. "Where are the other ships for the traders, or other Chosen?"

"The other ships, they drop off Chosen here, then

head around island." SeaFarer snatched the back of a deck hand's shirt as she ran by. In a language Cayan didn't understand, the grizzled man yelled out something. The woman nodded and turned back the other way. To Cayan, he said, "That other Chosen—the Inkna…" The man spit onto the deck in distaste. "He dropped off a countryman, then went around island, eh? Stayed a while. Waited to see what happen to his man. Cowardice, that."

"And has he gone in?"

SeaFarer shrugged. "Don't know. By now, probably. There is much unrest on the island. I hear Shadow Lord is not happy about some goings-on with trials. Lots of killing in Trespasser Village, too."

"Trespasser Village?" Cayan asked as those cliffs loomed closer.

"Trespasser. That's what they call people waiting for Chosen. Not traders, so not useful—take up space. Huts in wood, only. Lots of death, there. If you pay, you stay in city. If I were you, I'd stay in city, eh? But then, you stay in city, you don't know what danger goes on in the underbelly. Hard decision, eh?"

Cayan glanced at Sanders, who nodded once and headed back to the passenger holds. He'd take that information to Daniels and Burson. Hopefully Burson's *Seer Gift* would become active and point them in the right direction. If not, Daniels would need to weigh up their options and choose the best place to stay. They'd probably just have to make the best of whatever situation they ended up in and adapt until Shanti made it through the trials.

He didn't want to send her into those trials alone. Anything could be waiting for her in there. She was strong, capable, and trained for it, but she'd be completely cut off. She'd have no one to rely on. No help.

Cayan balled his fists and looked out over the water, pushing away an uncharacteristic feeling of helplessness. He hated things being taken out of his control, and that had been happening more and more on this journey. His destiny, and that of his people, was not only being decided by another; it was completely out of his hands.

"Have you heard anything more about the trials?" Cayan asked.

SeaFarer rocked back on his heels and then to his toes. "Only what you have, eh? Someone goes in. No one comes out."

"And have there been many hopeful Chosen?"

"Oh yes. Very many. Good business, bringing them over. Sometimes you hear screams. Sometimes a great roar, like a beast. That is if you get close. Most times, though… nothing."

"You can get close?" Cayan turned to the middle-aged man.

"There is a barrier, eh? You cannot see, no. But you can hear sometimes. Sometimes at night, screaming drifts over city. Terrible stuff, this. Why they do it, eh?"

"Some people have no choice," Cayan said in a low voice, his gaze once again settling on the back of Shanti's wheat-colored head. She hunched over the rail now, watching the opening in the rock grow larger and larger. Rohnan was pushed right up against her, his body stuck to the side of hers. He would be watching her go, too. The man had been selected to guard her at all costs, had almost died for her already, and he could be sending her to her death. Just like he was doing himself.

There was nothing any of them could do.

"Well. She's first woman," SeaFarer said. "I've seen hopeful Chosen of all kinds—old, young, rich, poor. All kinds. Most are a bunch of fools with a tiny bit of *Chesnia*. This is first woman. Women are not so dumb as men. And she is not dumb, this girl. Desperate, yes. I *believe* she have no choice, which makes me believe she's real thing, eh? But she won't be enough. No one person be enough, that's what I think. I think this is trick. Shadow people are cunning. They stack the storm, that's what I think. Stack it up good, too. Make it nearly impossible to get through. But... that's just me."

"You know them pretty well?" Cayan asked as a weight settled on his chest. SeaFarer was speaking sense.

If Cayan were in charge of a people that elected its battle leader, he'd make sure it was damn hard for someone to take his place. Damn hard. He'd test their strength, both mental and physical, he'd test their battle awareness, their strategy...

Impossible sounded right. Regardless what the scrolls said, people changed, and their customs changed with them. No one wanted to go to war, and if they had to, no one wanted a stranger leading them. Now more than ever, this seemed like a fool's errand.

"There's nothing we can do," Cayan said through gritted teeth, not waiting for SeaFarer's thoughtful answer. "There is no way around this."

SeaFarer rocked back and forth again. He clasped his hands behind his back. "That be true. And yes, I know them, after a fashion. I been trading a long time. I've stayed on this island more than most. I've no friends here but they are good people. Loyal, honorable, solid... and deadly. Do not underestimate deadly. You wrong them, and they kill you on spot. I seen it happen. And they have many with *Chesnia*. Many, many. An island full of them. All sorts, too."

"Chezna... is that mind-power?" Cayan clarified, stumbling over the sound of the foreign word.

"Yes, yes. Not just mental war, like them filthy Inkna. Healing and fighting and—all sorts. I not tell most people this, but I see truth in her. In you, too. You don't want to be here—that is smart. Sometimes we need do what we do not want to do, though. And here we are."

"Yes, here we are." Those cliffs reached out to them. The ship slid between the jagged, rocky teeth into the placid waters of the harbor. Three figures waited for them, all dressed in a shiny black material. One was on the docks, one on the muddy beach, and one stood back in a grassy area in front of a large arch, sculpted from heavily thorned plants.

SeaFarer turned to face Cayan. His brown eyes were sharp. "Foreigners will try to kill you. You look like a good Captain—a strong Captain. Weak don't like the strong, and the weak in city are rich. They pay good men. They try to kill you and your best men, eh? I do not know why—it is how it has always been. Maybe that is norm where they from—games of wealth and power. But you be vigilant. It will be poison in your food, or a knife in your ribs, or a beautiful woman in your bed. Do not trust anyone that is not Shadow. If your men can be bought, do not trust them, either. That place is twisted. A smile and a kiss will turn into a forked tongue and a deathbed. Be on your guard, eh?"

"Sounds like a real treat," Sanders said as he walked up. "Burson has some answers for you Captain, but first we need to see Shanti off. The old man is in a dither, I'll say that much. If he were a dog he'd be pissing all over the place. I've never seen him like this."

"It's all coming to a head, now. The future depends on her making it through those trials." Cayan watched Shanti as she looked ahead.

"That woman is too damn hard to kill. These Shadow ghosts aren't going to do it," Sanders said, looking behind him, then barking, "Rachie, get the hell away from there! Next thing you'll fall over the side, then where will you be?"

"Drowned, sir," came Rachie's voice.

"Idiots," Sanders muttered as he shook his head and turned to the front.

The ship drifted closer to the dock, which stretched out from the land in a bobbing, creaking, tilting string of boards. SeaFarer started forward, barking commands and ordering his crew. Shanti's head turned slowly the closer they drifted. Cayan could tell she was studying the man in black waiting on the dock.

"Ho-ly shit. They could be countrymen," Sanders murmured.

Cayan switched his gaze to the man on the dock. Wheat-colored hair peeked out from under a shallow, black hood. Cayan couldn't see the eye color, but his pale skin and thin frame gave him a build and look similar to Rohnan. A longsword handle peered out from behind his back, and knives hung low on his hip.

The ship's anchors dropped and a single rowboat

was lowered over the side. Shanti straightened up and turned. Her violet gaze bore into Cayan as she glided across the deck with Rohnan right behind her. She stopped in front of Cayan. "This is it."

"I don't like you going alone," Cayan said softly. He wrapped his *Gift* tightly around hers and sunk deeply into her mind. Her power surged his higher even as her apprehension drowned him.

She reached up and traced the pads of her fingers over her amulet, still hanging around his neck. "If I don't make it out—"

"You will," Sanders said with fierce determination. "If I have to barge in and get you, you're coming out."

A smile ghosted Shanti's lips as she glanced at Sanders for a brief moment before letting her gaze return to Cayan. She reached behind her neck and unfastened her father's ring. Rohnan shifted, his jaw clenched in disapproval, but he said nothing as Shanti fastened the ring around Cayan's neck.

"If Sanders can't find a way to barge in and get me—" she said, interrupted by Sanders grunting. "Take this to the Shadow Lord and appeal for their aid. They won't be forced to follow you, but they may aid you. It is said that just one of their fighters is equal to five average fighters. You'll need them."

"Don't you need this for the trials?" Cayan asked, his heart heavy. She was giving away all her possessions, expecting death. Throughout her whole journey she'd had this same expectation, and now she was facing it.

"A ring is easy to steal, and easier to lose. The trials won't be bent on a ring. A leader won't be chosen by a piece of metal, no matter its origin. But it might help with bartering. I don't know."

Cayan's jaw tightened. "Don't give into this, Shanti. You were made for these trials. You are more prepared than anyone alive. You heard what Burson said—Xandre has tried to recreate you, and he can't. You are the one for this mantle."

Her middle finger slid down the gold of her amulet before she raised her hand to Cayan's chin. "Please be careful. Keep everyone alive. And if I don't come out, don't go in after me. Find another way. You are the best hope against Xandre—you have the battle know-how, the leadership ability, the power—"

"I need you to use my power," Cayan interrupted, grabbing her shoulders. "You *will* make it through."

SeaFarer cleared his throat. "If we wait too long, they are liable to kill someone, eh?"

Shanti let her hand slide down Cayan's neck and stop on his pec. Heat radiated through his body. She then traced around his muscle before lowering her palm to his stomach. Her grin turned evil. "You do have a great body, though. I should've taken it for a ride."

"She just felt him up!" one of the boys exclaimed

behind them. A grunt indicated he'd been elbowed.

"You can teach him some things when you're back out," Rohnan said as a tear slid down his cheek.

"What is with the tears and that man," Sanders growled. "This is stupid. Shanti, the sooner you get in those trials, the sooner you get out and we can all go home. You're a pain in the ass that won't die. There's no way a bunch of tests will change that."

Shanti laughed and shook her head. She reached toward Sanders, making him flinch before realizing she planned to hug him. When she was done, she moved on and hugged each of the boys. "Okay, I have to go."

They stood in silence as she checked her weapons before moving toward the railing. Rohnan trailed behind. He watched her climb down into the boat, never taking his eyes off of her. Cayan felt his suffering. Rohnan was watching the last of his family walk away.

As the small boat made its way to the dock, a pang of unease gripped Cayan. Something about this felt wrong. Her leaving like this didn't seem like the right course of action. Everything in his person said he should be going with her.

He took a step before noticing Rohnan staring at her. He was probably thinking the same thing. Hell, they probably all were.

Cayan gritted his teeth and watched as she made it to the dock, climbed up, and then walked right by the man in black with her head held high. Cayan took a few more steps, feeling that tug to go with her. Hating that he was letting her walk away for a second time. His muscles flexed and his stomach filled with butterflies. Their mated power stretched and thinned. The power turned from a bubble into a simmer before settling down deep inside of him. He watched her solitary figure exit the dock and approach the arch. Without him.

No matter how loudly his gut screamed that this was wrong, he couldn't see an alternative. It was out of his hands, now.

CHAPTER 2

SHANTI'S FEET SANK INTO THE mud as she stepped off the dock. A light drizzle shimmied through the air and settled on her hair and her face. A tall man with light hair waited for her beside an arch made of thorny vines. His hazel gaze tracked her progress up the slope, noticing her weapons, pausing on various areas of her body that held the most muscle, and finally settling on her eyes. If he was surprised at their color, he didn't show it.

She stopped in front of him.

"Why do you come?" he asked in the Eastern-Common language.

"I have come to proclaim myself Chosen," she answered in the native language of the Shadow people. She'd studied it extensively, back when she was being groomed as Chosen, to lead these fierce fighters out of the Land of Mist. She knew it as well as her own tongue.

Again, if he was surprised by her near-perfect accent, he didn't show it. Instead, he glanced behind her. She refused to turn and look, knowing she'd see the ship getting ready to set sail and leave her behind.

"Once you enter the arch, you will either emerge the Chosen, or die in the process. Once in, there is but one way out." This time he spoke in his language.

"I understand."

His light gaze came back to rest on her. "Then please, enter." He turned and held out a hand, silently gesturing her into the arch.

Unable to help herself, she glanced over her shoulder as she took the few steps under the arch. The rowboat was turning the large ship to head back out to sea. Rohnan and Cayan stood side by side at the railing. Cayan's large arm-span spread across the wood. He leaned forward, as if about to propel himself over the edge and fly to her.

Her heart beat and her power pulsed, wanting him closer. Her power's mate was being ripped away, and it physically hurt through her middle. It felt like something was tearing, dislodging from her insides and ripping out through her chest.

She pressed a palm to her sternum, never having felt this before. She'd been away from Cayan often enough, and all that had happened was that her *Gift* lost some of its potency and settled deep into her core. Confused, and a little wary, she watched him drift away.

"The big man leaves you behind," the Shadow man said in a conversational tone.

"That is how this works, yes. Or am I allowed spectators and did not know it...?" She tore her eyes away from the handsome face framed by that shining raven hair. Sparing just one agony-ridden glance for her brother, she turned toward the arch.

Time to fulfill her duty. Cayan and Rohnan couldn't help her now. She could only hope they looked after themselves and the others and made it off the island alive when this was all over.

"Usually men crave the power of the title. We have never had a woman through here." The man followed closely behind her.

"Trust me, I would've rather sent him."

"No. I don't believe that is true."

They walked through a green tunnel made of large bushes cut to admit no more than one person at a time before revealing a clearing within a large grove of trees spread out in a circle. She could barely see the thorny wall reaching out to the sides, closing them in before it disappeared behind the green. It was half her height again, jagged, and offering no handholds that would not rip skin from bone. A natural but effective barrier.

A woman sat on the wet grass in the middle of the clearing. A tray holding a teapot and two cups lay beside her. To her right was a pile of what looked like tarps or clothing.

Shanti's *Gift* opened up and spread out, blanketing

the clearing and the trees beyond. As she expected, minds waited, out of sight and utterly still.

As she had also expected, they all had the *Gift*. Every single one was extremely strong in it, from half to three-fourths of hers. If they were Inkna, Shanti bet this was a group of elite, and killing them would be a severe blow to Xandre's forces, since Inkna didn't seem to produce many high in the *Gift*. Shanti had no idea what normal was for Shadow people, though. If they were like her people, there would be many more with *Gifts* this strong.

She greatly hoped they were like her people. She and Cayan needed as many mental-workers as they could get.

As she walked toward the woman, her *Gift* started to warp. Twisting and turning in on itself before once again growing and spreading, it pushed away from her deft touch and sought to join the trees and natural things as well as the *Gifts* radiating around her. It demanded a looser hold and more freedom, like a headstrong child. When it was given, it blossomed into something that stole her breath and blended so perfectly with the world around her she stopped mid-stride and put out her hands, almost able to feel the beating heart of nature.

"This is a special place for one such as yourself," the man said as he stopped beside her.

His *Gift* flowered like hers, weaving in and out of her power, blending, and then darting away again, like it was alive. Playful.

"What is this place?" Shanti asked in awe, looking around at the trees and flowers, feeling a kind of peace she'd never experienced before. One she had never had growing up with the constant threat of war looming over her. Even though that threat should've been more evident now, she couldn't help laughing like a child at the soft warmth that had settled into her heart.

More than anywhere else in the world, this place felt like home. Her *Gift* belonged here in a way it had never belonged anywhere else.

It took a few moments to remember the gravity of the situation. Slowly the joy and wonderment drained away. She started forward again.

"You let go so soon?" the man asked as he shadowed her movements.

"Time is a luxury I've never had, least of all now."

Shanti approached the woman, sitting peacefully in the drizzle. She looked up with a smile and beckoned Shanti to sit beside her. Her pale blue eyes reminded Shanti of tranquil waters in the early hours of the morning when the sun was just glancing over the horizon. Her mind was patient and soft, sensitive and caring.

Shanti gasped at the type of the woman's *Gift*.

"Greetings," the woman said with a kind smile. "You know our language well, but by your pale skin and light hair, you must be from the distant west. Is this correct?"

"Yes, but your hair is also light. As is his—" Shanti gestured at the man standing behind her.

"Yes." The woman continued to smile, but said no more on the subject. Instead, she turned toward the kettle on her right. "Would you like some tea?"

"Is it hot?" Shanti asked, feeling the cold and damp settle into her body. A shiver was not far away.

"It is. Well… warm, by now." The woman poured two cups and handed one to Shanti. With her gaze fixed on Shanti, she took a sip. Shanti did the same, enjoying the floral essence of the lukewarm liquid.

The woman put her cup down and entwined her fingers in her lap. "I would like to ask you some questions, but first I am obligated to tell you that you are likely to die within these trials. While you have the full dose of the Divine Endowment, what we call *Therma*, it is not enough for you to pass through unscathed."

"And what is your basis for comparison?" Shanti asked with an even voice.

The woman laughed softly. "That is a good question. A *present* question. I am not at liberty to say more, however. I can offer you the option to bow out gracefully."

"A quick death, you mean?" Shanti clarified, feeling someone in the trees shifting locations.

"You are the first person to draw that conclusion. You must have had a hard journey to think in such a dour way."

Shanti stared, waiting for the answer.

The woman gave the slightest of nods. "Yes, a quick death. With your power level, you are likely to die in great pain during the trials."

Shanti smirked. "At least you're honest. But no, I don't wish to take the easy way out." Shanti took another sip of her tea.

"You very much do, I think. You beg for it with your whole being to end your suffering, unless I am mistaken."

"You know you aren't mistaken." Shanti could feel her irritation rise. She hated being read like this, and she also hated wasting time. That other Chosen was almost certainly in this place somewhere, and Shanti needed to cut him down before he reached the end.

If she didn't have enough power though, how could he? How could anyone pass these trials? Before she could ask, the woman said, "Why did you enter?"

"The duty was assigned to me. Whether I believe in it or not, I owe it to my people to follow through."

"You are determined, but you expect to die. How dismal." Troubled, the woman turned and picked up the bundle. "Within this waterproof tarp, are warm and waterproof clothes. We have also supplied a fire-resistant container and a fire-starting stone. You may carry your knives, but not your sword. We have two rules—you must stay within the defined area, and cannot kill anyone."

"How will I know the defined area?" Shanti asked, taking the bundle.

"To escape would be to cut through a natural barrier of the worst thorns in the land, or to swim shark-infested waters. We fish off those waters—anyone seen in that area is killed immediately, traders and visitors alike."

"Sounds charming."

"Within the trials, you should have no problem finding food and sustenance. This land is plentiful."

"Wet and plentiful," Shanti said, feeling the warm fur inside the jacket provided for her.

"Yes." The woman re-clasped her fingers in her lap, staring intently at Shanti. "You have failed before you've begun."

"Well, you're a real treat. I bet you're not invited to many parties." Shanti rose.

The woman rose as well. "I have heard of you. The violet eyes. You are a pinnacle of hope as well as ardently sought, and yet you are not dead. I know something of your struggle, and feel the pain eating away at you. You want to be dead, but you are not. Someone has kept you alive—nurtured you. You are surprisingly hard to read."

Shanti sighed and started to strip. This woman could give Rohnan a lesson or two on unwelcome observations. "I've had practice disguising my thoughts in order to maintain privacy."

Surprise flitted through the woman as Shanti slipped into her pants, lovely and warm, and shrugged into the coat. The material was soft and flexible, something Shanti could fight in as well as keep warm. Once she found shelter, she could start a fire and find something to eat. Without cold biting at her fingers, surviving in a land like this would remind her of her youth. She couldn't wait to start.

"So, I just start walking?" Shanti asked. "Is there a path or guide of some sort to the various trials?"

The woman smiled. "The trials are different for everyone. This land was chosen by our settlers for its mysterious properties as it works with *Therma*. Challenges will present themselves to you, some with our help, some as products of your fear and your environment. The worst will take advantage of your hope. It is a perilous place."

"Have you been through it?" Shanti stretched out the tarp. It was a square with each side almost as tall as her. They were giving her help in making a shelter.

"I have been through the natural parts. Most of my people have, if their *Therma* is strong enough."

"So the actual danger is from your people. Sounds about right. I wouldn't want a stranger leading me, either." Shanti made a pack with the tarp, took off her sword and handed it to the woman, before tying the pack to her back. "Cheat to win. Stack the odds in your favor so you can keep your home and your peaceful life. Can't say I blame you."

Shanti nodded at the woman and turned to the man. She gave him a hard stare. "You are out of time. Stacking the odds keeps you on your own. Xandre has his eye on you, and he will not stop until he has you in chains. The fate of your people can easily be the same as for mine. The trials and empty titles aside, you need to ally yourself with Xandre, or against him, and now is the time. In a week it might be too late, if it isn't already."

"But if we ally with this leader of men, we will not be in chains," the man said with a smile. The sentiment did not reach his eyes.

Shanti huffed, scanning the way ahead. "There's no other way with Xandre. Friend or foe, he will put you in chains. Your only decision will be if they chafe."

Shanti started off toward the tree line, alone. The man didn't follow, and the woman didn't say farewell. As she threaded through the trees, she heard, "Which side have you chosen?"

"Dumb question," Shanti yelled back.

As she worked her away through the trees, she felt the minds drift in the opposite direction. They were moving toward each other, probably to discuss their strange interview with her.

Before Shanti could think what that might be, her *Gift* cut out. Just as if Burson was suffocating her ability, she suddenly couldn't *feel*. A shot of adrenaline hit her as she prepared for what might be about to come.

CHAPTER 3

CAYAN DISEMBARKED WITH THE REST of his men at the large harbor on the other side of the island. Here boats loitered, anchored in the large bay and bobbing in the swell of the tide. The docks were busy with traders and fisherman, loading or unloading cargo. One ship was allowing passengers to disembark; wide-eyed and smiling spectators, no doubt hoping to catch a glimpse of the Chosen.

Within the crowd were people that were, without a doubt, Shanti's distant kin. Blond and light-haired people with pale skin and unusually light eyes, they moved through the crowd like silent predators, their bodies honed, swords slung at their sides, and eyes watchful. Their high cheekbones and slim noses meant many of these people could've been Shanti or Rohnan's brother or sister. With many generations since their people's split—not to mention the long journey east—the blood lines should've been diluted. Maybe they were and it was just that the blood of Shanti's people continued to assert itself. Cayan didn't know, but looks this similar could not be imagined.

"They watch the docks closely," Sanders said as he moved closer to Cayan. The men gathered behind them on the gravel path just above the winding and floating landing places for boats and ships.

"With so many strangers, some of them out for personal gain, things can easily get out of hand," Cayan said.

"SeaFarer didn't say what's got the Shadow people all riled up?" Sanders' gaze darted all over, pausing on some longer than others.

"No. Something is wrong with the trials, and there have been more killings in the city and the Trespasser Village than normal. Other than that, he didn't know much."

"And this Inkna went into the trials?"

"Early yesterday, apparently." Cayan stopped a few paces from the docks as a wide path led away from the harbor along a copse of trees. He gestured for Leilius to join them. When the youth, dressed in the plain gray he often used for sneaking around their city, was standing right beside him, Cayan said, "Now is the time. I don't want you interfering with anything, I just want you wandering around the huts. Find out who is where, find out who seems dangerous, and notice if any of the Shadow people are around."

Leilius frowned before nodding. "I won't let you

down, sir."

Sanders snorted.

Cayan patted the youth's shoulder. "Good. And stay safe."

A tall woman with blonde-white hair passed them. Cayan felt a light presence touch his mind. Her face turned slowly. Shapely eyebrows sank minutely over her luminous green eyes. She passed without uttering a word, but a lingering question haunted her steps as her mind pulled away. She was one of many strongly *Gifted* minds in this area that Cayan had felt.

"They know my mental power level," Cayan said softly as he started walking again. "I'm confusing them. I can feel it. I'm constantly getting light mental touch-es."

"Why would that be confusing them?" Sanders wanted to know.

"I don't know."

"Where's Burson?" Daniels asked from behind Cayan. His voice was tight with strain. Cayan's oldest commander adapted quickly and efficiently, but they'd seen more than one Inkna on the docks, and heard about many others spread around both the city and huts. Based on the looks they were receiving, the Inkna knew who Cayan and his men were. Cayan's men viewed the Inkna with just as much hostility. It was going to be an extremely tense few days while they waited for Shanti.

That familiar ache sounded through Cayan's middle as he thought of leaving her. A strange ripping tore his insides. He couldn't shake the feeling.

Making his way up the gradual incline to the large brick walls of the city, he said, "Burson is scouting out the area on his own."

"We could use his input," Daniels said.

"He doesn't have any. Not since we left Shanti." Cayan felt the mental touch again. A man stepped out through the trees ahead of them. He held a bow worn from use, with a sword strapped to his trim waist. A dagger adorned his other side. His light-brown gaze shocked into Cayan as the mental touch turned into a *poke.*

This man was strong with power. A little over three-fourths that of his own, and sharp with it. Cayan could feel his menace, riding on the threat of violence. Those same attributes etched every movement of his body. He stood at ease, but perfectly balanced, as if expecting to pull his sword at any moment.

The small hairs on Cayan's neck stood on end as Sanders stiffened beside him, but he ignored the mental contact. He didn't know the protocol of this place and the last thing he wanted to do was incite a fight. Harder to ignore was the challenging stare. Cayan knew exactly what that was about, and he wasn't in the habit of backing down.

"Bring Rohnan up," Cayan barked, pulling his eyes away from the man. If he let his gaze linger any longer, he'd offer his own challenge.

Cayan glanced at Daniels. "Burson is having three different competing... choices, I suppose. He told me what he's sure of, but something happened that pushed us into murky waters. He's... afraid. He thinks being on this island is going to decide our fate, but there are so many paths, and so many outcomes... he can't make enough sense out of them to help."

"We were doing just fine without him," Sanders huffed. "We'll figure it out."

"Yes, Captain," came Rohnan's quiet, sing-song voice, lilted with his foreign accent. Sorrow and trepidation still ruled his thoughts after leaving his sister, but his strength was coming back. He had a duty to perform, just like her, and pushed ahead with everything he had. Cayan admired him for it.

"Do I allow a mental touch from these people?" Cayan asked, seeing another light-haired man standing beside a large wooden gate that marked the entrance of the city. His hands hung loosely at his sides, but he stood ready for any problems. Cayan could feel it in his emotions and read it in his stance. He must've been a guard, though he dressed no differently from any of the other Shadow people.

Suspicious eyes scanned Cayan and his men as they passed. A large square opened up before them with a kind of stage at the rear, currently bare. Lining the square were stalls selling food or other items. A spicy smell wafted toward them, cut with an occasional whiff of horse manure. Many people loitered, some talking amongst themselves, some simply standing and looking around. A building rose up behind the structure, two stories, square, and fortress-like. A window overlooked the city's entrance from the second story, showcasing the shadowy outline of a lone person standing within.

Answering Cayan with eyes darting, Rohnan said, "If it is an Inkna, attack immediately. Cripple, but do not kill." Rohnan's voice took on an edge. "The Inkna want kill us all. You, most of all." He still had trouble with the subtleties of the language.

"Those Inkna tried to kill me once. Didn't work out so well for them." Sanders grimaced as he spotted one of them and stared him down.

"I figured," Cayan said as they veered to the right, following SeaFarer's directions.

Burson had told Cayan they should all stay in the city, saying that SeaFarer should arrange their accommodations. Surprising Cayan with his readiness to take on the extra duty, SeaFarer wasted no time, finding them a place to stay shortly after docking. He'd only needed to speak to the nearest Shadow person he saw.

That was it.

Seafarer might not be friends with the people who ran this island, but he was trusted by them. That could only bode well for Cayan and his men, since the coarse sea captain seemed to be rooting for them and Shanti.

"And if the Shadow people make mental contact?" Cayan persisted.

"I not sure—so far you have surprised them with your *Gift,*" Rohnan answered, only occasionally looking at someone he passed. "With that well of power within you, more available to you now that you have accessed it twice, you seem to have more than a full dose of the *Gift*. At least, so history would have us believe. I also surprise them, but more for my appearance."

"You look like one of their siblings," Xavier said from somewhere in their crowd.

"The question of distant kin is no longer an issue. If only it help." Rohnan's voice was dry and somewhat brittle.

"It might." Sanders pointed at a square building with unfamiliar writing above the large door. "SeaFarer said the blue, brick house. Why someone would paint brick that God-awful blue, I don't know."

"Can you read the writing?" Rohnan asked as Cayan pushed through the door. Cayan didn't hear a response until Rohnan said, "Now can you imagine why someone would paint one of fifteen of the visitor living quarters blue?"

"I see being an asshole runs in the family," Sanders grumbled.

Cayan climbed the stairs and sought out the first blue circle above a brown, nondescript door, which SeaFarer said would be his quarters. He turned to the men gathered in the hall. "Sanders, break everyone off in pairs. Two people per room. I want an experienced man with a non-experienced one."

"What about the girl, sir?" Sanders asked.

"Put her with Marc."

"Why me?" Marc whined from way in the back.

"Because you won't peek at her, you idiot," Sanders said as he started walking down the corridor. "And if you do, she'll beat you bloody."

"Ruisa," Cayan said as she passed. The young girl stopped in front of him and looked up. Unlike the boys her age, she showed no fear of his presence or his status. The girl was a tomcat, tough and unflinching. She had been an excellent choice, despite her lack of fighting experience.

"Yes, sir?"

"I want you and Marc to talk, not only about what you know, but what he knows. Every night I want you talking. If you run into anything that looks… dangerous, try to get a sample and analyze it. I want you both familiar with antidotes, and if we need it, I want your guidance with… attacks. In the day, you two are to separate in case there is a problem. If someone needs help, one of you will need to administer aid quickly, so I want one of you with each group at all times. Also, never—and I mean *never*—are you to be alone, do you hear me?"

Cayan's power blasted into her as his gaze turned intense, demanding her attention. With wide eyes, and losing all the stubborn determination of youth, she nodded. "Yes, sir."

"I will be telling Marc the same. You two will be sought and killed for the part you play. More importantly is that some people here are living without fear of the law. They'll take what they want, when they want it. A pretty, young girl is something a great many men want. Maybe you can fend off one, but not a couple. Have someone with you at all times."

Ruisa gulped. "Yes, sir."

Cayan nodded. "Good. Now catch up with the others. And tell Marc what I said about talking. He is shy to a fault—he'll need encouragement."

Ruisa's expression darkened.

Realizing how that had sounded, Cayan added, "Shanti used to kick him in the head to encourage him. If words don't help, try that."

A relieved smile graced Ruisa's lips. "Yes, sir," she said. She turned and ran down the hall to catch up with the others.

Cayan turned to his own room. He took out his sword before opening the door. He entered quickly and ducked to one side in case someone had made it here before him. No knives or arrows flew through the air and landed in the door behind him. That was a good sign.

Quietly, he shut the door and moved through the sparse space. The room was half the size of his bedroom back home, with a simple bed, simple wood chairs, rugs and paintings on the wall. Cayan checked under the bed before he rolled his eyes at his ridiculousness and filled the room with his *Gift*. There were no minds in there save his.

"I have one of the most powerful minds in the city, and I don't think to use it to see if there's an intruder in my room." Cayan shook his head as he dropped to the wood chair. His voice sounded loud in the empty room.

He allowed himself one moment of rest before he started to think about their situation. With so many Inkna present, the island was festering with enemies. Never mind keeping people out of trouble—how was he going to keep them *alive*?

LEILIUS DRIFTED IN BETWEEN TWO huts and leisurely passed by a water spout where two men were leaning close together and chatting. Leilius adopted his unassuming walk toward the nearest tree, and then loitered behind the trunk, letting his body go still and his mind slow down. Almost immediately, he was rewarded with, "I heard a woman went into the trials today."

The man was using the trader speech Sanders made sure that every army person and trader in their city knew. Leilius had hated learning it, thinking he'd never be asked to go on trading ventures, but now he was thankful and determined to ask Rohnan to teach him other languages. A big part of being a spy would be understanding people from different places—S'am would want him learning everything he could.

"So did I," the other man said. A squeak sounded, the water spout being used. Water gushed into a bucket, masking the voices for a moment, but soon Leilius heard, "—eyed girl. Has to be. Who else has all that mind-power, eh?"

"Don't know. She didn't waste no time, though, from what I heard. Right off the ship. Didn't even stop in the city."

"Well…" A pause filled their conversation before a lowered voice continued. "If she had stopped there, they would've killed her, sure as I'm standing here. From what *I* heard, them Graygual want her something fierce. Probably safer in the trials than here or in the city."

"Not anymore." Leilius heard a throat clear. "Good

mornin'. Er, afternoon, I mean."

"That one's always creeping around, that one is," the other voice said a few moments later. He must've been talking about whoever passed.

"Yarm saw some men takin' that Inkna-Chosen out of the bushes."

"What'd you say?" came the other's shocked exclamation.

"Shut up, if you know what's good for you!" the first hushed. "Yarm done said it, and Yarm ain't around no more. So you do the math."

"What do you mean, though, takin' him out of the bushes?"

"There ain't no fence keepin' around them trials—just some thorny bushes. Well, Yarm reckoned there was a hole in them thorns. He saw that damn Inkna walkin' out."

"Ain't no way. Ain't no way he did."

"That's what I heard he said. That's all I'm sayin'."

"They only get a knife," the disbeliever scoffed. "I seen them thorns. No knife is getting through that, I don't care how sharp."

"He weren't alone, you wool-headed son-of-a-goat! He came out alone, but there was a few men waitin' for him…"

"Oh." The squeak of the water spout sounded again. Water punched the bottom of a fresh bucket. After a moment, the disbeliever said, "That can't be right. If they're trying to get that Chosen thing, they need to finish the trials. Not sneak out of 'em."

Another throat clear. "I don't know 'bout that," the first said. "But that's what Yarm saw. He came running into the hut and blurted it out. Said he was going to go tell the Shadow people—thought he'd get sum'in for it. Only, his dead body was found strung up on that thorn fence the next morning. His tongue was cut out and dick cut off. Now, that could'a been them Shadow, right as rain, but they ain't usually vicious. They'll kill a man, but they don't make a show of it. Naw, that could only be whoever he was tryin' to tell on."

"You think it's *him?*"

"Now, I don't know that he would be here, but he wants the violet-eyed girl. How do you get the girl, and keep your man? Well, you cheat. And we know that kinda guy cheats, so… Now, it probably isn't *him*. No, don't see how it could be. *He* wouldn't be here. But he's got lots of workers…"

"Hello Farley," the disbeliever said in a cheery voice.

"What are you two hamming about?" came a third voice.

"Just taking some water and being on our way. Pity about the rain, ay? Awfully sloppy out here."

"Get on whit ya. I gotta fill my bucket," said Farley.

Leilius drifted away with a tingling in the base of his

spine. He didn't know who this *him* might be, or who these men were that waited for the Chosen, but cheating was bad news. So was this Inkna-Chosen not being in the trials when S'am was trying to kill him.

Rather than running immediately to the Captain, however, Leilius walked toward the outskirts of the camp. He needed more information.

He soon realized that the inhabitants in this Trespasser Village were nearly all men. A few women wandered around, but they had their bosoms almost completely on display, and led with their hips in a way that had Leilius' face turning red.

He listened in on one conversation after the other, hearing "violet eyes" often. News of S'am's arrival traveled really fast. It also seemed that the people in these parts hoped she would dispose of the Inkna-Chosen. Every one of them respected the Inkna if they passed one, and nearly fell over themselves bowing to a Graygual, but when they thought no one was around, they were rooting for S'am.

Yarm's name came up a few times, but exactly what he was supposed to have seen was mostly conveyed with large eyes and lifted eyebrows before people looked at their feet. Few were brave enough to recount the story.

After a while, when nothing else noteworthy could be heard, he decided to head back up to the city. He was wet and cold and didn't want to get sick. He hated being sick, especially because he wouldn't be able to bitch about it with Sanders around.

He drifted toward the city with his unassuming walk when a group of men passed in front of him, heading toward the huts on the outskirts of the camp. Most huts out that way were vacant, and in bad shape. Still, this group was moving in that direction.

Leilius veered right so he would be able to see these men in more detail. There were five of them total. Four wore shiny, black material that kept off the rain—the same kind Leilius had seen often since they'd landed. Loose arms, hung from broad shoulders, swung at their sides. They moved, stealthily and quiet, their eyes sliding from one side to the other.

Leilius felt tingles crawling up his back as fear settled in his gut. He didn't know these men, but the way they moved, the look of their swords, and the sharp edge in their eyes, made him think *killer*.

In the middle of their group strode a man completely their opposite. Short and bald, he walked in a floppy sort of way suggesting he was no fighter. His skin was pale and he wore a shiny, blue shirt with shiny, red pants.

Leilius' mind raced as he veered left again. This group was silent, and they were beyond dangerous. They were not the sort of men Leilius needed to get messed up with, even just to snoop. The Captain or

Sanders could handle guys like that!

Then there was that guy in the middle. He was free to walk, so he was no prisoner. With men like these around him, he had to be someone important, like that Hunter stalking S'am. Or someone worse.

Fingers tingling and really wanting to run, Leilius remembered what S'am had told him about fear. If he showed it, it would alert the predators. Spies were in dangerous places all the time—the spies that lived were the ones that didn't act like they were ever in danger. They acted like they *belonged*. Confidence would keep him alive. Hopefully.

Leilius adopted a dumb-puppy expression and a loose-limbed stride. He'd play up the young idiot persona that Sanders always strapped the Honor Guard with. It's what people expected, which meant it was the best way to blend in.

Not a moment too soon.

The gaze of one of those men swung his way. Fear pinged through Leilius' body as dead and hollow eyes honed in on him.

"What are you doing here, boy?" came a dry rasp.

The man broke away from the rest, walking closer with the smooth slide of a deadly predator on the hunt. None of the others bothered to glance Leilius' way.

Leilius' legs went numb as the fear overcame his senses. His foot hit something, tripping him. He fell, face-first, into the wet mud, scraping his cheek against a rock.

"I'm sorry," he muttered, not sure what else to say.

A hard boot smashed down on the center of his back, pinning him painfully.

"I said, what are you doing here, boy?"

"I-I was just trying to find my pa," Leilius stammered, playing up a more rural speech. "He were supposed to be in one of these huts, but I can't find him. He took the wine we was supposed to trade for our supper."

The boot ground into Leilius' back, grazing skin and bruising bone. He heard a *pop* before agony seared up his spine. He cried out, squeezing his eyes shut. "Please," he begged. "I didn't mean no harm."

"Your pa isn't around here. See that you aren't, either." Without warning, the weight lifted. Tears of pain dripped from Leilius' eyes and coated his cheeks. He stayed frozen, not sure what to do. Not sure why the man was hovering over him. The cold seeped through his skin, making him shiver violently. His teeth chattered, crunching grains of dirt that had flown into his mouth when he fell.

After some minutes, still shaking with fear, Leilius finally looked up to see that the man was gone. He'd walked away through the mud and gunk without a sound.

A flood of relief washed through him. He dropped his head for a brief moment, thanking God for his life, not caring about the cold or the agony of his back. Just happy to be alive.

Slowly, painfully, he climbed to his feet, not caring about the whimpers of pain he couldn't contain. Hobbling, he made the long way to the city, thankful to be alive. Only when he was almost at the Captain's quarters, drawing eyes and pitying expressions, did a greater fear wash over him.

He was alive, but if they were responsible for helping the Inkna-Chosen, and for shutting up Yarm, how much longer would S'am be alive?

CHAPTER 4

SHANTI OPENED HER EYES SLOWLY. She'd been standing in the same spot, with her eyes closed, for an extended period of time. Listening. If there was anyone there, even a master at stealth, Shanti would either have heard him, or felt his presence. She didn't have her *Gift,* but she'd grown up in the wood. She'd trained, snuck, spied and got up to mischief in thick trees amongst some of the best fighters in the land. The *Gift* could be a crutch, so Shanti's people made sure they were well-versed in doing without.

The dwindling day remained quiet and serene. A lonely bird sang high in the trees. Raindrops fell in a smattering of plops. Nature produced the only sounds.

Mentally blind, Shanti continued on her way with soft footsteps. Knife in hand, eyes always on the move, she looked for signs of someone passing before her. A broken branch off to the right at shoulder height indicated someone unskilled in tracking or stealth had gone that way. The break was old, though. The exposed wood of the branch had darkened through exposure to the air for some time.

A few footprints filled with water from the rain were also old, made with a heavy boot with hard soles. The Shadow people had been wearing waterproofed, soft-soled boots. This imprint was typical of Inkna, but there was no telling if the full-powered Inkna-Chosen had made this tread, or one of the minions who'd been put through before him.

She reached a fork in the trail. Glancing first to the right, then the left, she couldn't see any difference in the paths. Heavy trees crowded the walking space as branches reached overhead. Glistening moss grew on rocks and rough bark lined the outside of trunks. The heavy boot tread went left. Another, fresher boot tread went right. Both were probably Inkna.

Shanti went right.

Through the gaps in the trees overhead, rain sifted down. In other spots, the collected water on the high branches turned into plunks of fat drops. Still she walked, scanning. Listening. Noticing the slightest changes in the foliage.

Her stomach growled. Beyond the branches, the sky was darkening.

She needed to take care of the basics of survival in the wild while there was still light. The elements could kill as easily as the Inkna-Chosen—probably more easily.

With that in mind she increased her pace, identifying possible areas for shelter. Her garments would keep her warm thanks to the Shadow people, so she needed only the bare minimum, including a fire and a few provisions. Without delay, senses always alert, she sought out the things she needed.

AS THE DAY DWINDLED, SHANTI sat down under the tarp, which was strung along the tops of a shallow rock outcropping. Two large trees rose to either side of her with a thick canopy overhead. If the rain turned heavy, her open fire would remain mostly protected.

She boiled rainwater that she'd collected, cooking wild vegetables in it. A small bird roasting on a spit was almost done. The woman had been right: this wood was plentiful, and sustenance was not hard to find. With the gifts of the tarp, clothes, pot and firestones, surviving would be easy—at least until the trials began.

Shanti scanned the quiet wood. She hadn't seen a boot tread in some time, but she *had* seen some soft imprints, crossing the path from the grasses beside it. Those, she bet, were made by Shadow people.

I can't kill anyone, she reminded herself as she stirred the pot. *Let's just hope the Shadow know when they're defeated. Otherwise, I'll have to maim, and that won't be much fun for them...*

As she removed the bird from the spit, thinking about how she would do the same with the hot pot, a *snap* sounded away to her right.

Shanti froze, immediately closing her eyes to cut out the distraction of sight.

The tiny sound of a branch moving reverberated in the silence. A bird gave a shrill cry, announcing someone in its midst, before the beat of wings suggested it taking flight. Silence once again reigned.

Thinking fast, Shanti used her old, damp garments to remove the pot, setting it on some grasses and mud. In silence, she scraped up two handfuls of dirt and slid behind the rocks that made her shelter. After smearing mud on her face and tucking any visible hair back into her hood, she settled into a hiding place and waited.

A slushy sound of watery mud came from the left. A slosh of boot announced someone approaching. A small movement twenty paces in the opposite direction drew her attention. A branch wiggled, as if caught by wind.

But there was no wind. Not even a breeze.

Goosebumps crawled across her skin. She removed a knife slowly and waited, eyes scanning the area in front of her. Nothing stirred.

She let her awareness expand out behind her. Almost immediately, she was rewarded with a slide of soft material on rock.

Adrenaline dumped into her body as she spun and

threw her knife. A *fffuuuwwww* sound reached her ears, making her duck out of the way. A dart bounced off the rock beside her. A body, a man, staggered into a tree five paces up the incline. His hand reached for the knife in his shoulder.

Shanti ran at him, leaping over any rocks in her way. The man brandished a knife in his good hand. She dodged his first strike, then blocked the next, her forearm clashing against his. He slid his hand away, aiming the knife down toward her. She flinched back, shifted, and pushed the hilt of the knife in his shoulder, driving it in further.

The man grunted. His lips pressed, fighting the pain as his knife slashed at her. Her tarp shook, as if someone was brushing by it in a hurry.

Help was coming, but not for her.

She yanked the knife from the man, blocked his thrust, dodged a strike, and stabbed him in the leg. He cried out and bent, but she didn't pause to reflect on a solid hit. Clutching his tunic, she yanked him toward her, then used his momentum to use him as a shield.

Another *ffffuuuwwwww* announced the dart right before it lodged in the neck of the man, barely three inches from her face.

These people had great aim with their darts. Thank the Elders for granting her luck.

"If that is poisonous, you'd better see to your man,"

Shanti called out in the Shadow Lands language before shoving the man down the hillside. He staggered forward, limping badly on his leg, as she ducked behind the nearest tree. "You shot it into his neck—he may not have long."

That is not my kill!

"It's a sleeping agent—you've passed this trial. Please, stand down so that we may collect him," a voice echoed from behind her shelter.

Adrenaline pumping, not totally believing the words, Shanti peered out from behind the tree in time to witness a tall man with brown hair hook a shoulder under that of his countryman. The injured man leaned heavily before his head started to roll. The sleeping agent worked fast.

Another man, with flaming red hair and brilliant blue eyes, came around the rocks of her shelter. He assessed the damage to his countryman for a brief moment before wiping his hands and stepping closer to help carry him. Taking his weight, he looked up. His eyes, only ten paces away, were piercing yet sparkling, full of jest and humor. He winked. "Your bird needs salt."

"Care to supply any?" she asked, still keeping most of her body behind the tree. She had no idea if these people could be trusted.

"Next time. Enjoy your wet night. You might use

the rain to wash your face."

"What if I hadn't avoided the dart?" Shanti called as the men turned and started back the way they came. "Why not have it tipped with poison? Otherwise, you're just promoting failure."

The flame-haired man stopped the progression and shifted so he could turn his head toward her. "You're the first outsider to avoid the dart. If it were poison, our fun would end shortly after it began. How can we train when we kill everyone right away?"

"Had I known I was helping you train, I might've devoted some time to following your trails and catching you unawares. You might step softer, if you want to stay hidden."

A flash of smile crossed his face. "I see the old adage is true—women are infinitely harder to impress." Laughing, he helped drag away his man who was now completely limp.

So the trials for the would-be Chosen weren't so much about finding a future leader as they were for training. It probably hadn't started that way, since the Chosen was prophesied, but the years of false-Chosen making their way through the trials had given the people of this land everything they needed to hone their skills. Since the Chosen couldn't kill, there was no danger for the Shadow. Their only problem became the duration of worthwhile training. Hence the sleeping agent instead of poison.

An entire people had been given the task of making sure she failed.

"The woman at the beginning told me as much," Shanti muttered, returning to her dinner. A large bite had been taken out of her bird. She shook her head. "Thieving fool."

She'd be lying if she said she'd ever expected to make it through these trials. It had always seemed like too big of an undertaking for one person. But then, she'd never expected to make it this far, either. The important thing was finding the Inkna-Chosen and killing him. After that, she'd give 'em hell as best she could. They might've stacked the odds against her, but she'd traveled too far, and endured too much, to roll over and play dead. She'd follow the rules as long as she could, but when Death came to collect her, she'd take as many down with her as she could.

CAYAN CAUGHT SIGHT OF THE natural arch at the first light of day. After Leilius had limped painfully into Cayan's room last night and revealed all he'd seen, a blast of fear had suffocated Cayan. That itching, clawing certainty that he should've gone into the trials with Shanti returned. The pull, the ache—he almost ran from the room straight away.

Instead, he'd used logic. Mistakes happened when decisions were made in haste, and mistakes would get his men killed.

Keeping his calm, he'd called a meeting of the company, explaining what he'd learned, what that might mean, and what he'd have to do. Everyone was allocated their roles. The chain of command would remain well-established.

He impressed upon them all that the most important thing was to stick together. Stay alive *together.* Against an army trained to be individuals, like the Graygual, Cayan's men needed to be a tight unit, working for each other. Helping each other. Relying on each other. They were infinitely stronger that way.

As Cayan was leaving before the sun did more than lighten the horizon, Burson stopped him. "The choice you didn't make yesterday was to go with Shanti. That choice led to a much harder road, fraught with death. The choice you make today rights the wrong. It tips the scale closer to balance. There will still be death, but you have made a wise decision."

Cayan's anger rose immediately. "Why didn't you mention this yesterday?"

"The choice had to be made by you. If I had told you, it would've been disastrous. Keep her grounded. She is prepared for death—give her a reason to fight for life."

Cayan would've loved to hang the man up by his feet and shake him, but that wouldn't have solved anything. Instead, with the need to join Shanti clawing at his gut, he'd just shaken his head and started out.

He met the gaze of the man who'd greeted Shanti yesterday. With sleepy eyes and an untucked shirt, it looked like the man had barely made it here before Cayan. It meant the Shadow were watching the city closely, and word spread quickly.

He wondered if they were watching the Trespasser Village, too. It seemed unlikely, not with the hole in the thorn fence and the gruesome killing put on display. That was a level of viciousness that had been left unchecked. If it was allowed to continue running rampant, it would only grow into something nasty. The worst of the Graygual were in that Trespasser Village, Cayan had no doubt. And his sole purpose was keeping that danger away from Shanti.

"Why do you come?" the man asked as Cayan stopped before him.

"I seek entrance to the trials," Cayan stated in a flat voice.

"Do you proclaim yourself Chosen?"

"No."

The man's light eyebrows settled low over his confused eyes. "Only those who proclaim themselves Chosen may enter."

"Is that a rule?"

The man's head tilted. He paused. When he answered, his voice wasn't hesitant, per se, but he certainly hadn't been confronted with this situation before. "To enter, one must proclaim himself Chosen…"

"Fine. I'm Chosen. Let me enter."

"Once you enter the arch, you will either emerge the Chosen, or die in the process. Once in, there is but one way out."

Cayan felt his impatience rise. "Obviously there are two ways out—alive or dead. But I wonder if you've found the third. Regardless, I understand. Let's move along."

The knot between the man's eyebrows deepened as he gestured Cayan in front of him. "This is not… a standard situation."

"I agree, but I came with a woman who does nothing the standard way. It's rubbed off."

Cayan walked through the thorny, green tunnel and saw a woman sitting on the wet ground in the middle of a clearing. A small movement to the left caught his eye. He barely caught a shoulder slip behind a tree trunk.

As his mind reached out, he picked up others, hiding within the trees, waiting to rush out should he try to kill this woman sitting on the ground. Cayan wondered if Shanti had received the same audience, or if this was because he was a man with an agenda.

He stopped in front of the woman, not bothering to sit. He then let his gaze sweep away towards the only trail, and figured that Shanti would've headed that way. He pushed out his mental reach, trying to find her, but once he reached a certain point and only felt emptiness, his *Gift* wouldn't penetrate.

He refocused on the woman. Catching his gaze, she put her hand out in front of her. "Please, sit."

He was about to tell her he would remain standing, but his *Gift* warped and bent, trying to pull away. He paused, struggling for control. It swirled out from under his grasp, and then blasted out, scouring the minds hiding in the trees. He tried to rein it back in, tried to follow Shanti's fastidious training over these last few weeks, but no matter what he did, he couldn't stop the torrent of power ripping out of him.

"Please, shield," the woman prompted, touching her temple with a squint.

"I… I can't…" Cayan said, trying to work with his power. Trying to collapse it down, or direct it up. Trying to do *anything* to stop the leak.

Then he felt it. That cover over the deep well of power, his safe-hold, lifted. Like worrying away a scab, the strange feeling in this place, the warp on his *Gift*, had that cover rocking. Peeling away.

More power leaked out. Then more. Surging, pushing up into him, dumping into his body, the power filled him. Fear pooled in his gut.

"I need to get to the sea. Or a place with no human life. Please—" Cayan squeezed his eyes shut, clamping down on that cover. Trying to contain the searing, burning power that was crawling up his insides. He could feel it searching for its mate.

Cayan took deep, lung-filling breaths. He tried to relax. He tried to let the power come so he might be able to expel it. But the more it pooled into him, the more it blistered his insides and scorched his mind. He didn't know how to control it.

Panting, his hands balled, he staggered in the direction he had come from.

"You cannot leave once you have entered," the man behind him said through a strained voice.

"The pain you feel right now is nothing," Cayan grated. "That's the power I can usually control, after a fashion. What's coming will kill you. I can't control it and I don't know how to link with you to get help. It'll kill me first, then explode out and kill everyone in this clearing. You need to let me attempt to direct it to the sea."

The man hesitated, but Cayan didn't wait for an answer. He pushed past him, staggering toward the arch. His body bounced off the razor sharp sides, but he felt no pain. Not through the blaring, blistering agony welling up within him.

He fell to his knees on the muddy bank, grabbed as much power as he could, felt like he was gasping for air, and then *EXPELLED*.

In a huge gush, the power ripped out of him. His scream scored his throat. The power raked his insides. A low rumble blasted out to the sea but also curled around him. A backlash shot out behind, small in comparison, but still dangerous. Another scream sounded, filled with both pain and surprise. The mind did not wink out, even though agony flashed strong.

As the power dwindled away, the only sound was the lazy lapping of the waves against the dock. Cayan took a huge, lung-filling breath and wiped the tears of pain from his eyes. It felt like he'd swam the length of the island underwater.

Getting painfully to his feet, he turned to find the greeter with a pale face and wide eyes. Cayan wiped the sweat off his forehead. "Yes, I just broke protocol, but I am going into those trials. If I were you, I'd get out of the way and pass me through as quickly as possible. I don't know what strange flux is in that clearing, but I can't control my power when I'm in it."

"We've never experienced this before," the man said. He couldn't control his shaking voice, or maybe he just wasn't trying.

"That doesn't change the fact that I need admittance."

The man held open a hand toward the arch. "I am not in charge of who goes through."

Cayan stalked back into the clearing, fear clawing at his insides. He had no idea how long it would take that power to build up again, but he had a feeling it wouldn't be long.

On the other side of the arch, the woman was wide-eyed and grim. "You did not mean to harm us," she said. "And so you are forgiven. You have enough power to pass these trials, but you do not have the control. You will die in these lands."

"No, I won't. May I pass?"

"Even without the trials, that power will kill you. It is not a weapon, it is an explosive death sentence for the wielder."

"Only when I don't have help. Is that bundle for me?"

"You are not here for the title of Chosen. You are here to protect the one you love."

"Astute. You should meet Rohnan; the two of you would drive each other crazy."

"Usually, after revealing you won't make the trials alive, I give the offer of a quick death…"

Cayan stared down at her, feeling his power slip sideways again, then flop back. It felt like trying to hold onto a fish. The other power was already building, deep within him. That cover keeping it contained was there, but it was loose. It wouldn't hold.

"Are all of the trials like this, with this strange fluctuation in power?" Cayan asked, feeling the urgency to find Shanti.

She shook her head before gulping. "No. This particular place is mirrored in a few others, but it is not the norm. You seem to have a hard time with control—you hold your *Therma* too tightly. Your fear of letting go suffocates you."

Cayan realized what Rohnan had told Shanti the first time they'd all worked together. She had been right—knowing would hurt more than help, and he didn't really want to know.

"Listen, you have your standard way of dealing with this, I'm sure," Cayan said with impatience, feeling his power rise. "But I don't have much more time."

The woman stood with the bundle and went over what each item was. When she was finished, she said, "If you do not find her soon, you will probably starve in these woods. You do not have the know-how."

"Helpful." Cayan raised his eyebrows as he took the pack. "Is there anything else?"

"Since you require her assistance with your power, you are now grouped with her. Our rules as they concern her extends to you. If you break these rules, you will be ruining her chances of success. Those rules are simply: do not try to escape the trials, and do not kill anyone."

Cayan grinned. "She's here out of the duty placed on her by her people, so she'll follow the rules you set. I'm here for her, so in order to keep me on a leash, you pair us. Smart. That's fine. I'm not interested in protecting her from your people."

"Then who are you here to protect her against?" A man with long blond hair cascading in a sheet over his shoulders stepped out from the trees. His classically etched face and symmetrical features lent him a beauty rarely seen in men. Not even Rohnan could boast the flawless appearance of this man.

"The Graygual." Cayan started off at a fast walk. As he reached the trees, he said, "You best start preparing for war, because it's landed on your doorstep. These games you play are about to end."

PORTOLMOUS WATCHED THE MUSCULAR MAN disappear into the trees. One person having that much power was foretold, but it shouldn't have been possible. It had nearly killed the man and he hadn't a hope of containing it.

But he had said the woman could, somehow.

"He was completely genuine throughout the whole interview," Salange said as she, too, stared at the receding back of the man. "But I forgot to ask for his sword."

"His power is the woman's mate," Punston said, still wary from when he'd watched the man's explosion of power by the water's edge. "He alluded to it. He doesn't want the title, and I bet he's not interested in our warriors. She knows she needs us for her schemes, but he knows he needs her. Is that right, Salange?"

She gave a small shrug. "She knows she needs us, that is true, but she doesn't scheme, unlike the others. She's here to request aid, and this is how we mandate she do it. Our system is as barbaric now as it ever was, and through it, we might kill our hope of a future."

"That wasn't the question. We don't have time for fluffy sentimentalities," Punston cursed.

Salange squared her shoulders with a scowl. "She is here for us, he is here for her. He said as much, and I validated his statement. Only a simpleton would have missed that."

"I've looked into him," Portolmous said, cutting off Punston's reply. "He's the Captain who took down the large Inkna settlement we heard about, with the help of the woman."

"And he wore the ring," Punston said.

"How could you know it's the right one?" Salange asked.

"Her features, and that of her countryman, could've been born on this island. I saw her put something around his neck on the ship, and I've seen the painting countless times. That man's neck was right below my eye-line. I got a good look. It's the right one."

"Why would she give it to the man?" Portolmous asked as he made his way out of the clearing.

"She didn't think she would survive these trials," Salange said. "She needs aid and he seems like a great leader of men with a lot of power. Perhaps she thought the ring would create a pathway for him to negotiate with us."

"It's impossible to say," Portolmous said. "But these trials aren't just for our benefit. They're to determine if someone is worthy of being our ally and leading our armies into the great battle. What that man said is true—something unpleasant is on our doorstep, and the Graygual have brought it. Since the Graygual bring nothing but war, we must assume it's finally stretched across the land. There are whisperings of a threat on this island, but so far we have been unable to turn up much. We cannot find the last three Inkna, even with our *mind-search*. They're either dead, or hidden in the areas our *Therma* can't reach. It's worrying."

"What's to be done?" Punston asked.

"Speed up the trials. Hit the woman with the beast now, before the man can join her with his sword. If she survives, then start laying on the most essential of our tests. This is no longer a training exercise. I want to know if she is the one."

"It will be *they,*" Salange said softly. "She hasn't enough power, and he hasn't a proper use of the power that is enough. The Chosen has always been a title, not a person. It is a force, and together, if their power *Joins,* they could be that force."

"We're stepping into the unknown," Portolmous said quietly, feeling a weight settle in his stomach. "We have Graygual on our doorstep, we have the violet-eyed girl, and now the title of Chosen is taking on a new meaning. I have a feeling we may not like where this leads. We need to fortify our defenses."

CHAPTER 5

SHANTI TREKKED THROUGH THE DENSE forest, breathing easier now that her *Gift* had returned and was spread out to cover ground. She felt animals scurrying here and there, and the occasional person lurking far back in the trees, always alone. No one had engaged with her yet, though.

What were they waiting for?

She was also concerned that she hadn't seen any more Inkna tracks. If the Shadow weren't killing those in the trials, she should've seen that someone had walked this way.

Yet she'd seen nothing, let alone any signs of violence.

A growing unease niggled at her as she made her way. Where was the Inkna-Chosen?

A snuffling up ahead cut through Shanti's reverie. She honed in with her *Gift*, getting the impression of a larger animal. It would be safer to kill a smaller animal, but with a larger one, she could pack up more meat so she didn't have to hunt again for some time. The extra weight would be worth the time it saved.

Dropping her pack, Shanti grabbed a knife with her left hand to compliment the one already in her right. Quietly she approached the clearing, focusing on that mind with her *Gift*. Larger animals took more power, which would leave her vulnerable if a Shadow attack came shortly after. Subduing the larger animal with her mind, and then running a knife across its throat, usually worked out just fine.

She crept to the edge of the clearing and crouched in tall grasses. A light breeze stirred her hair from behind. She was upwind, but hoped it wouldn't matter.

As she peered out of her hiding place and into the clearing, her stomach dropped.

It mattered.

Flak!

In the clearing, sniffing the air, was a great creature, the like of which she'd never seen before, not even in pictures. Eight feet high at the shoulder, the animal moved on giant paws tipped with long, curved claws. Its body looked a little like a giant bear, but its head was flatter, ears larger, and its teeth noticeably bigger. Huge canines emerged from black gums and ended just below the jaw. Its black nose twitched as it sampled the air currents. It lowered its great head and small brown eyes looked in her direction.

Please be a stupid animal. Please be a stupid animal.

The animal gave a huge, guttural roar as it lifted its head. The sound alone shook Shanti's spine.

She backed out of the area quickly to snatch up her pack. That thing was too dangerous to take on her own if she didn't have to. The question was: did it hunt humans?

Another roar sounded in the clearing. Followed by movement.

"Flak," Shanti mumbled under her breath. She jogged through the trees, cutting through small spaces and increasing her pace to a run when the trunks were further apart. Branches broke behind her. Leaves crunched. A huge body rammed through foliage and scraped against trees.

It was following her.

"Bloody—" Shanti cut left, running on instinct. There was no outrunning that thing. Few four-legged hunters would be slower than a human. Could she outthink it in time to get away?

Loud grunts sounded close behind her. Tearing plants and heavy paw-falls stole her breath. It was gaining on her.

"Death's playground, that thing is fast," Shanti huffed, trying not to let panic overcome her.

This had to be a trial. There was no way that thing was roaming around these woods without the Shadow people controlling it, or they'd end up dead too. If she outsmarted it and escaped its notice, it would stalk her. Failing that, the Shadow people could just lead it to her again.

Making a quick decision, Shanti cut left, back to the clearing. She needed room to work. To move. Dodging plants would only slow her down, especially because that thing didn't seem to dodge anything. It just tore through.

"This is not fun," she grunted, jumping into the clearing. A growl sounded right behind her as the huge body crashed in after her.

Outsmart it? She couldn't even get a moment to think about where to run from it.

She turned as a massive paw raked in front of her eyes. She struck out mentally as she rolled to the right. It roared again before standing up on its hind legs. Shanti's mouth dropped open as the giant beast stood before her, over fifteen feet high. Massive.

Not wasting another moment she mentally struck again, harder this time, as she dodged in and swiped at its leg. The blade opened up a red line in its fur, but despite the force she put behind the blade, it didn't open up much flesh. Its fur was too thick.

The animal landed on all fours with a growl. She rolled out of the way and sunk her blade into its hind-quarters. It spun, faster than it should've for its size, and swiped again. One claw sliced through her coat, scraping her shoulder. Pain stung her arm.

"Flak!" she swore. She *slashed* at its mind as she ran around the beast, looking for a way to get closer to its body without that claw gouging. *Twisting* and then *stabbing* only had the beast hollering. Its mind had some natural defense against the brunt of her power. Her *Gift* was having little impact on the creature.

The animal stood again and roared. Fear simmered up Shanti's spine. It lunged as it came down, right over her.

She threw herself to one side, barely dodging snapping jaws. Searing pain bit her leg where claws snatched at her. Ignoring the pain, she scrambled to her feet. Panting, heart beating fast, she rushed in to its side, stabbed twice with each knife into its soft underbelly, and ran out before it could turn.

Hot blood ran freely onto the wet ground, but the beast didn't slow.

It lumbered after her, covering a large distance in just a few strides. She dodged to the side, but its movement cut her off. It swung its paw, swooping toward her head. She rolled again, slashing with her inadequate knife. The blade cut into the soft tissue on the back of one leg.

The beast roared.

Its paw came down beside her. Its other rose for a blow. She stabbed down into the planted paw, dove toward its body, and came up with both blades to its chest. She stabbed as the creature backed up, howling. She stabbed one more time as a paw caught her broadside, throwing her to the side. Her limbs splashed against the soft ground and her head cracked against a hard rock.

Dizzied, she rolled to her stomach and tried to climb to her feet, but the world careened around her. The beast lumbered toward her, dripping blood.

"What in all of Death's humor are you?" she muttered as she rose, staggered, and prepared to meet it head on.

It lunged again, the paw blurring in Shanti's vision as it sped toward her chest. She hit the ground, bounced up with a knife swipe, and dived beneath the next paw. Chest heaving with fatigue, vision slow to clear, she rushed in and dug her blades into the beast's rump. It cried in madness as she *speared* its mind with a full dose of power. She couldn't get out of the way in time. It hit her again, knocking her down once more. The world swam. Its huge, brown body bounded toward her. She rolled from a raking claw, but not far enough. A gash opened up on the side of her back.

She screamed as agony seared her.

I've spent my life learning to fight the Graygual, and an overgrown bear will be responsible for killing me. Super.

She dug into its mind again as she rose up, digging her knives into its throat.

The beast howled, but like a bear, the fur at its throat was thick. The knives hadn't pierced deeply enough to kill it.

"Just die!" she yelled, ripping her knives out for another strike. Blood gushed down onto her as it howled a second time. Its head came up and its body turned away from her.

She launched another mental assault as hard as she could, when she felt her power swell, and then surge. The spicy feeling erupted in her middle as her *Gift* gained in potency. The beast howled again, trailing blood as it lumbered after someone else.

Cayan.

What was he doing there?

Shanti continued her mental assault, *stabbing* and *tearing* as much as she could, while she limped forward, her body on fire. It struck out in front of it, whining as it moved. She caught up and dug her blades into its rump. It tried to turn back, but hesitated as a sword glinted in the sun before swinging toward the beast's body.

An agony-ridden howl erupted from its throat. Its huge paw lashed out at the larger blade in front.

Shanti hacked into its legs from behind, using Cayan's distraction.

This time, the howl was more of a whimper.

The animal lashed out again before turning. Baying with pain, the beast took off, limping away.

It wasn't a stupid animal. It knew when it was outmatched.

Thank the Elders for their mercy.

Shanti looked to her help. Cayan stood straight and tall, holding a sword and a knife, with blood splattered down his chest. His blue eyes flashed as his muscles rippled, looking like an avenging warrior.

Gasping for breath, Shanti sank to her knees. "Swords are cheating," she said, falling onto her hands. "But I'll overlook it this once. Think it'll come back?"

Cayan ran forward. He dropped his sword and knife beside her and straightened her up. Without delay he stripped off her coat and laid it to the side. His gaze traveled her wounds before he bent to examine her leg.

"Ow." She winced as he touched the shredded material, which brushed against torn skin. "That thing was fast."

"Yes. I've never seen one before. You'll heal, though. Have you seen any healing plants?"

"Who do you think I am? Rohnan?" The mind of the creature winked out. Not dead, she bet, but in a *Gift*-free part of the forest. That, or they had someone with a Gift like Burson.

As she should've expected, Cayan tossed her coat

over his shoulder and scooped her up.

"I can walk, Cayan," she said, pointing at her pack at the edge of the clearing.

"Can, but would rather not, I'd wager."

It was true. And she didn't feel like arguing.

He jostled her, but retrieved her pack without putting her down. He carried her out of the clearing, and started trekking through the dense trees.

"Where are you going?" she asked, her mind open. She didn't think the Shadow people would want to finish her off without more sport, but had no idea of what to expect from them. She certainly hadn't expected that animal.

"I passed a hollowed out tree on my way to you. It'll be good for shelter and warmth."

"My, my, learning to live without leather couches and giant beds filled with big-breasted women?"

"You're just jealous."

"Yes, actually, on both counts. Although, I'd prefer to *have* the large breasts, not play with them."

Cayan chuckled as he threaded between trees and paused in front of a giant trunk, hollowed out as he had said. A huge storm would eventually bring this mammoth down but for now it was sound.

"Nice find," she said as he ducked inside with her and set her down on a cushion of leaves and grasses. There was some scat in the corner, indicating he wasn't the only one to make use of this great shelter. It was old, though, and with a fire right outside, they shouldn't have any unwelcome visitors.

"Not that I'm ungrateful, but why are you here?" Shanti asked. She shivered as she stripped out of her shirt and breast binding to assess the damage to her shoulder and back. Blood dripped from her gashes, but the wounds themselves weren't terribly deep. The deep, painful scores in her legs would take a little longer to heal, even with her *Gift* speeding up her rate of healing.

The problem wouldn't be the loss of blood with these wounds, it was the risk of infection.

She felt his shields lock into place with her question, drawing her eyes out of the opening. She couldn't see his body.

"I decided I couldn't let you have all the fun," he said.

"What's the real reason?" she asked in a firm tone.

He hesitated before answering, "Someone cut a hole through the hedge. People are dying in the Trespasser Village. Word is, someone was taken out of the trials."

Tingles crept up Shanti's spine. "Do the Shadow people know?"

"If they do, they're keeping their mouths shut."

"They must." Shanti paused in thought, working through the implications. "They must know he's gone. They use this as training for their own people. They have their *Gift*, they track… they *must* know. Did they kill him?"

"We would've heard if they had."

Shanti bit her lip, a frown working at her features. "Then someone is sheltering him, because they wouldn't just let him go. There are only a few who have the ability to shelter someone on the Shadow people's homeland."

"I think those people are in the Village," Cayan said before explaining what Leilius had heard the night before.

Shanti listened with growing concern, making Cayan repeat some of the details about the group Leilius had seen, of the man they surrounded, and of the man who walked in mud in silence. By the end, her stomach was in knots.

"It's him," she breathed, sweat beading her brow despite the cold. "It has to be. There is no other power like him—no one else who would be guarded by men like that."

"Surely there could be." Cayan's voice remained neutral.

"Yes, okay—there *could* be another man out there matching Xandre's description with guards matching the descriptions of Xandre's Inner Circle. Yes, that *could* happen. However, why would that person set up camp in a place he would never be noticed while an

Inkna is entered into, and then rescued from, the trials…"

"That is why I'm in here with you. The Graygual aren't playing by the rules, so there's no reason you should, either."

Shanti ducked out of the tree to find Cayan setting out materials with which to make a fire. The way he laid everything out, slowly and methodically, before picking up the fire-starting rock and analyzing it, meant he hadn't much experience.

"Do you need help?" she asked with a grin working at her mouth.

He glanced up at her with a furrowed brow. He shook his head and looked back down. "I haven't done this since I was fifteen or something, and even then I used slightly more… advanced methods of starting a fire. But it can't be that difficult."

"Yes it can."

"I'll figure it out," he said with determination as he struck the rock to see its effects.

The grin turned into a smile as she watched him try to best the rock. A moment later, though, their situation withered her humor. "Xandre must know his Chosen would never make it."

"Then why go through the charade of putting him through just to raise eyebrows by pulling him out again?"

"Simple. To get me in here. To keep me put."

Cayan looked up. Those blue eyes flashed. A surge of power sprayed Shanti before she slammed down her mental shields. He said, "Then we'll find that hole and get out. We shouldn't be in here waiting for him to come get you."

Shanti shifted, then winced as her pant leg brushed against her wound. She heaved a sigh, trying to ignore the burning pain. "I can't. I need the Shadow army, and they won't follow me unless I get through these trials. If we leave now, he can just scoop me up. I'm sure his men vastly outnumber your own. The Shadow people will do nothing to stop him as long as we are outside the city." Shanti brushed the hair from her forehead as determination kindled deep in her gut. "No, I *have* to make it through these trials if I want to make it off this island with my freedom. I may not have much hope, but it's the duty my people assigned me—I have to at least try."

"Well, they've let me in and tied me to you to help themselves. They changed the rules. We can work together and still get you that title."

A rush of gratitude stole Shanti's breath, thankfully hidden behind her shields. She'd always been stronger with him. She'd always evaded death when he worked by her side, even when she worked alone and he picked up the pieces. If she had any hope at all, it was with him. And yes, the Shadow people had changed the rules.

They changed the rules. That meant he was right: working together was allowed.

"Maybe Xandre turning up was good news—otherwise you would've just lounged in the city and put your feet up, getting fat."

"Getting fat?" Cayan smiled as he struck the stone above some grasses.

"Yes. That stomach of yours brings all the admirers. A fat man would only bring the money-grubbers."

"Money-grubbers?" he asked, dimples showing with his smile. "Only until they heard of my prowess in bed. Then I'd have to turn women away again."

He glanced up. His blue eyes sparkled with fire. The answering heat burned deep in Shanti's core. Sweat beaded her brow for a second time, but not from fear.

She took a step back.

"How about that ride?" he pushed, his smile showing even, white teeth.

Oh yeah. That. A momentary case of *loose lips* and now he had ideas.

"I'll go gather up some things for dinner and something for my wounds, shall I?" she asked, grabbing her ripped coat.

Eyes twinkling in mischief, Cayan held up a coat similar to hers but larger. On his body he wore a slick sort of black, shiny material. It must've been something he had picked up in the city.

"They had something to fit you, huh?" Shanti asked, taking the garment.

"No. My shoulders pull at the seams, it won't close over my chest, and the sleeves don't reach my wrists. What I'm wearing is fine for the day, and your body heat will be enough for the night. I'll be fine."

Shanti's core tingled before the pain on her side stabbed her. Without bothering to comment, she turned and started off. "Keep mental contact with me. I'll blast a shock of fear at you if I get in trouble. Otherwise, I shouldn't be long."

"And Shanti—"

She turned back. His eyes had lost the heat and humor. Warning now etched his face and dulled his gaze. "They are going to hit us with everything they have— both these Shadow people and whoever is pulling the strings for the Graygual. Everything they have. We *have* to be able to access my power easily. To do that, we need to work on it. *We* do, because it would take a lifetime to control that much power, which you have and I do not. We need to work on it if we hope to use it when we need it."

Uncertainty and fear wormed into Shanti's body. She remembered the feeling of delving deeply inside him, and then letting him delve just as deeply into her, creating a level, solid balance in which their combined power would build. She remembered that sweet rush of something so powerful it fluttered her eyes and stole her breath. Then the heat; the blistering heat that she wanted to turn into something sweaty and messy until they forgot about their surroundings and just reveled in pleasure.

She also remembered the intense, deep feelings that went with all that. She'd thought about that often. And just like the last time, Romie's face hovered into view. Not the Romie with the pale, lifeless face, but the one she'd fallen in love with. The sweet, charming boy with a slow smile and soft eyes. She couldn't remember the same feelings in all her time with Romie. Not the rush of lust, the heat of passion, or the burning, aching need consuming her body. She didn't remember wrestling intellects, fighting for dominance, or even the confusing arousal of submission.

Shanti turned away, uncertainty eating away at her. She didn't want to give in. She was still lost, but now she was fighting what that meant. Deep inside, she knew it was a fight she'd already lost.

"Okay," she said softly before she was limping away. She'd have to face Cayan soon, and once she'd given away her soul, she'd have to fight Xandre. She didn't know if she was up for either.

CHAPTER 6

"WAIT A MINUTE," MARC EXCLAIMED, closing the door to his and Ruisa's room and turning back to Ruisa. The Captain had left them that morning to go help S'am, and for most of the day Marc hadn't done much more than study the maps and try to get the lay of the land. Now, at suppertime, Ruisa was trying to talk about how they might best work together. That had also meant revealing quite a few ghastly secrets. "You mean to tell me that women in our city run around, willy-nilly, poisoning guys at random, and you think that's *okay?*"

Ruisa sighed as she strung a satchel over her head. "The art of poison has been—"

"The *art* of *poison?*" Marc cut her off. "Are you *listening* to yourself?"

"It's been passed down for generations. Men can protect themselves, no problem. And sure, they like to say they'll protect their family, but when they go out and fight wars, who's left? And who protects the family from the men?"

"The law, for one," Marc said with his face red and

fists clenched. He couldn't believe what he was hearing.

"Back in the day, the men made the law for their family. Is it so wrong that women have a defense?" Ruisa shifted, sticking out one hip and adopting an expression Marc had already come to realize was stubbornness. "You can use swords and knives and muscles, and we're supposed to… what, be totally fine in our vulnerability? We aren't allowed to look after ourselves because we have vaginas, is that it?"

Marc winced at the word—female anatomy was still mostly foreign to him. Even the words embarrassed him.

The bigger problem was having to share a bathroom with her. She'd come out wearing just a breast binding and pants earlier. She hadn't thought a thing of it, and apparently she didn't realize how aggressive the male imagination could be. Now when he looked at her, all he saw was her toned midriff and the outline of her round, perky—

Marc put a palm to his forehead and squinted his eyes, trying to chase away the image.

"C'mon—we need to get to the food hall before a *man* poisons our guys." Ruisa gave Marc a hard stare. And then, apparently thinking Marc was dense, elaborated with, "Because men poison, too. Or didn't you know?"

Marc scowled as she walked toward him, all temper,

violence and mysterious femininity.

An image of her body and round breasts flashed into Marc's head again. He knew he wasn't supposed to be picturing that stuff, and didn't move as fast as he should have. Ruisa reached him and shoved him out of the way. She pulled open the door, glanced to her right looking for lurkers, and then stalked left down the hall.

"So… if you have… that capability," Marc said as he caught up to her. They took the stairs down to the alley. "Why are you bothering trying to learn to fight?"

Ruisa pushed through the door. When they entered the busy alleyway, she steered them toward the right and hunched slightly, trying to blend in like Leilius said they should.

"I don't want to be left behind," Ruisa said in a quiet tone, eyes darting from side to side. "I want to protect my home, not wait until the worst happens and try to salvage a bad situation. I come from a warrior nation, just like you. Is it so strange that I want to take part in training too?"

Marc shrugged, feeling eyes on him. A tingle crawled up his spine as two Graygual passed within five feet, their hard gazes staring Marc down. Buildings seemed to close in, crushing Marc as he and Ruisa made their way. Panic ate at his nerves.

Marc and Ruisa had purchased the raingear sold to tourists in great quantities, now looking like most everyone else, but it didn't seem to matter. The Graygual and Inkna knew who the Westwood Isles people were, and it was no secret how much they wanted Marc's crew dead.

"I'd rather just doctor," Marc said through a trembling voice. "I didn't want to be here at all."

"Well, I do want to be here." Ruisa pushed him to the right, still violent, but her voice shook just as much as Marc's. The harsh stares, and hands on sword hilts, scared her, too. They shouldn't have stayed behind to talk about poison. They should've gone to the eating hall with the more experienced fighters.

A Graygual, large and broad-shouldered, passed too close to Ruisa. His body bumped hers. A sneer creased his face. He made a kissing noise. "I have plans for you, little girl."

"Are you sure you want to be here?" Marc asked with a hard hold on his sword, ready to rip it out. He sent a hard scowl after the swaggering Graygual.

Ruisa raised her chin as she placed her hand on her sword like Marc had. "I will not cower. Shanti has seen so much worse, and she's still kicking ass. I can do it."

They left the alley and into a thoroughfare. There were all kinds of visitors passing through, from the obviously rich with velvet robes and attendants shadowing them, to those without any means at all, sitting beside poorly erected stands selling their badly created wares. Shadow people stood along the walls dressed in well-made fur coats or animal hide with their light hair and eyes, watching silently. Providing protection.

Marc heard Ruisa echo his sigh of relief. "Okay, here we are," she said as she pulled open a heavy door to a square, nondescript building. The furniture inside was sparse and simple, durable and well-made, but with no flourish. Marc wondered if it was just for visitors, or these people didn't put much value on creature comforts.

The eating area consisted of rows of long tables with benches to either side. Rich and poor alike could sit next to each other. A counter at the back sectioned off two people who took orders, and through a door behind them lay a kitchen. Only Shadow people were supposed to be in the kitchens and taking orders, guaranteeing tamper-free food. Still, Ruisa insisted, and Sanders agreed, that everyone should eat at the same time, in case any substances found their way into the food.

"Damn it, they're all around Sanders..." Ruisa swore.

At the side of the room in the back, a long table was taken up with all the men. Rohnan sat at the end, eating his meal while scanning the room. Burson sat at the other end, chewing while frowning into his plate. The rest of the guys were quietly talking amongst themselves while inconspicuously glancing around the room.

Sanders was in the middle with his familiar scowl.

"Why shouldn't they sit next to Sanders?" Marc asked.

"Because the Inkna know him. Everyone around him will now be targets, too."

"Were you sleepwalking to get here—we're all *already* targets. They know who we all are!"

"Maybe, but the guys are shoving that in the Inkna's faces," Ruisa murmured as her gaze swept the room.

Marc shook his head in frustration, but didn't push the issue. "What are you looking for?" he whispered.

"People who study the art of poison take their craft very seriously. They're knowledgeable and detail-oriented. And they always have their supply close at hand if they plan to use it. Many only specialize in that one trade. Killing is in their eyes, cunning, but their body doesn't say *warrior*. There are a few such people here, one of them a Graygual. He'll make the first move, I bet. With poison, I mean. Then there are the rich people with staff for hire. They won't take any customers until they get a firm handle on the different sides, though."

"We're outnumbered—I doubt they'll choose our side."

"True." Ruisa bit her lip, honing in on one seedy-looking character with black clothes and a black hat, hunched over his plate, his eyes peering up through his lashes. "He's trouble—the one with the pockmarks all over his face. That was an experiment gone wrong, I bet."

"Oh my God, Maggie Jensen has pockmarks—I thought it was a rough puberty," Marc mumbled.

"Yes, she figured out how to make a certain formula of powder blow up after a handful of seconds. Unfortunately, she hadn't gotten the reaction she'd been trying for, and the concoction spit acid at her." Ruisa shifted, one hand drifting to her sword hilt again. Her eyes took on a worried look. "Look at his eyes—calm but lethal. Cold and distant, but calculating. He is scanning plates and food—dangerous, that one. There is no way I'm as good as him. Not yet. We might be in over our heads, Marc."

A FEW HOURS AFTER DINNER Sanders leaned against a corner of the large building that loomed over the main square in the city. Twilight was falling and merchants within the square were packing their wares, ready to head to the Trespasser Village or elsewhere for the night. Fewer wealthy visitors strolled through the open space as night rolled in. From the mutterings Sanders had heard, the villains came out at night, trying to hide their misdeeds from the Shadow people.

Sanders spat as he watched another group of

Graygual saunter through the open gates as if they owned the place. Each had at least two bars on their breast, but only one had four, and none higher. Low-level scum, but with some ability with their swords.

Men like this had been oozing in all day, stepping onto the island by the boatload. Inkna, too, filled out the ranks, walking around like they couldn't smell the Being Supreme's shit on their upper lip.

Sanders glanced at one of the Shadow people standing beside the gate and noticed the woman staring back. Pretty little thing, too. Slight and sinewy with long legs and a heart-shaped mouth. Her weapon was shiny, the leather on the handle worn, and her face advertised no-nonsense. She'd give you a wink and slice your dick off, Sanders bet. Deadly and humorless, like the rest of the Shadow people he saw loitering around.

Her gaze went back to the group of Graygual.

She'd been standing there as long as Sanders had been in his spot, taking over from a thin man with a scar across his forehead. If Sanders read her right, she was observing the changing of the tides just as he was. An army leader didn't stuff all his men into one place without a plan in mind. That plan usually involved either keeping the peace, or taking the stronghold.

There were already peacekeepers. The Graygual had other things in mind, and the extra troops were taking their positions.

Sanders glanced at the dimming sun. Full nightfall was probably an hour away.

He shifted his position as he grinned at a passing Inkna. The grin didn't hold any humor. It held a promise.

A shot of pain blasted Sanders' face. His eyes watered as he forced himself to stay on his feet. His grin turned into a silent growl.

The Shadow woman shifted. Suddenly, the pain was cut off and the Inkna staggered in his steps. The Graygual around him looked over in confusion, wondering what the problem was, when three Shadow people strode up the road toward the square. Their gazes were trained on the Inkna, sinking to his knees and clutching his head.

"Mental warfare is forbidden in the city!" one of the Shadow people said in a harsh voice as they descended on the Inkna.

"There's no problem here," a Graygual said. He bore three slashes across his breast. With a hand out and a placating smile, he stepped in front of his Inkna to block the incoming Shadow. "I'm sure this is a misunderstanding."

The Graygual gave a shriek and sank to the ground. He grabbed his head as those around him started groaning or screaming. They all withered to the ground.

The Shadow people reached the Inkna. Without

wasting time, the one in the lead brutally punched the Inkna in the face, knocking him out. He bent and hauled the unconscious man up by the shirtfront and handed him to the two Shadow behind. As a unit, and without another word, the three turned and dragged the Inkna back the way they had come.

"You will regret that!" the lead Graygual called as he climbed uncertainly to his feet. "You are nothing compared to my master!"

"What just happened, sir?" Tobias strode up with some of the others clopping behind.

"One of those filthy Inkna used mental warfare on me, probably to send a message, and the Shadow people dealt with him hard and fast. They do not like their laws being flouted."

"In the city, maybe, but I heard that three people died in the Trespasser Village, today. Had their tongues cut out along with their innards. Someone said they heard the shrieks—like the poor sods were alive when it happened…" Tobias shook his head with a grimace as he noticed the woman across the way watching them. "What's up with that one? She got a thing for your ugly mug, or what?"

"Trying to suss me out, I'd wager." Sanders pushed away from the wall.

"Sir… you probably know this…" Marc cleared his throat with a bright red face. "But Ruisa thinks we shouldn't be together all the time, even though the Captain said to work together. People know where we came from, and that we came with Shanti, and… well… that might work out badly for us."

Sanders grunted. "It'll work out badly if we hide in fear, sure. I don't hide, son, and I *don't* show fear. We got a lot of Inkna and Graygual slinking around, playing dirty. Tonight we're going to flush them out. There's a new terror in town, and that's us."

"Even the score, ay sir?" Tobias said with a grin.

"Less Inkna to try and kill us on our way out of here," Tomous said in a quiet voice.

"My thoughts exactly, Tomous. You're not as dumb as you look." Sanders looked down the road toward their dwelling.

"You are," Tomous said, huffing a small laugh that didn't turn into a smile as he stared at yet another group of Graygual coming through the gate. The kid had a hard time of it a few years ago—Sanders could see the scars in the kids' eyes. But he was a fighter, and he was starting to come out of his shell. Sometimes all a man needed was a purpose, and Shanti had given him that. Sanders was letting it blossom.

"Where the hell are Burson and Leilius? They're holding us up." Sanders growled.

"Burson's coming, but he told Leilius to stay behind," Marc answered in a wispy tone that meant he hated being noticed by Sanders. Sanders knew that tone well.

"Said Leilius wouldn't come back if he went out tonight," Tepson volunteered. "I was there. Told the younger boys to stay away from the pretty girls, too. Told them to listen to Ruisa in whatever she said. He didn't do that weird smile or look at the sky, once. That guy is pretty wound up."

"He's trying to keep us on track with a constantly changing situation." Sanders nodded and adjusted the knives at his belt. "He say anything about the Captain and Shanti?"

"Muttered something about how they were nearing their biggest milestone," Tomous said as he glanced at the Shadow woman still staring at them. It was starting to get irritating. "Said they were holding up their path, or something, but we were a gaggle of field-mice herded by cats, and we could tear it all down."

"Helpful," Sanders said with a sarcastic tone. "And did he happen to mention when he'd be along?"

"Here." The older man walked up with dark circles under his eyes, a messy gray halo of hair around his head. "I wanted to speak with Rohnan before he went out."

Sanders nodded and started forward.

"If you leave, you are without protection," they heard as they neared the gate. The voice was high and squeaky. Girlish, almost. The Shadow woman followed them with her gaze.

"If you continually lock yourself in your city, *you* will be without protection," Sanders shot back as he left the gate.

"Do you think they know what's coming?" Tomous asked quietly.

From what Sanders had picked up, Tomous was fully expecting the Graygual to declare war and take the city any day. He thought they'd do it before Shanti emerged from the trials so they could greet her with shackles. Sanders had to admit that it sounded likely.

"They don't seem stupid to me," Tobias said. "They have to know something is happening, especially with so many Graygual coming in. But they sure aren't acting on it."

"No, they aren't," Sanders growled. "Otherwise, they'd figure out what's going on in that Trespasser Village."

"Are we going to wander through?" Xavier asked in a nonchalant voice. He couldn't hide the adrenaline fueling his words. He was still new to all this. Fighting real enemies had the kid as jumpy as a whore talking to God.

"No," Sanders said.

Before he could elaborate, Burson added, "Whatever festers in the darkness needs to remain there for now.

Bringing it into the light will alter all our lives."

"Hard to argue with crazy," Tobias muttered.

Sanders had to agree, but that crazy had also steered them here safely, so Sanders didn't plan to throw stones.

AN HOUR LATER THEY FOUND themselves walking in the shadow of the briar fence separating the trials from the rest of the island. They'd passed by the docks, checked in with SeaFarer, and heard that three ships full of Graygual and Inkna had landed. The contents of two ships had gone toward the Trespasser Village, and the rest headed into the city. Strangely, the senior officers had veered toward the Village.

SeaFarer commented that that wasn't normal. Sanders had to agree, unless the Graygual needed secrecy away from the watchful eyes of the Shadow people.

Sanders looked up at the massive wall of horribly prickly briars. Not even a sword would hack through, and no one was going to climb that thing and survive. Sanders was no gardener, but this type of plant looked like someone had experimented on it over the course of a lot of years, and taken great pains to breed and grow the thing just right. It was an excellent barrier.

Except...

He stopped in front of a gaping, black hole. The sides were ragged, as if someone had chopped their way through with an axe. Through the opening, big enough for two to walk abreast, Sanders could make out more thick forest. Hard boot prints made a rough path through the center of the gap. More than a few people had come and gone, as evidenced by the ripping away of grass and moss, leaving small and bare stones in the wake.

"This isn't good," Tobias said into the din.

The rest of the men spread out, facing outwards. All had swords in their hands.

"The Shadow people must know about this," Tomous said.

"If they do, they aren't doing a whole helluva lot to guard it," Sanders growled, tempted to go inside and find the Captain. If he did that, though, his men would follow, leaving half their party exposed to whatever was going on in and around the city. It would also put them all in one group, which would make them easy to take down.

Sanders had to keep his position on the outside to keep the way clear for the Captain and Shanti to emerge. That was the best way to play this.

He also had to kill every Graygual and Inkna he could find. If they kept flooding the city, they'd dominate in number. That was a no-win situation.

"Okay." Sanders turned around and faced the deep night. Only splinters of moonlight pierced the canopy above. "Let's head back. We have work to do."

Sanders turned around, the rest falling in line silently. Their footfall barely made a sound, and the swish of their clothes deadened quickly.

If they hadn't been followed, all that would've meant something.

"Three *Sarshers*," Burson said in a quiet warning. "Twenty paces out. I am now masking your minds. They know you are here though."

"How many others?" Sanders asked, dodging behind a tree. The rest of the men peeled away to the sides, hiding behind the nearest trunk.

"I can only feel those with mind-power. I'm not like Shanti," Burson whispered.

The creak of wood announced that someone had drawn a bow.

"Can you keep their power off of us so we can cut them down?" Sanders asked as he peered around his tree. Another bow creaked in the quiet forest.

"Yes. But I cannot kill them."

"They can't fight, anyway—if they run, though…" Tobias let the comment linger.

"Then we kill them before they reach the city—" Sanders cut off as a footfall fell in wet mud. Leaves rustled. Another boot sloshed in the darkness. Then more.

Not training those Inkna how to fight was a blessing

for Sanders' side.

A black shape moved into the space between two trees about ten paces away. Two more joined it, directly behind. A beam of moonlight splashed down on the leader, revealing dark hair and a high-necked tunic. A sword flashed at the man's side before he was nothing more than a dark shape on a darker background, hard to define.

Sanders glanced at the tree where Tobias waited patiently with a half-drawn bow in hand. Tobias was waiting for some sort of signal. Sanders pointed off to the left, then made an arc with his finger, telling Tobias to walk around the outside of the cluster and try to get behind. The moonlight was dim, but it had been enough—Tobias silently moved away.

Sanders turned the other way, but all he could see was Xavier. A moment's hesitation ended in Sanders trusting the kid. He wasn't great, but he was good. He could do it.

He waved his hand, drawing the kid's attention and giving him the same instruction, sending him the other way around. Xavier nodded. His footsteps were as silent as Tobias' had been.

The leading Graygual moved through speckled moonlight. He had ten at his back. Three more followed way behind, and though they were still in the darkness, Sanders bet those were the Inkna.

Sanders and his men were outnumbered. Grossly outnumbered if he took away Marc and Burson, the non-fighters. He could tell everyone to melt away into the darkness, to hide and then to run. With Burson to mask their minds, they could make it.

With the number of Graygual that had landed, though, they'd always be outnumbered. If they didn't make a statement, a hard, vicious statement, it would look like they were afraid.

Bullies thrived on fear. Might as well wave them on for a second attempt.

A boot splashed into an unseen puddle, less than ten paces away. Sanders' hand tightened on the hilt of his sword. Adrenaline spiked in his body and blood pounded in his ears with the nearness of the enemy.

He glanced behind him. Everyone had shifted to be able to see him. Waiting for the command. Ready to fight for their Captain and their cause.

He connected eyes with Burson. It was now or never—the call to fight was upon them.

Burson nodded slowly. He adjusted his body slightly. A bow edge stuck out from the tree.

Sanders turned with bent knees, crouching. He put his thumb up so everyone could see—*we fight!* Then an open hand took its place—*wait for my signal.*

The boot falls moved closer. The sound barely carried within the crypt of the trees. A silhouette came into sight, staring ahead, sword out. Creeping. Trying to be silent. More came behind, moving past Sanders, completely oblivious.

Sanders' hand was still raised. He did not move. His heart hammered in his ears.

More bodies moved past, working into the middle of Sanders' men. As the last was visible, Sanders made a fist with his hand and dropped it in a quick motion— *charge!*

He burst out toward the closest man, a silent shadow. His sword-thrust pierced soft flesh, stabbing a kidney. The man screamed. He fell before he knew he was dying. Sanders was on to the next, stabbing a knife into a man's neck before he could react to the scream. Sanders ripped the knife out, blocked a sword strike, and jabbed his knife in an eye. Liquid spattered his face. He pulled the knife out before thrusting his sword through his gut, just in case the Graygual thought he'd fight through his dying gurgle.

A bowstring rang through the night. Someone to Sanders' right screamed. Another arrow's release was followed by another scream.

Yells broke out as the Graygual realized what was happening. Black shapes sticking to dark patches filed out from the trees. Moonlight showed glimpses of shiny material, wet with rain, and occasionally a sword flashing, before more Graygual screamed. Sanders' men knew to attack silently.

Sanders ran at the next Graygual, stabbing through his back, making him arch before pushing the body to the side. As the scream died, he turned to the next, slashing with his sword before plunging his knife into a hard chest plate. It took a moment to yank the blade free.

He spun. The moonlight caught metal high in the air. A Graygual was descending on him. The sword swung toward Sanders' head.

With no time to block, but needing to be inside that sword strike, Sanders barreled into the man, knocking him to the ground. Mud flew out around them. Sanders stabbed the man's side with his knife as his opponent struggled, then slashed across his sword wrist.

The man bellowed, thrashing. Sanders stabbed again, and then once more, until the man weakened. Sanders rose to his feet, then feinted to one side as a blade barely missed him. Reacting, he caught the next sword strike with his own, then lunged forward, plunging his steel into the man.

Sanders looked for the next as the last dying scream wrenched the night. Muddy, or bloody—it was hard to tell in the low light—and winded, Sanders' men stood tall with swords in hand, waiting for the next strike. A quiet tally indicated they'd all made it, and they'd all fought, including Marc and Burson.

The former was the only one looking awestruck that he was still alive, however.

"Any wounds?" Sanders asked, looking behind him in case more came.

"I just need a few stitches, but I'm okay," Xavier said, shrugging off something that probably hurt a lot more than he was letting on, judging by the strain in his voice.

"You going to bleed out?" Sanders asked seriously, turning his attention back to the kid. Marc had already moved to Xavier's side.

"No. I'm okay," Xavier reiterated.

"Sounds like it stings a little," Tepson said, chuckling as he bent to the body closest.

"What about the Inkna?" Sanders asked.

It was Tobias who answered. "They were sitting ducks. Just waiting back there wringing their hands. They looked spooked."

"They could not access their mind-power. They have not trained for vulnerability," Burson said.

"This Graygual looks like he's got two slashes," Tepson said before looking at another body. "Hard to see, but looks like two over here, too."

"This one has only one," Tomous said, staring down at his feet. He held his sword with a tense body, still ready to take more vengeance.

"They are low ranking," Burson said as he looked

out past Sanders. "They have been following us since the city."

"Thanks for letting us know," Tobias said in a dry voice. "Really helpful."

"The outcome was better by keeping my silence," Burson said, starting to walk out of the area. "There were five possible outcomes. I hope I chose the best. There are always a great many outcomes with every decision on this island. I don't often get time to discuss the possibilities before the decision is upon us."

"Are we following him, sir?" Tepson asked Sanders.

"You can stay, but I would advise against it if you want to live," Burson called as he continued to walk.

"That answer your question?" Sanders quickly bent to clean his sword and knife on a Graygual uniform before briskly following Burson.

"What I don't get is," Tomous said in a low voice as they cut through the forest on the fastest route toward the city. "Why wasn't that hole guarded? Anyone could've found it. Anyone can still find it. You'd think whoever has used it would've been protecting it."

"The person who made that hole is a marked man, though," Marc said as he wrapped Xavier's forearm while they walked. "Leilius said that the Shadow people are really scary when their rules are broken. Anyone guarding that hole would probably be killed..."

"Or would at least be called in for questioning," Tobias said in a thoughtful tone. "Doesn't mean someone wasn't watching it, though. If I cut that hole, I'd want to know who knew about it. Then I'd want that person silenced before they went telling anyone else."

A chill worked up Sanders' back. The rest of the men fell silent, no doubt thinking along the same lines. Plenty of people had been horribly murdered recently and had their tongues cut out. Silenced.

As they walked through the trees, the branches closing in on them, the silence pressing down, Burson said, "And now we show that we are capable of beating large odds. We have sent a message. Now we will see what is done with that message."

CHAPTER 7

THE DAY DAWNED HAZY AND white. A low-lying fog shifted through the trees and skimmed the ground, making visibility minimal. Shanti stoked the fire, making it burn brighter, turning the mass of white around them a flickering, pale orange. She straightened her back and once again closed her eyes, sucking the essence from the natural life around her. Her *Gift* was completely rejuvenated, and with Cayan so close stronger than ever in this strange place, but her body still ached and burned. Her muscles had been taxed and her skin would take a while to heal. She recovered faster than others with the help of her *Gift* feeding off of the natural energy around it, always had, but healing wasn't an act of magic. It still took time.

"What's the plan for today?"

Shanti jumped as Cayan's deep voice broke the tranquil silence. She sighed as the spike of adrenaline subsided and waited for him to pull his dry tarp from the tree, place it across from her on the wet ground, and sit. He wiped the sleep from his puffy eyes but didn't pat down the raven-colored windstorm of hair sticking up at odd angles around his head.

With a grin, she indicated the rainwater she'd collected last night in his container. "Drink. It'll help clear away the sleep. I didn't realize you weren't a morning person…"

He grunted and reached for the container.

"I don't want to go far today," Shanti said, thinking about what lay ahead. "The salve I made last night is working fast on my wounds, but that animal gave me a couple nasty scrapes. I want a day to let it heal before I confront whatever the next nasty surprise might be."

"I didn't realize you had such a thorough understanding of healing." Cayan wiped his mouth as he lowered the empty container.

"All my people did to some degree. A fighter gets hurt—she needs to know the basics of healing. Nature gives us most things we need for that. Rohnan would've been able to make something much better, but I know enough to fix myself up."

He nodded and blinked down at the happily dancing fire. Flames crackled as they engulfed the wood. "And you make a warm fire."

Shanti huffed out a laugh. Cayan had had trouble getting a flame going last night, and when he did, it was a paltry thing. She'd tried to stoke it up when he wasn't looking, but the foundation of the fire had been laid poorly—it wasn't burning hot enough, and with bedtime close, it wasn't worth fixing. This morning she'd started from scratch, though. Much better.

"I have more experience in the wilds than you. I'm good at surviving."

"And here I thought I was better than you at everything."

"Imagine that," Shanti answered in a dry voice.

Cayan yawned and stretched out his arms. He scratched his chest and sighed, blinking a few times before widening his eyes. He glanced off to the side in a dopey, unfocused stare.

Shanti couldn't help a lopsided grin as she watched him slowly wake up, hunching in his seat like a child. It was hard to believe that this was the same man who would walk into the practice yard with a straight back and brawny shoulders and demand the attention of every hard, fighting man there. He was just so… cute when he first woke up. So… grumpy and dopey. It was obvious he'd always awoke in safety and comfort, never being startled out of a shivering sleep in the bushes in a strange land by a worrying sound. His warm fires and servants preparing breakfast had spoiled him and it showed.

"I could use some tea," he said, looking down at the fire.

Shanti let the grin blossom into a full smile at the

proof of her thought. "I'll collect some more herbs now that you're up."

He nodded and stared across at her. "So what do we do for the day?"

"Access your *Gift* and defend ourselves if we have to. We'll see if the Shadow people come knocking on our door."

"On our tree…" he corrected absently. His hand rubbed his stomach. "We need food. I'm hungry."

"Death's playground, Cayan, can you sit in silence for one moment? You're worse than a kid with all your demands."

A smile tweaked his lips. "Make me breakfast, woman. Do your job."

"Ah yes, these defined tasks your people are so fond of. The men flex while the women do all the work. What a treat to be a woman in your land."

"I can show you what it's like firsthand if you marry me." His blue eyes sparkled with the jest.

Shanti rolled her eyes as she moved his empty container out to a more open area to catch rainwater. At the moment all they had was a drizzle, but it'd probably pick up soon. Unfortunately.

"Speaking of which—" she heard.

Cayan unclasped her father's ring from around his neck and stood so he could move around the fire. Shanti moved her hair to the side so he could fasten it around her neck. "You should hang on to that. I'm not the rightful owner."

She ran her finger along the gold chain before touching the ring. Without warning, memories of laughing faces from home sprang up. She could remember so many times when they'd sat around a fire deep in another wood, just like she and Cayan were. It had always been easy and lighthearted, despite the hard training that would always follow. Team and family.

She smiled with the memory.

"What is it?" Cayan asked, watching her intently as he sat back down.

She didn't bother to shield, allowing him to catch her bittersweet mood at the memories. He'd get these and much more before long—hiding things wasn't an option when she accessed Cayan's sublevel of power.

"Just thinking of home," she admitted. "We had some good times when we trained. We were such a cohesive unit. Anyway." She wiped the thought away and focused on the present. "You can go check the snare I set last night. I'm sure it'll have something. I assume you know how to clean and skin an animal— that being a *man's* work, and all."

His dimples made an appearance as he stood. "I should be able to manage that, yes."

"Wonderful. I boiled the roots already. They're staying warm by the fire. So we're just waiting on you."

Shanti pointed to the starchy tubers laid out on a rock a small distance from the flame.

Cayan's smile burned brighter. "You make me feel like a novice."

"Because you are a novice. Chip-chop. Get moving."

"It's chop-chop," Cayan laughed as he moved away. "And yes, ma'am."

AFTER THEIR BREAKFAST, THEY MOVED back into the tree where they were completely sheltered from the dripping leaves and clinging wet of the fog. The heat from the fire gave them enough relief from the cold that they could remove their coats. When ready for the inevitable, they sat opposite each other. Their knees brushed in the confined space and their gazes locked.

They were completely shielded in anticipation of trying to open up and let the other in.

Shanti gave a nervous laugh. "This isn't a great way to start."

"I didn't think anything could be ten times more intimate than sex."

Shanti's brow furrowed. "Sharing your soul is what makes sex intimate. Otherwise it's just a pleasurable exercise."

"I'll take your word for it."

"Your women aren't much for talking?" Shanti

badgered, stalling.

"This isn't fair. I can't pick on you because of your past. But yes, some of them were. I was more interested in their breasts than how their day went, though."

Shanti smiled, then felt the familiar pang. Time for the first revealing: "I don't think I shared my soul with Romie. I thought I had, and I loved him very intensely, but... Knowing what I know now..."

"He didn't have as powerful of a *Gift,* though, right?" Cayan asked in a soft voice. "We cheated, when you really think about it. We stole each other's secrets; we didn't share them over years of getting to know each other. It's a forced intimacy, which is why we both resist it."

Shanti's smile was sad. "I *had* years, though. We didn't even scratch the surface. Rohnan knows more about me than Romie did, and I'd just as soon punch Rohnan as hug him."

Cayan's smile was slow. "Different situation. Romie was the product of young love. Adults share intimacy differently than kids do. Kids are all about first-times and secrets. Adults are jaded—they only realize intimacy is upon them after their soulmate somehow pries them open without their knowledge and learns all their secrets before they can defend against it."

"You sound wise."

Cayan laughed. "I do, don't I? Pretty good for

someone who is repeating everything secondhand."

Shanti shook her head and grudgingly let her shield down. She felt exposed, knowing what was coming. Raw, almost. Bare. "I've made the first move, which you can't feel because your shield is still up."

"I'm getting there. Don't rush me." Cayan's smile made those dimples stand out, but his eyes were wary. He'd been pushing for this, but now that it was upon them he wasn't as eager as he'd let on.

"So you proclaimed yourself Chosen?" Shanti asked patiently.

"After a fashion. I tried not to, but I don't think they'd encountered someone who wanted to enter without the glory of the title. Then that strange clearing messed with my power—I lost control and blasted them."

"With all your power?"

"Kind of. I felt it rising up and ran back out to the bay so I could release it. They caught the backlash."

"So, you tried to enter the trials without proclaiming yourself Chosen, then you left the trials, which is supposed to result in death, before scouring them with a painful release of power? No, they probably hadn't encountered anyone like you before. And after all that, they still waved you through?"

Cayan shrugged. "Mostly, yes. But they've paired us together. I agreed not to kill anyone or leave the trials only because if I didn't, you'd be disqualified. They tethered me to you to make me behave."

"Ah." Shanti sighed and shook her head. "We do nothing as it should be done."

"Of course not. I make rules, I don't follow them."

Shanti huffed out a laugh. The expression dwindled as she remembered her conversation with the woman in the clearing. "They said I don't have the power to make it through. That I'd die in here."

"They said I had the power, but without the control, I would die. I told them they were incorrect. It was nicer than telling them to go to hell."

"They can only grant one Chosen." Shanti threaded a lock of hair behind her ear.

"Fine. They can grant you Chosen."

"But what about you?" she asked softly.

"They'll either ignore me, or they'll attack and die as a result. They'd be stupid to attack, though, and before long they'll realize that. With the Graygual on their doorstep, and that nameless power gaining entry into the trials by breaking the rules—they'll want power on their side, and they know we have it. Only a fool would kill a potential ally in their hour of need. Judging by how they monitor their city, they aren't fools."

"And the sword?" she asked, knowing he spoke logic, and hoping the Shadow people employed it.

Cayan's brow furrowed as he glanced at his weapon,

lying at the edge of the space to be out of the way, but still within reach if someone approached their shelter. "What about it?"

"They let you keep it? They took mine—part of the rules."

His expression became a quizzical smile, with his mouth slightly twisted upwards but the brow furrow still in place. "A bit of an oversight on their part."

Shanti laughed. "Seems like it. Did you not wonder why I didn't use a sword on that animal?"

He shook his head, his smile slipping a little. "I didn't think about it. I arrived in that clearing after hearing the roars—all I saw was blood and a giant monster trapping you on the ground."

Cayan's eyes intensified. She felt his mental block lower until concern and a haunting fear bled out of him. Fear of losing her.

One of his shoulders ticked upwards in a small half-shrug. "Might as well do this now. You'll pick up all these emotions eventually, anyway."

It was definitely forced intimacy, and that's what made it so hard. If sex wouldn't completely complicate everything, she'd suggest trying to find their way into intimacy that way. It was hard to be guarded right after a great orgasm. Assuming he could inspire one.

Shanti's face heated at the moment his mind touched hers. Her desire and suddenly aching core flowed into his mind unhindered. The embarrassment at having been caught thinking about him leaked over shortly after. His eyes sparked with heat.

"Let's try that again," Shanti said hastily, pulling back and taking a deep breath. "Sorry, it's been a while. My mind wanders when in close proximity with the opposite sex." It was only a half-lie.

"Your hands can wander, too. Just let me know what you want to touch."

Clearly he knew it was a half-lie.

"Focus, please," Shanti berated.

"I am. And imagining…"

Shanti struck out. Her fist clipped off his chin, jerking him to the side, his reaction late because his mind had been in his pants. He laughed and put up his hands. "I submit."

The way he said it, low and raspy, had her fired up again. Had her imagining the fight they'd have before she *forced* him to submit, and then what that might yield.

"Damn it—" Shanti rubbed her temples. "This is hopeless. And I can't fight it out or I'll undo all the healing I've done so far. *Why* did I get strapped with the burden? Of all the people in our village, why did the Elders choose someone who would struggle every single step of the way—including stuff like this that should be so easy."

Cayan's smile dwindled. "That's the root of it, isn't it? You've always wondered *why you?*"

Shanti touched his mind with hers, expecting it when he pulled her in tight. Their *Gifts* entwined, and then wove into something even tighter. Shanti put out her hands. Cayan took them, his skin warm, his touch gentle. Their power delved deeper, merging to the point of pain or bliss—it was hard to define. The world started to dim, hazy at the corners. His heat, and his presence, created a warmth through her middle that spiked the simmer of spice and power. Their *Gifts* throbbed to the beat of the other's heart, pulsing within them.

It wasn't deep enough. This was what it was to mate powers, but she wasn't deep enough to reach that hold within him, which meant there were more levels to traverse. They were barely halfway, and to be effective, they needed to submit to each other totally.

Pausing, because she didn't want to go any deeper, and she didn't want him as far inside her mind as he already was, she said, "Yes, I've always wondered. Always. I was different from everyone else, starting at age five. My eyes are different, which is the physical reminder that my power is different. I could use nearly full power early. I chose a Chance that should've been a healer. I committed myself to a man my complete opposite without experimenting like fighters generally did, casting myself out further. I learned to fight differently. I tweaked things in a way I thought made more sense. I hated my position, I constantly caused problems… If there was ever a person *not* meant for a leadership role, given the task of saving her people, it's me. And don't get me started on the amount of times I messed up in the journey East."

"Those that don't follow the norm usually make the best leaders," Cayan said seriously. His thumb stroked hers. "Getting into trouble taught me how to stay out of it. It made you excellent at silent stalking. Your style, altered, made you the best fighter. Your Chance uses his skill in a way that elevates him above others. And naming a sibling—even though he isn't a blood brother, he's as good as—as sensitive as he is, makes for the most loyal, devoted guardian. All the things that set you apart made you ripe for the role you have. *That* is why you have it—because you aren't normal. You are exceptional."

Shanti felt tears well up from some place out of her childhood. Some place rough and painful; a place comprised of uncertainty and fear that constantly hounded her with thoughts of not being good enough. Of not being enough, period.

She hung her head, desperate to believe him.

He unthreaded a hand from hers and gently lifted her chin. His smile was supportive. "Take it from the master of uncertainty, *mesasha*. You are in the role you were meant for. And if you didn't second-guess yourself and always strive to be better because of it, you would've been dead a long time ago. It's the doubt that makes your mind agile. It is determination, love and loyalty to your people that makes you push on. Sanders is a hard bastard who thinks people are generally idiots, but he would follow you to the death. There is only one other person that has claimed that loyalty as a leader from him. All those men and boys would follow you, too. All the people you meet along the way that see something of you in themselves, broken and in pain, but pushing on, need you to focus on. To remind them that there is still a fight to fight, and there is still a victory to win. Believe in that, Shanti. Believe in it."

A tear rolled down her cheek. She nodded silently, not trusting her voice. His eyes drifted to her mouth, but he backed away. His hand fell back down to hers. "Now it's my turn, I guess. I think you unwillingly let me in a little deeper."

Shanti closed her eyes and felt his presence within her. It wasn't just in her mind anymore. It felt like he'd stepped into her body. The spiciness overcame her senses and the tingling warmth floated through her.

It was… pleasant. Comforting. Like a warm blanket and a trusted stuffed animal during a raging storm.

"I'm okay with this—the… presence. It's almost

peaceful," she marveled. She ran her hands over his arms, feeling the difference between the physical touch, and the mental. "Share your power with me."

"I can't access it." A brief note of strain entered his words. His *Gift* fluxed in the small space.

"No, not that power. The surface level power—the everyday-use *Gift*."

She felt his light-hearted humor well up. Immediately, his stress drifted away and tranquility filled them at the same time, easily rolling back and forth between one and the other. His power tumbled into her like a fluxing, tumultuous storm. The electricity of it energized her, sparking her *Gift*. The wildness, the raw abandon…

She felt a smile drift up her face as the glory of battles won raged through her. Sweat and blood and working in perfect harmony with those you've trained with all your life bolstered her. Besting the enemy. Obtaining victory.

Her *Gift* rose up then, overshadowing Cayan's. The crisp, clean smell of the first rain invaded her senses right before the crack of lightning rained down. Pure and sweet, she recognized this feeling as second-nature. It was the feeling of her power, fresh and light, agile and precise.

Cayan's hands lifted hers, feeling her *Gift* in its purity for the first time. He put their palms together, and rethreaded their fingers. The hold was tighter. His thumbs still stroked hers, but the touch was more intense somehow. Each run of his skin shocked into her core, invigorating. Taking part of her and holding it inside, as she did with him, and then feeding it back to her.

Everything started to spin. Round and round, her head felt dizzy. She leaned in, clutching onto his shoulders as he responded in the same way. Their powers played off each other, two parts of a storm merging into one mighty system. His thunder rolled, her lightning filled them with electricity. Their *Gifts* danced, circling each other.

She sank totally into him, then. Deep, deep to his core. She filled his body as he did hers. It was hard to tell where one ended and the other began. And still the power spun, circling them. Crashing onto them, and then *into* them. The power started to burn as the cover came off his deep well of power. It welled up, searing. Boiling their bones and pricking their skin.

Shanti gritted her teeth against the pain. It wasn't rising up in him and spilling over this time, it was rising through both of them at the same time. Climbing slowly. Building. Bubbling up.

"I can't do much more, Shanti," Cayan groaned. He pulled her closer, dragging her body into his lap and wrapping his arms around her, needing something to hold on to. Needing an anchor. She could feel that need as if it was her own.

Or maybe it was. It was impossible to say.

She clung onto him too, letting the power engulf them. Knowing, without understanding how, that they needed to let this happen. They needed to wait out the agony as the power filled every inch of them, cementing them into one plane where they could harvest the power and then work it.

Her wounds had ripped open when Cayan pulled at her, but that pain was nothing compared to the tearing, scorching power. It raked their insides and ate through their flesh like acid. Still the power built. Still it pooled.

Shanti squeezed her eyes shut and gritted her teeth, clutching Cayan's shoulders with clawed fingers. His fingers, in turn, dug into her.

With a flash that had Shanti screaming in agony, everything cleared. The blistering pain and slow build of something so destructive it should've given them terrors, melted. Shanti gasped in the sudden absence of torture. And then gasped a second time.

Like a field in spring, their merged powers melded together and blossomed. It flowered up, as peaceful and drifting as a light summer breeze. Soft heat rolled, and then built to ecstasy. Pure, balanced bliss sparkled between them. Cayan's great power had merged with their mated halves, and now it rolled from one to the other peacefully, tranquil and light.

Shanti felt a smile take over her face. She recognized part of the foundation as hers. The thing that had sparked and boiled at age five, and then became a part of her, made the base of this giant power. She also recognized the other power, sturdy and steadfast, like the roots of a great oak; Cayan was equally mixed in this blend. Their *Gifts* weren't just entwined, they'd been fused into one. The fizzing joy, hinting at aching pleasure, spread between them.

Before she could help herself, she grabbed Cayan's hair and yanked downward, tilting his face up toward her so she could look into the brilliant blue of his glowing eyes. Her lips met his, hot and needy. Wanting more of this. Wanting to feel *all* of it. All of him.

His hands slid up her chest and stripped away the material. Hers did the same, feeling his hot skin and cut muscles. Their kiss deepened as that spicy feeling returned, heightened now with the increased power. The euphoria took over her senses as his hot kisses trailed down her neck.

Needy hands stripped away the barrier of clothing between them. She rose up, her lips on his, the feel of him all she could focus on. She lowered herself back down. The breath rushed out of her lungs and her eyes fluttered as his heat pushed into her.

Everything outside of his touch disappeared. All she

could feel was him; his body inside hers; his hands on her skin; his sweet breath on her face; his power surging within her; his slow and deep rhythm. She held on tight, the pleasure aching through her body in a way that belabored her breathing. Higher and harder they climbed together until the eventual climax stole her breath, as sweet and pure as their merged power, and just as forceful and intense. Her limbs melted around him, draping across his body, shimmering with sweat. Her lips fell against his hot neck where his pulse reassured her that they were still alive, despite Xandre's best efforts so far.

Basking in the feeling of the moment, she almost didn't feel the presence stalking closer to their location.

CHAPTER 8

SHANTI JUMPED UP AND PAUSED for only a second as she saw the smears of blood coating Cayan. She looked down at her body, seeing her gashes opened and weeping. Cayan crawled out of the tree so he could fully stand, his eyes distant, focusing on the people creeping up to their tree.

"Five of them," Cayan said quietly, looking down at her once she'd joined him outside. A small knot formed in his brow as he scanned her wounds. "You can't fight like that."

"I've fought with worse." Shanti bent to her clothes but Cayan stopped her with a hand on her arm.

His eyes lost their focus again as he said, "There are five, but only two have the *Gift*."

Shanti followed his trail of power, marveling that it seemed like it was an extension of her own. They weren't pushing and pulling at each other, riding with one or carrying the other, they were just... a unit. She could *search* out one way and he the other, and they could feel through each other what lay out there. It was…

"Miraculous," Shanti breathed with a smile. "We have so much power, but it's not overpowering us at all. It's just a calm… oasis, flowing between us. So tranquil."

"Hey…" He brushed a thumb against her jaw. She felt his urgency, immediately clearing her mind and focusing on the problem. He turned for his own clothes. "Can you tell if they're Shadow or not?"

Shanti focused on the minds, the closest at about thirty paces out. A flash of intellect touched her and Cayan's merged *Gift*. It was nothing but a feather, but with the added power, she felt it easily. The newcomers weren't tracking, they were using the *Gift* to scout out her location.

"Six males," Shanti said quietly, analyzing the types of minds. The three non-*Gifted* seemed observant and cunning. They also seemed non-emotional. There was no thrill to sneak up on prey, no firing of intellect like she would expect in training, and no love for those around them. They didn't seem a tight unit with the others in their group. The *Gifted* seemed intent but slightly nervous.

This didn't smack of the Shadow people, but she barely knew them. Half of what she thought she knew might be based on tall tales she'd heard as a child. The simple fact was, those sneaking up on them could be anyone.

"I can't tell," she said softly, bending to her clothes again. Cayan stopped her for the second time, earning a scowl. He'd slipped on his clothes and sword while she was assessing what came their way.

"We don't need to fight, *mesasha,* not with the added power. There are only five—we can take them easily."

"What does that name—" Shanti shook her head, trying to focus past the pain from her wounds and the strange new power vying for her attention. "We can't kill them, Cayan, and we haven't had a chance to work with this power yet. I've been with my *Gift* so long using it is muscle memory. I could swat them mentally, only to have them drop dead."

"You can't kill any Shadow people. But Graygual and Inkna? They shouldn't be in here, anyway. And if their bodies are never found, what's the loss?"

Shanti squinted at Cayan, crouching near the opening of the tree, dead serious. She debated, chewing her lip. What he said made sense—what was the harm in ridding the world of rule-breakers? They couldn't be counted as part of the trials, so the trial rules shouldn't apply to them.

The problem was, *they* would be making those rules—Shanti and Cayan—and they were already bending enough rules as it was. If the Shadow people didn't find their reasoning solid, making it through the trials might be forfeit.

Shanti shook her head. "I can't risk it, Cayan."

He assessed her for a moment before nodding once. "Then here's the plan. Let me assess who they are. They're moving slow. Whatever they've found with that mental touch has them worried. I'll take a glance and report back. Then we'll decide what to do next. But until then, let those wounds air out. I shouldn't have…" He stood with a furrowed brow. "Just wait for me, and then we'll decide what's next."

Irritation welled up at him handing out orders like she was one of his army men. She swatted it down, though. He'd need to be taught that *working together* didn't mean one person assuming control, but that could wait until after this threat was stamped out.

He was right about the minds—they'd almost stopped. Fear emanated from the one that had touched her and Cayan's minds a moment ago. A Shadow person wouldn't be afraid—they'd know she would follow the rules. They wouldn't be concerned for their life.

Shanti gave the assenting nod before re-entering the tree and bending to her salve, stored in a pile of goop on a few large leaves. She scooped up the thick substance as she monitored Cayan's progress, moving around their tree and into dense foliage. Lathering the stinging concoction onto her wounds, she glanced at the available garments that might make a good bandage for if she had to fight, and also for when they had to move on from this location.

Cayan stopped halfway between her and the intruders. His mind stilled for a moment until, like a clap of thunder, his mind blasted out a warning. Graygual and Inkna, it had to be.

He started back toward her a moment later. As he entered the tree, he said, "Graygual. Three officers, two with three slashes, one with four. Three Inkna, one who seems like he's trying to convince the others to retreat. He was lagging back, whispering furiously, and motioning them back the way they came. The others didn't seem to favor his desires."

Shanti glanced up, holding the binding for her breasts. She paused in putting it on. "He read our power level and knows we can take them all out. We could give them a scare, send them running, but they'll just get reinforcements to overpower us." She blew out a breath. "They're probably wondering about the rumor of a colossal power. News of how many we killed must've reached them by now. I bet that Inkna has confirmed it. If we let them leave, we're giving them information."

"Information, and time in which to make use of it. While we're stuck in here for however long, they can bring over an entire army to take the whole island.

What's to stop them?"

"Fuck," Shanti swore. "We need to nearly kill them and somehow leave them for the Shadow to find. I wish they'd given us rope."

"We can make rope out of vines, or didn't your people teach you anything?" Cayan's humor filtered through her mind, though it didn't show on his face.

"Is it worth sneaking up on them?" Shanti asked seriously, letting the binding material fall to her side. "We'll have to use our *Gift,* anyway, with the Inkna. If we accidentally kill one, we might as well kill them all."

"I'll let you lead."

"Amazing. And here I thought I'd have to teach you a lesson in sharing command…"

"You can still try. I don't mind embarrassing you."

Shanti ignored him as she painfully sat down and closed her eyes. What was once effortless, now would require all her concentration to keep the power contained.

"Do you need my contact?" Cayan asked, still crouched in the mouth of the tree opening.

"No. I have too much power as it is. I don't even think that would help. I'm still deeply embedded in your mind without skin contact. Whatever we did with the power, it seems permanent. At least while we're close." Shanti felt the minds, creeping toward them. Slowly, though. Wary. Fear still pumped out of the one who was hanging back the farthest. He knew what awaited them.

She hated to disappoint.

She clutched the minds of the Inkna. Screams sounded through the trees, agonized and panic-stricken. "Shit." Shanti eased back, reducing the amount of power until the screams turned into loud whimpering. She eased back even more, finally sighing into the silence. Both Inkna were writhing on the ground still, but whatever sounds they made were too low and far away to hear.

"The three are—" Shanti started.

"I got it," Cayan cut her off, ducking away from the tree.

"—running at us," she finished for the sake of completion.

She sucked the energy from the Inkna, who were trying to break free from her hold but completely powerless to do so, and focused on the Graygual. She *slapped* their minds with a soft hand, testing the waters.

A shriek sounded through the still air. It sounded almost as if she'd startled someone.

She tried it again with more force. This time, a wail echoed through the trees as Cayan reached them. She applied more pressure to the Graygual minds, trying to make them sluggish to make Cayan's job easier.

Instead, one of the minds winked out.

"*Flak!*" she swore, pulling back yet again. It almost seemed like she'd have to re-learn using the *Gift* all over again at the absolute worst time to do so.

Concern wavered into her mind from Cayan. A moment later, she felt his relief.

Hopefully that meant the Graygual was still alive and just unconscious.

Another mind winked out, and then the third, Cayan physically knocking them out. It was definitely safer that way.

Shanti continued to monitor Cayan's progress until he appeared outside the tree carrying two Graygual, one over each shoulder. He dropped them in a heap and left again, coming back with two more, and then a final trip to grab the last. She ducked out of the tree with parts of her body on fire from the salve.

Cayan glanced at her wounds before looking out at the trees. "I can grab the vines."

Shanti smirked. "You have no idea which ones will work for this. The ones I bet you're thinking of, which are close, will turn brittle when they dry and break. I'll go."

Cayan's gaze returned to her body. "Not that I don't enjoy a naked woman wandering around in full daylight, but it's cold. You should cover up."

"Oh, *now* you want me to put on clothes. I needed to air out when there was fighting, but when it comes time to gather, suddenly I'd better cover up..." She squinted her eyes at him in faux-suspicious anger.

Cayan's lips tweaked up at the corner, a smile he obviously couldn't help. "It is your job, after all. As the woman..."

He glanced back down at the Graygual before seriousness crept back in. His grin faded.

Shanti looked over the fallen men. "I could use some more wrapping—help me with this officer. Usually the higher officers keep clean—maybe he has an undershirt or something I can rip up. I don't much care if he catches the 'flu."

Cayan bent to the man immediately, stripping him and holding up the shirt under his uniform. He smelled it and paused. "It smells clean, but..."

"It's been against his skin. Let's see if any of these others dressed in layers..."

It turned out one did, another of the officers. His undershirt was over a vest-type piece of fabric. Shanti got to work making the necessary wrapping for her wounds. Neither she, nor Cayan, bothered to redress the men. If the cold killed them, then Shanti was still in the clear, and there would be a few less Graygual and Inkna to worry about.

"I wonder how long it'll take the Shadow people to come calling," Cayan asked as Shanti readied to go scout for some durable vine.

She shrugged, glancing out through the shifting sheets of white fog. "They've been pretty good at keeping an eye on me. I can't imagine it'll be long. I just hope they pass on the knowledge that the Graygual have breached their trials. Otherwise, I'll be ripping all the scabs again when they come to attack."

"Let's hope," Cayan said in a low tone as he bent to stir the fire. "Time will tell."

PORTOLMOUS SAT AT HIS DESK at the back of the city looking over the reports from the docks. The setting sun shone through the window, turning the room orange. The man had been in the trials for two days and one night now. He had found the woman yesterday, Portolmous had been told. He hadn't heard much else, though.

The waiting continued.

He drummed his fingers on his desk as he read the numbers from the docks.

A huge influx of Graygual had arrived and were being dispersed around the island. Many had gone to the city and Trespasser Village, but some went beyond to areas not inhabited. Based on the report that lay in front of him, patterns in the ways they had spread out were organized. The news did not bode well for what might be to come.

He glanced up as his brother entered the doorway. The man, younger by two years, leaned against the wall nonchalantly. It was impossible to tell if he came bearing news, or for social reasons. Sonson had never been one to stand on ceremony.

Portolmous looked back down at his report. "You should do something about that hair, brother," he said. "The vibrant red is bad enough, but letting it run wild around your head disagrees with your face."

Sonson cracked a smile and sauntered further in. "I'm the best swordsman on the island—the ladies don't even notice the hair. They just wonder what else I'm the best at."

"Then I do not envy them their inevitable disappointment."

Sonson barked out laughter. He sat in a chair facing Portolmous. "Thought I might pop in and fill you in on the trials."

Portolmous clasped his hands on the desk and looked up at his brother. "I would ask for good news, but in this situation, I don't think that's possible."

"Why? Because someone might be making it through the trials and that will throw our world into upheaval? Or because someone is dead within the trials and the signs indicate we will be lost if we don't find this foretold, powerful Chosen soon?"

"Both. Have you noticed all the Graygual and

Inkna?"

The humor melted off Sonson's face. Seriousness erased the twinkle in his bright, blue eyes. He crossed an ankle over his knee. "I've heard rumors that someone extremely powerful is crouching in the darkness. Anyone who gets close goes missing. So far that has not included our people, but then we haven't really gone to investigate."

"We have, actually. I sent someone this morning to look into the corpses displayed around the Trespasser Village. I expect him back any time to report on his findings."

"And the talk of a hole in the thorn barrier around the trials?"

Portolmous nodded, indicating that was part of the scouting objective. They should've looked into it long before now, but the emergence of the woman, and then the man, had pushed back the need. A terrified hopeful-Chosen hiding in a spot where *Therma* was dimmed was not uncommon. Portolmous and Sonson often let them hide for a few days, staving off the inevitable. With everything else going on, though, and that rumor, they could no longer deny a possible escape. A hopeful-Chosen had gone missing, and signs pointed to a breach in the wall.

"What of the trials?" Portolmous asked.

"Well, first thing—I would've appreciated a note

that you let in a man with power to shake the whole island. One that doesn't care about the Chosen title and therefore doesn't have the proper respect for our ban on killing. With his fighting prowess, he could bring down a great many of my force before we stopped him."

A ghost of a smile graced Portolmous' lips. Sonson's fighting prowess often went to his head. He was the best in everything, had been since his teenage years, and rarely met a challenger without a yawn. It had stunted him in many ways.

It had taken Portolmous one glance to realize the skill in the foreign man would easily rival his brother. The difference between the two men, however, was that the foreign man's outlook remained open. His mind was fast and agile, and if Portolmous had to guess, he'd say the man sought out opponents that challenged him, trying to better himself. The foreign man would continue to get better, whereas Sonson had plateaued.

If only Portolmous had been able to see his brother's face when he realized he was no longer the best. What a wonderful expression that must've been.

"Ah, I see," Sonson said with a sour face and contrasting twinkling eyes. "A joke. I didn't know your personality allowed such things."

"Only when you're the punchline, brother."

Sonson's eyes ticked upwards in a facial shrug. "Anyway, he helped the woman take down the beast. I'm not sure she would've done it on her own. While she caused it serious injury, and almost had him, she was in a precarious situation when the man showed up with his sword…"

Portolmous winced. "The sword, yes. The meeting with him was… unusual. Taking the weapon completely slipped my mind."

Sonson gave him a level stare. "Of all the men who could've made that detail slip your mind…" Sonson shook his head. "Anyway, he got in a hack or two, and she continued her assault, until the beast ran off."

"And how is Bonzi now?"

Sonson's face turned grim. "Lost a lot of blood. His mate won't leave his side and his brood whine all day. He's cut up pretty bad."

A weight settled in the pit of Portolmous' stomach. They imported that breed of animal from a distant land based on the suggestion of a *Seer* who had passed through looking for someone she called the Wanderer. The woman had been so persuasive Portolmous not only did as she said, but he brought in a mate for the beast as well.

At first it was a perilous venture, with the animal trying to kill everyone in its sight. Fires and spears had been needed constantly to keep it confined. Soon, though, the animal showed signs of domesticating. Now, after working with him and his mate, Yari, for a few years, he was almost as docile with his handlers as a big dog.

A very big dog.

Unleashed on strangers, though, the animal wreaked havoc. He was usually the last thing a hopeful-Chosen saw.

"She has completed another milestone, then, the only one to do so," Portolmous surmised.

Sonson let his foot fall back down. "She had help, though."

"We'll discuss that later. What else? Anything?"

Sonson's eyebrows fell, but he didn't push. Instead, he said, "She and the man have *Joined*."

Portolmous leaned forward in a rush. "How do you know?"

"An hour ago we wandered close to the tree in which she and the man are taking shelter. She's letting her wounds knit together, and I am letting her. We've never pushed the hopeful-Chosen. I want her to take the trials at her own pace."

Portolmous impatiently gestured his brother on. He knew their tactics.

Sonson continued, "She felt us coming, as you would expect. I felt her mind assessing ours. It was the man that came closer, though—probably to keep her from aggravating her wounds. He asked our intention in utter fearlessness, with an express warning that he and the woman would defend themselves mentally, but did not have a firm control of their power level. *Their* power. I could feel the rolling, surging, raw strength of this man's *Therma,* and I could feel her essence below it. I've met enough people to know when two individuals are *Joined*—just never with so much power. He informed us that we would be in peril, and to proceed with caution. It sounded as though he was running the show…"

Portolmous couldn't help a grin at his brother's scowl. "He might have the same self-confidence as you." He'd wanted to keep that statement a lighthearted joke, but his unease bled through.

From what Portolmous had heard, that man wasn't from a great nation. He had some solid fighters, and was rumored to have a prosperous, well-run city, but it was fairly small. Yet, the man assumed control of those around him as a birthright. He had no fear, and no pompous ego—he conducted himself with unfailing confidence and an unfaltering leadership style. It would be easy to assume he was a great battle commander. The Inkna seemed to think he was, based on his previous exploits.

A man like that would have no problem assuming control of the Shadow Warriors. What's more, Portolmous had every assumption he'd do the job well, managing not to ostracize the already-established leadership.

These were more indications that their peaceful life was coming to an end. War was upon them. They needed to know who to trust.

Sonson gave him a flat stare before saying, "We gave a truce. We were then told of a team of three Graygual and two Inkna that attacked them earlier today."

Portolmous stood as a warning tingling began in the base of his spine. He crossed to the window and looked out over the wild lands, his mind racing. "They entered the trials and sought the woman?"

"Yes. They were not killed—the woman didn't know if that would violate our laws. They were rendered unconscious and tied with vine."

Portolmous turned back to stare at his brother. "I hoped you righted that wrong…"

"Yes, they are now dead, of course. Xandre's interest in the violet-eyed girl is real, and he must know she's here. If he's not the one hiding somewhere on this island, with his minions running interference, it's one of his trusted few. If he captures her, only a fool would assume he'll then leave the island. No, he'll set his sights on us, next. Or maybe at the same time. Time has run out."

"She has to make it through the trials, though. The scriptures are very clear on that point."

Sonson stood and braced himself in the middle of

the room. His eyes flashed and the fiery color of his hair seemed to glow with the light running through it. "I've never cared about those old records. Titles handed down by scriptures mean nothing, not when war is upon us. I am in charge of the warriors on this island, and I am telling you that the power that man and woman possess is myth incarnate. They now yield one of the mightiest mental weapons this land has ever seen. I will not kill them—not when they can assist us."

"She or they *must* complete the trials," Portolmous pushed.

Sonson opened his mouth to interject, but was stopped by a guard striding in with harried steps. "Sirs," he said, offering a slight bow. "Startess went missing. We believe he was on the outskirts of the Trespasser Village before he disappeared. And we've found a hole in the barrier."

CHAPTER 9

MARC SLINKED INTO THE COMMON room at the entertainment hall after midday, right behind Sanders. They'd been on the island for barely four days, and in that time had killed about forty Graygual and a handful of Inkna. Whether it was from meeting the enemy randomly in the city and killing them before they could kill, or venturing outside the city walls and seeking them out, Sanders was determined to cut down as many as possible.

Unknowingly, he had also been determined to stir the pot and add some heat. Menace now boiled between the Graygual and Sanders' men. Marc could see it in the enemy's eyes and in their stance. Shadow people hung around each of the groups, ready with swords and glowing eyes that meant they were accessing their mental power. Things were getting dicey.

Most of Marc's group sat in the far corner, sipping ale and chatting while scanning the crowd. Ruisa stood in the opposite far corner, removed from the others, wearing baggy clothes and a surly expression. Even as

Marc noticed her, a man dressed in velvet approached her with a drunken swagger and a suggestive movement.

That was the problem with being a young and pretty woman in a place with horny, drunk men. She was always being bothered.

The first couple of times she was propositioned, Marc and the other guys had immediately come to her aid, shoving the stranger away forcefully. Soon, though, they learned that she could deal with the strangers as Shanti might've. She glared at them, waited a moment to see if they would go away then gave them a sound uppercut followed by a kick. She did this in front of Shadow people without batting an eye.

The Shadow people never even stepped in her direction, let alone tried to punish her for violence in their city. Apparently, as far as they were concerned, a young woman defending herself was only exercising her right. It was sound logic.

The man in velvet staggered toward Ruisa, hands out at breast level. When he was close enough, she brushed his arms to the side and punched him on the nose. Even from across the room, Marc heard the *crack*. The man hollered, covering his face as he fell against the wall, turning away from her. Blood dripped from under his hands and down his chin. She'd broken his nose.

"That's my girl," Sanders said in approval as he

worked through the laughing, jeering men to his army. As he passed a card table, a woman turned and smiled in a sultry way. Her hand reached out to pet Sanders across the chest.

Marc reacted. He grabbed the woman's wrist, wrenched it away, and shook until the palm lay flat. He stopped to analyze her fingers—no needles, no fake tips, and no other means of destruction. This woman had simply wanted to touch the man rumored to be vicious and utterly fearless.

Women liked the strangest things.

"Sorry," Marc mumbled, releasing her hand.

"Ow." The woman's pouty mouth turned down into a scowl. Her large breasts heaved, nearly falling out of the bodice that barely confined them. Marc gulped as she shook out her hand and turned back to the table.

Ruisa gave Marc a nod from across the room.

"The girl beats up men, and you beat up women, huh?" Sanders asked with a flat voice.

"The women in here are more dangerous than the men," Marc mumbled with a red face.

Marc had become just as paranoid as Ruisa, mostly because she badgered him into it. So far, it had been for nothing. They'd seen plenty of knives, had arrows shot at them a couple times, and been attacked with swords, but no poison.

Ruisa said it was coming, though. Marc wondered if

she just wanted a reason to belong.

"Where's Xavier and Etherlan?" Sanders asked as he and Marc reached the collection of worn, round tables gathered into a cluster in the corner.

Rohnan stood against the wall, his eyes scanning the room. His mind-power had saved them more than a few times, identifying those who wished them harm before they made a move. Burson sat close to him, looking at the ceiling.

"Etherlan was getting it on with a girl last night," Rachie said with a grin. "She was really loud."

"Yes, boy, but where is he *now?*" Sanders growled. He didn't bother to sit down.

Rachie shrugged. "I left early because they started up again."

Sanders' face closed down into an unreadable mask, which wasn't a relief from the flash of anger he'd shown a moment ago. It meant something worse than his temper might be happening. "You haven't seen him since?"

Rachie's smile melted off his face. "No, sir."

"And Xavier?" Sanders asked in a gruff voice. His body flexed and his hand moved to his sword.

"In the back." Tobias threw a thumb in the direction behind him.

The door opened at the far end of the room, and stayed open. Marc turned to look, and then gaped when five Shadow people dressed in light green walked in with measured, even strides. All were men except for a woman bringing up the rear, letting the door close in her wake. Two men went right, staying close to the wall, and two left. They spread out so they were spaced evenly within the room, one stopping only ten paces from where Marc stood. The woman wandered to the middle, walking slowly, scanning the crowd with focused eyes.

Rohnan sucked in a breath. At that moment, the woman's gaze swung their way, hitting Rohnan with a flat stare.

Something happened. Marc couldn't see anything, but he could feel it. Like a charge of electricity, Marc's small hairs stood on end. Rohnan went rigid and his eyes widened. The woman didn't move.

Burson smiled like a madman. "This bodes well."

"What?" Marc asked as he noticed movement from Ruisa out of his peripheral vision.

She nearly sprinted across the floor, pushed between two huge men, knocked over a beer, and snatched a woman's hand out of the air.

"Hey!" the woman screeched, a curvy thing with breasts completely exposed while leaning way over Xavier. The hand that wasn't captured by Ruisa was inside Xavier's breeches, slowly stroking the hard thing she'd found there. The movement didn't stop as she stared up at Ruisa.

"Xavier!" Ruisa yelled into the hypnotized man's face.

Xavier blinked slowly through hooded eyes. Ruisa's voice didn't disengage his stare from those perfect breasts. The woman's hand picked up speed.

Marc shifted uncomfortably, his pants a bit tight in the groin, as Ruisa looked closer at the woman's fingers. She snatched something out of the woman's lap.

"What you think you doing, *feassa?*" the woman spat as she yanked her hand out of Xavier's pants.

Ruisa glanced at a small pouch as the woman started to struggle out of Ruisa's grasp. Xavier finally looked up, anger written plainly across his face. "What the fuck, Ruisa?"

"She means him harm—take her," Rohnan said, his gaze turning toward the scuffle.

Sanders was moving before anyone else. He walked to the back table in quick, even strides. One of the large men Ruisa had knocked into had stood up. His angry, red face turned at Sanders' progress.

"Dat your girl, man?" the man barked in a gruff voice. He reached out to grab Sanders by the shirtfront.

Sanders grabbed the hand, ripped it around, and shoved it behind the man's back. His other hand flew in, striking the man's throat then glancing across his eyes. He released the man, gave two solid uppercuts to the midsection, and continued on as if he hadn't been interrupted.

The man sputtered out wheezing coughs, falling against his table. Glasses fell over. Beer gushed across the wood surface and splattered to the floor.

A Shadow person intersected Sanders next.

"I got no beef with you, blondie, but that is my man over there, and I will be getting him."

The Shadow glanced up at the woman in the center of the room. He received a nod before he said to Sanders, "Proceed."

Sanders brushed by the Shadow. He reached Xavier and hauled him up by an upper arm. "Pull up your pants, son."

Red-faced, Xavier still stared at Ruisa as he followed instructions.

"What's going on here?" Sanders barked, grabbing the struggling, spitting woman by the hair and yanking her away from Ruisa.

Ruisa held out a small leather pouch. The woman snatched at it, but Ruisa pulled back before the grab could land.

"Looks like sugar," Ruisa said, giving the bag a tiny shake. "She had Xavier suck her finger before dipping it into the pouch. She then returned the hand to put her finger into his mouth. I don't know what it is yet, but it's not good. Only a whore or a drunk woman would stroke a guy in public while exposing herself, and this sober woman wasn't looking for money. She was distracting him so she could feed him whatever is in this pouch. He was too stupid to catch on."

The closest Shadow man looked behind him at the beautiful woman in the center of the room. She nodded. He turned back and took hold of the woman's upper arm as he said, "I will take her."

Sanders let go, but as the Shadow man reached for the pouch, Sanders stepped in the way. "We need to look at that. We need to make sure we can counteract it. You fellers don't do a bang-up job of policing this place."

The man's hard hazel eyes stared at Sanders. Sanders stared right back, unflinching. Finally the man said, "I will give you a sample, but I need to evaluate the contents to judge a punishment."

Ruisa dug in her pocket for a little pouch. She poured some of the crystalized material in, which did look a lot like sugar, and then handed the pouch over.

"I had to!" the woman cried. Tears welled up in her eyes before overflowing down her face. Black from her eye-paint ran down her cheeks. "I got no choice. I work or I get killed. I got no choice!"

Someone near the door got up, drawing the notice of the closest Shadow man to the door. As the stranger tried to exit, the Shadow man went running to intercept.

It had just become clear who this woman was working for. Ruisa stared in that direction with squinted, contemplating eyes.

"I got no choice!" the woman wailed again as the Shadow man yanked her to the side.

"A pretty woman like you always has choices," the man said in a low drum as he dragged her toward the exit. "She just has to be courageous enough to make them."

"Let's go," Sanders barked, shoving Xavier in front of him. "We need to find Etherlan. Good work, Ruisa. You've probably just saved this numb-nuts' life."

Face burning red, Xavier passed through the space with a lowered head. The others got up from the table and filed out, expressions solemn, except for Burson who was smiling.

Rohnan filed out in front of Marc, and as he passed the Shadow Woman, slowed. His gaze rested on hers. "Do you come with the violet-eyed woman?" she asked.

It took Marc a moment to realize she was speaking in Marc's home language—not the common trader language so popular here. Marc had no idea why, since that wasn't Rohnan's language of origin.

"She is my sister," Rohnan said softly as he stopped walking.

"And you believe she is the *Chulan*."

"As do you." Rohnan turned to the woman. Marc stopped with him, curiosity getting the better of him. Everyone else streamed around them. "I did not think I would ever find my *Gift's* mate."

A smile touched the woman's lips. "We are rare. As is one with full power. I am Salange."

"My name is Rohnan, and I think we are rarer still."

The woman nodded slightly. "Yes. But it is a big land, and I have explored little. Maybe there is a whole army of us."

"I have traveled much, and if that is the case, I have not heard it."

"Not that it would matter," Marc heard himself saying. The woman's gaze flashed toward his. Violence crept into her stare. Marc bowed in on himself and stared at the ground. "Sorry—it's just that, an army of you types would really only help sick, right? I mean, against warriors, what would you do? Point out who was the most determined? That wouldn't help."

"Marc, let's go!" Sanders barked from the exit.

"I must leave. It is perilous for us here," Rohnan said to the woman.

"Your sister has now hit three milestones none before her has reached. The big man has *Joined* with her. They are being viewed as a single unit, rather than two individuals. I thought you should know." The woman smiled. "You are happy for her. But your faith remains as it was. She is wise to keep you close."

"I am wise to keep her close. You'll see why before the end."

"A terrible menace lurks on this island. Watch yourself," the woman said in a whisper. "We've now had two disappearances, and the Graygual are starting to walk with a swagger. They are working on outnumbering us. Soon, they will."

"Push the Chosen," Rohnan said in a plea. "She doubts. The Captain will bolster her, but if she's allowed time to reflect, she'll deteriorate. Push her. Hit her with constant milestones. Challenge her and she will shine. We are running out of time."

The woman nodded as Rohnan stared at her.

Marc shifted uncomfortably, but his way was blocked by a couple of huge guys with beer stains down their shirts. Finally, Rohnan said, "I'll see you again."

She gave him a slight smile with glittering eyes. Her face took on a light hue of red before she dropped her gaze.

Marc had seen that look before. Women did that when someone they liked told them they were pretty.

Rohnan turned and walked toward the door. She glanced at him leaving for a brief moment before she went back to scanning.

"So… she was pretty," Marc prodded in a quiet voice as they made their way through the room.

"Extremely. And full of love and light. She likes to laugh often. The trials in the city are scaring her, though. She fears she will lose loved ones. And meeting us, she knows that is correct."

"Don't tell her you know all that. That'll just scare her away."

"She has same *Gift* I do. *The* same *Gift* I do. She knows what I know. And I know what she knows. There can be no hiding between us. I now know how people feel between me."

"Around you, you mean. She also speaks my language a little better than you do. Maybe you can ask for help…"

"You are helping. I will ask her for other things."

"Good God. A bit forward," Marc mumbled. He left the entertainment room behind Rohnan and stopped dead.

Sanders and his men had fanned out in front of the establishment, staring across the small road at a line of lounging Graygual. A few were officers, standing straight and tall, but the rest were what Shanti called grunts—low-life men with sneers and crinkled uniforms. Three Shadow people dotted the way, standing in the middle of the road, staring out at nothing.

"Can't they send more Shadow people?" Gracas asked quietly. He had a knife in his hand.

"No Inkna. Three Shadow is probably plenty.

They'll bring everyone to their knees." Sanders pushed Xavier in front of him. "Let's go—this is just a scare tactic. As soon as we're out of eyesight of the Shadow, though, kill at will."

Graygual eyes followed them as they moved down the road. Knives came out. More than one tapped a dagger against their belt as they watched Sanders' crew passing. One man drew a sword, sneering at Rachie, who was closest to him.

"They are waiting for the same thing," Rohnan said in a low tone. His hand rested on his sword. "The Shadow people know this. Their wariness has increased tenfold. Their people are starting to disappear."

"That woman say anything about the Captain and Shanti?" Sanders asked, staring at a Graygual who had stepped forward.

"The temperature is turned up, and the forces are converging. The Chosen will emerge through the fires of need." Burson took a knife out of his belt. "But war will come to those most loyal before it scours the island. We are in for a bloody few days."

"A few blessed days of silence, and he comes back with that," Sanders growled.

They turned into the alley and saw one, lone Shadow person in front of their building. The Graygual hadn't followed, probably knowing Shadow lurked in here, too.

Sanders stopped beside the door to the building containing their many rooms. He watched the guys going inside—making sure everyone was there, probably.

Rohnan stopped beside the Shadow woman. "This is not a good place for you. We'll be followed shortly, and then you will be outnumbered."

She glanced at Rohnan. Her eyebrows dipped in confusion for a moment, before a grin tweaked her lips. "I recognize your power. I cannot say it is a welcome one, but very useful." She stepped away from the wall. "I will take your warning. Be careful when leaving."

As the woman walked away, Tobias said, "Why are you scaring away the help? We could use one more fighter with mind-power."

"He has saved her life, and further entrenched us with their people," Burson said as he passed into the building. "I can't keep up with the choices before us now. Luckily, the Wanderer has brought only the noble to her cause so far. It is making my job much easier."

"You're making mine harder," Sanders said. "I think it's time we paid a visit to the higher-up in this place. Shit's about to get real. First, though, we need to find Etherlan."

THEY TOOK THE STAIRS QUICKLY and spread out around

the door to Rachie's room. Sanders walked to the front as Rachie reached for the handle. Without a word, Sanders grabbed the kid by the shirt and ripped him to the side. He stepped up, his hand on the handle, cold to the touch. Tobias, next to him, took out a throwing knife. Rohnan, on the other side, did as well.

Sanders stared at Rohnan for a moment. "Feel anyone?" he asked softly.

Rohnan shook his head. "But there are many barriers in the way. It hinders my ability."

Sanders rushed into the room. A cluster of black shirts greeted him, spread out and mostly lounging. Sanders threw his knife before peeling off to the side. A knife clattered against the wall behind him as Sanders rolled to a stop behind a chair. A quick blast of power scorched his mind before it stopped just as quickly.

Tobias and Rohnan ran into the room, each getting off a knife throw before ducking behind furniture. Xavier was next, doing the same. Someone grunted at the far end of the wall.

"Three are still up," Rohnan said in a loud voice.

Sanders popped up from his location and threw another knife. It struck a Graygual in the face, his own knife falling uselessly to the ground. Two more stood beside, one in plain black staring at the fallen at his feet, while the other yanked out his sword.

Sanders rushed forward, but Rohnan beat him to it.

Rohnan feinted, drawing the sword strike. He tapped the blade wide with his sword before slashing down. Blood spattered as Sanders reached the Inkna, thrusting his sword through the man's middle. The Inkna shrieked, having done nothing to protect himself once Burson had rendered his mind-power useless. The Graygual tried to strike Rohnan one more time, but the strength had gone out of him as he sank to the ground.

Sanders scanned the room for any other enemy. All he saw were two legs sticking out of a room to the right.

"Ruisa!" Sanders barked, making his way to that room immediately.

Etherlan lay on the ground with his face in a chamber pot. Vomit covered the floor and filled the bowl. Sanders felt small hands push his aside. He stepped away, allowing Ruisa into the room. She bent to Etherlan, placing two fingers on the side of his neck.

"He's got a pulse!" she said with hope etching every word. "It's weak, but it's there. Quick! Move him to the bed."

Ruisa ran toward the door as Sanders hauled the limp, pale man up. As he moved Etherlan to the bed, as gently as possible, he heard Ruisa demanding, "Where did that woman come from?"

"How should I know?" Rachie answered.

"What did she look like?"

Sanders tuned them out as Rohnan came over to

help with Etherlan. They laid him down. Rohnan felt his pulse and peered at his eyes. He sniffed Etherlan's breath. "He doesn't have long. It's a miracle he's still with us, but he's a fighter. He's clinging."

"He'll be fine," Ruisa said, pushing between them. She put a bag on the bed and jerked it open. "Rohnan, I need blood."

Rohnan lifted Etherlan's sleeve and stuck him with a knife. A small amount of blood welled up. Etherlan showed no sign of feeling the nick.

Ruisa collected the blood into a vial. As it slid down the side of the glass tube, she pulled out another bottle. Unscrewing the lid, she took out the dropper and squeezed some of its fluid onto the blood. As she shook it, the blood turned a black-blue color.

"She was an amateur, thank God." Ruisa dug through her pouch and extracted another vial with a blue lid, filled with a red liquid. "Either that, or she didn't want him to die right away. She dosed him with a pretty common rodent poison it looks like. There is a lot of it around this city. It's weak in case it's accidentally ingested. She probably gave it to him in water, and diluted it enough that his stomach would purge it before it could really take hold."

"Why would she poison him if she didn't want to kill him?" Tobias asked from the end of the bed.

"She might've liked him. He was attractive and great

in bed, or so I've heard."

"How have you heard that—older men is your thing, huh?" Rachie blurted suspiciously. Sanders thought it sounded like a case of sour grapes.

"Women talk," someone muttered. "Beware a scorned woman, too. The whole city will think you've got a tiny dick."

"Think? Or know?" Tobias didn't accompany the automatic quip with a laugh or even a smirk. His eyes were rooted to Ruisa's efforts.

"He was also kind and treated women with utmost respect, me included, even though no one thought I belonged here," Ruisa elaborated. "A lot of the women in this city have haunted eyes—they're property. The visitors, I mean. Meeting a man that treats you like a person… it'll give you second thoughts about trying to kill that man. Women's hearts speak louder than their minds in most cases."

"Then why go through with it at all?" Tobias asked.

"Because not going through with it would mean certain death. If she was anything more than an amateur, she gave him this out." Ruisa dribbled liquid into Etherlan's mouth. "And as I think about it, she must be, because a foolish woman would think Etherlan would protect her. If she'd asked, he would've tried. All of you would."

"Of course we would," Sanders said, his own gaze

rooted to his fallen man.

"A smart woman would know that that would be impossible. The whole city is ganging up on you guys, starting with the Graygual handing out money to people like her master. How could someone protect her when he couldn't even protect himself?" Etherlan coughed, his body's reflex to the liquid trying to work down the wrong pipe. Ruisa fed him more. "Plus, her changing sides would just bring more animosity. She'd become a target. No, she must've let him off easy. That's the only thing that makes sense."

"Women are too complicated," Leilius said from the corner.

"When we don't have dicks to distract us, we have the freedom to use our brain." Ruisa stood.

"So when do you start working for our side?" Gracas asked. "When do you start showing us that you aren't an amateur?"

"Gracas," Sanders barked, throwing a pointed glare at the boy to shut him up.

"I already have. You'll see my efforts in another day's time," Ruisa said in a smug tone. "I have breasts, too. They distract men just as well as this woman's. With Rohnan charming ladies and men ogling breasts, no one notices what the silly little lady's hands are doing, do they?"

Sanders quirked an eyebrow at Rohnan. Rohnan

said, "You left her in my care. I decided what the best use of our time was. Daniels agreed."

"And I would give the order again," Daniels said in a haughty tone, his gaze on Etherlan. No one wanted to lose a man, especially when the odds were so stacked up against them. "She had an extremely insightful, well-thought-out plan. The Captain was right in bringing her."

Sanders looked at the straight-faced girl, that smugness she must've felt not displayed. "Why wait?"

"If poison works quickly, people immediately look for the distributor. They go over who the victim had talked to, what he had done, what he ate—it takes a lot of effort to hide from that scrutiny. Time it to strike after a few days' time, and the traces are mostly gone. Also, the damage is done. They're infected before they can defend themselves. So, tomorrow, we will see a lot of sick people. If everything goes as planned…"

"Let's hope so," Sanders said, glancing out the window. "We are losing traction as more people flood this city. At this point, the Shadow people are sitting in a sinking ship."

CHAPTER 10

"LET'S STOP HERE FOR THE night," Shanti said with a sigh as she dropped her pack of garments rolled within a tarp.

Cayan stopped and looked back at the small area she indicated with a thick hood of branches over it. He glanced around them, picking out defensive capabilities. A small rock ledge stood behind Shanti's chosen shelter with thick trees lining it. If someone came from that side, they'd be hard pressed to get through the trees without making a lot of noise. In front and to the sides was the normal forest, with ground sodden with rain and green grasses dotted with large trunks. Visibility would be minimal if someone crept toward them, but that problem would exist in most places.

She was already setting up the tarp, not waiting for him to give his approval, and unlike with his men he felt no need to reclaim control or authority. Of course, he had no authority here. He was her support in this endeavor, and he had never felt that he had control over this woman. Even when he forced her to follow his commands, she did it because she chose to. When that desire ceased, she did as she pleased.

A large part of him respected her more for it.

Cayan put down his pack and helped her secure the tarp over the top of the shelter. He then laid the other tarp under, creating an area big enough for the two of them to lay in order to keep dry. They'd need to sleep close to each other, sharing both space and body heat.

"Food?" he asked as she laid out the fire equipment.

"We have the rabbit we didn't eat earlier. If we just scrape up some root vegetables, we should be fine. It seems like we've walked miles today, I'd rather relax then eat."

"I'll go get some root vegetables." As he left, she flashed him a thankful smile.

He wandered into the wood, listening while searching for the vegetables she'd been pointing out on their walk. This part of the forest was a dead-spot for their *Gifts,* so they'd have to listen for sounds of any stalkers creeping up on them. So far, they'd seen no one all day. Cayan figured they were probably letting Shanti heal—making a sport out of her—but time was always on his mind. The Graygual were getting ready to strike.

He bent to dig a carrot-like root out of the ground, hearing the soft rustle of an animal in the near distance. The rustle sounded again, and then a third time. An animal foraging for food, he'd bet his life on it.

And, in truth, he was.

He finished yanking the root out of the ground and moved on to another. When he had enough, he landed back at the camp, marveling at the welcoming fire Shanti had started.

"I don't know how you get them started so easily with all this wet." He sat down next to her, feeling the hum of her body so close. Their power gave a small surge at the proximity.

"Practice," she said, coaxing the flame higher. "It didn't rain nearly as much where I grew up, but we were close to the ocean. Everything had a dampness to it."

They sat in silence for a moment as the crackling of the fire grew louder and flame reached higher. Cayan said, "When do you think the next trial will come?"

She sighed and looked out at the trees. "Any time. I think they must let the candidates move at their own pace, but we were walking today. That probably says to them I am ready to keep going."

"What do you think is next?" Cayan watched the flame dance as she braced her elbows on her knees.

"They know we have a lot of power, and they didn't push when you warned them of it, so they probably know hitting us with that will take planning. They've tried to sneak up on me already, and they'd sent a strange monster-type animal after me. What's left but fighting?"

"Archery? Knife fighting?"

Shanti laughed. "Well, I don't have anything but knives, so knife-fighting is a definite. I'll just have to dodge the arrows."

"How do I factor into this?" Cayan shifted away from a rock. His knee touched and then stayed connected to hers for a brief moment. Electricity surged between them, tingling his base. She shifted, cutting off the contact. Running, as per usual.

It was as maddening as it was exciting.

"They bring more fighters, that's how. They've seen how you move. Not fight, no, but a good fighter can tell a lot by how people move. They'll prepare for it."

The light in the sky dwindled as Shanti started peeling the vegetables with her knife. The crackling of the fire and the slow slide of her knife competed with the soft dripping of water onto the tarp above them.

"Without you, I'd be cold and miserable this whole trip. And hungry. I could get by in here, but not easily." Cayan picked up the other vegetable and took out his knife.

"Without me, you'd be warm in your house tucked away in your city."

"Waiting for death."

"We are all waiting for death, Cayan," Shanti said in a soft tone. "It is how long we have before the inevitable that makes the difference."

"And how long is that?"

She shrugged. "The Elders only know."

AFTER EATING AND SPENDING A few moments quietly listening to the soft sounds of the forest, they moved further into the shelter. Shanti set out Cayan's unused garments, providing a small amount of comfort, and lay down facing the fire. Cayan moved in behind her, pushing up against her back and closing his eyes as he breathed in her scent, feminine and floral.

"How are your wounds?" he asked as electricity jumped from her body to his. His body stirred at the contact. He ran his hand up her thigh and over her hip before dipping it into her coat and resting on the warm skin of her waist.

"Healing. They don't hurt as much, and they've scabbed over now, so not as prone to infection, but they'll break open with the first battle." She removed his hand.

"Are we going to pretend we didn't make love?" Cayan asked as he trailed his lips across her neck. She shivered at the contact. A small sigh escaped her lips. He slid his hand over her hip again, unable to stop himself from touching her.

"No. In the heat of the moment, it felt right, but I don't want to get involved, Cayan. I can't afford to love again. I can't afford to let people get that close, because I can't stand losing any more loved ones."

"We're already that close. The Honor Guard, Sanders—all of us are already that close to you. We're your family now. The thing between you and me—we both feel it. Why not express it?"

"Because that makes it real," she said with a tremor in her voice. She flung his hand away, resorting to violence to drown out her pain and uncertainty. She closed down her shields, trying to shut him out, but their connection was deeper than that now. Whatever they'd done, they'd combined their *Gifts* and merged parts of themselves. Closing down the mind didn't stop the feeling from leaking from one to the other. It also didn't stop the aching desire.

He could let her run again, as she always seemed to do, or he could match her violence, and force her to submit. Neither would be permanent, but each would make a statement; both of his intent and her resolve.

It took a split second to make the decision.

He backed up and then pulled her shoulder toward him with a heavy hand, forcing her to roll his way. She winced, rolling on her wounds, but her eyes showed fire before they were lost to shadow. She jabbed him with an uppercut, forcing the breath from his lungs. He caught that hand. The next punch was hindered by her position, but when it hit the base of his neck, he choked.

Wheezing, he rolled onto her, as much to stop her hurting him as anything.

Pinning her upper body, and holding her hands with his own, he said, "No more running."

He expected a head-butt. Instead, her thighs slid up the outside of his as a slow burn sparkled her fire-lit eyes. He kissed her, a hard, bruising kiss. She matched it angrily. When she opened her mouth, he filled it, tasting her, but not slowing down. Not letting her fear catch up with her desire.

He let go of her wrists and pulled open her jacket. He slid his hands underneath her shirt and felt that smooth, hot skin. Her legs tightened around him. The kiss became harder, more needy.

He stripped her as she ripped clothes from him, movement difficult in such a small space, but actions firm and rough. When he entered her, she didn't hide her moan of pleasure. He took to her hard, giving her what she needed, matching her fight to overcome the memories of her past and those she lost. And also to claim her, because she was his. This was it. With their power, and their actions—he was done chasing.

His explosion matched hers. Then, his kisses softened. His movements slowed. His mood shifted.

What had started fierce and wild became slow and deep, but just as intense. Her hands shook as they snaked around his middle, palms splayed on his back. A tear flowed down her cheek in the firelight as she looked up at him.

"What does *mesasha* mean, Cayan?" she asked in a quiet tone as she accepted this new slow, deep movement.

"It is a term my grandmother used for my grandfather in her home language. It means heavenly beloved. In essence, it means there is only one. For me, you are that one."

He barely saw her nod as her arms moved from around his middle to around his shoulders. "I hate that you've forced me into this," she whispered.

"I know. But it was inevitable."

"I'll torture you for it," Shanti said as another tear rolled down her cheek. "I'm a hard woman to love, Cayan. People close to me seem to end up dead. I chew people up and then my duty spits them out."

"*Shhh*," he silenced her with his lips. Her whole body shook as she clung to him. "I'm as much in this as you are. I'd still be by your side if I hated you—and that place would be infinitely more perilous."

Her lips curled into a smile. "This will take time for me. I feel like I'm betraying another. But... *Heaven's Gates,* Cayan, you feel good."

"The Elders are in heaven?" Cayan asked, moving faster, feeling the build.

"No. We believe the Elders exist within the blanket

of stars, looking down on their children and helping point the way. But I heard Rachie say Heaven's Gates, once. It stuck."

"Hmm," Cayan said, losing the ability for words. Shanti did too, straining into him in the way she had recently strained to get away. When their explosion came again they entwined in each other's limbs, sharing heat and completely open. Their *Gifts* surged and flowed, despite the forest's limitations. It blossomed out from them, the foundation solid and unbreakable, the power as beautiful as it was terrifying.

In the aftermath they lay together, him curled around her with their clothes draped on top, sharing warmth. Come the morning, she'd probably try to run again, but they would both know it'd be in vain.

SHANTI STARTLED AWAKE. CAYAN'S WARMTH coated her back, his breath rising and falling in sleep. She listened. The soft patter of drops splashed on the tarp above. The fire, having died to a soft glow, only made a couple of light crackles. Leaves rustled in the falling rain, but otherwise all was quiet.

Shanti knew better than to close her eyes again. She'd been hunted for more than a year, and before that, trained in the harsh conditions her people conjured up. When her body awoke with a start like this, there was always a reason.

She sat up, wincing as pain lanced her leg and side. She moved out of the shelter so she could stand straight, shivering immediately with the cold.

"What is it?" Cayan asked quietly.

A light fog sifted between the trees, glowing white where the moonlight hit it. The deep black of the shadows contrasted, making depth perception and visibility nearly impossible. Her eyes were no good to her.

Her eyelids drifted closed and she centered her mind, letting the world around her soak into her awareness. A light breeze brushed against her skin, bringing with it the damp cold. The sound of raindrops fell away, ignored so she could focus on the small sounds lingering behind and between the definable.

She heard it. A soft crunch, then silence. A tiny slide came next, barely noticeable. Her small hairs stood on end, feeling something moving out there. Feeling an awareness creeping closer. Animal or human, they were both dangerous—especially with the animals in these woods.

She spun to her clothing, pulling them on hastily but making sure she made no sound. Cayan stood quickly, doing the same. She armed herself with what she had, then picked up the coil of vines. Loose rocks went into each pocket padded with wet leaves so they wouldn't make a sound. She loaded Cayan's pockets the same way. The extra weight was unfortunate, but they might be useful.

With a hand to his large shoulder, she applied just enough pressure to get him to bend toward her. He prepared for a kiss. She rolled her eyes and nudged his chin away so she could get her lips near his ear and whisper, "There's something out there. If it's an animal, we'll probably do enough to scare it away with loud noises. We'll need to stay upwind of it though, in case running would be best. If human, they are experts at stalking. I doubt Rohnan could be quieter. We'll distract them with the rocks before bursting down on them, either killing them, or..." She bit her lip and backed away. She had no idea what to do in that situation. Bonk them on the head? Say, "Gotcha!" and expect everyone to put their weapons down? Her shrug was probably lost to the dark, as was the nod she could feel him make.

Their merged *Gifts* were proving beneficial in these trials.

She started off to the right as fast as possible, still making no sound. Cayan stayed right behind her, trusting her judgment, and equally silent. They circled around until their scent was behind the faint sounds coming from fifteen paces away.

Suddenly, the sounds stopped.

Shanti and Cayan stopped, too.

The rain faded into the background again. Nothingness filled in the space in its wake. No movement. No sound.

It couldn't be an animal. She would hear snuffing if it had caught wind of something. Usually only a deer would stay still this long, and the sounds she'd heard were not from hooves.

It was human.

The question became, was it Inkna or Shadow? Either way might be death.

She let a thrill of fear alert Cayan to what she suspected. She felt a soft hand on her shoulder, and then he pulled away, walking ahead of her. She watched him for a moment, his large form somehow graceful in its stealth, not moving like a man with that much bulk should. He would get behind as she came in from the side. Smart.

She wished she had her sword.

Another faint footfall came from their prey. She didn't hear Cayan at all.

Keeping her breath even and deep, to keep her brain rich in oxygen, she waited until she felt a thrill of anticipation—Cayan was in position.

Balanced and patient, she stepped forward. With the fog and darkness, visibility was down to about four paces in any direction. Trunks loomed and then edged into sight. Branches made strange shapes in the fog until she could identify them. Jagged rocks, unseen, pressed against the soles of her shoes. Slowly, methodically, she closed in until those tiny movements, careful but vague, sounded just beyond her.

Movement assaulted her perception, raising goosebumps along her body and trying to amp up her heart's rhythm. A few people, not just one, moved in the night. Creeping. Stalking. Intending to catch their prey unaware.

A twig snapped. Sound halted.

Cayan's presence loomed off to Shanti's right. Stationary.

Anticipation started to rise in both her and Cayan.

She heard the sound of skin grazing fabric, she was sure of it. Which meant someone was lifting an arm or turning a neck.

A warning blast came from Cayan as she felt it herself. Suddenly, the night was action.

Someone rushed directly at her through the wall of black. A sword caught the moonlight, high in the air. She ducked around a tree as it fell, barely getting out of the way. She ran around the tree, sensing someone else coming her way. A sword clashed near Cayan.

She stepped in with quick hands, catching someone running by. Blonde hair streaked by, barely visible, but black camouflaged the body. Shanti swung her arm toward the chest, squishing against breast—had to be

Shadow. *Don't kill!*

With her knife, she lightly jabbed the person in the neck, only enough to break skin. With an intake of breath, the person dropped. Shanti's heart beat wildly in her chest, fearing she'd jabbed too hard, until she saw the woman kneeling. Out of the fight.

Her inner sirens went off. She ducked and moved as a blade swung past her head. She turned and struck out with the handle of her knife. The body moved to the side easily and countered. Her fingers locked around his wrist as she turned, yanking him with her. She pummeled him in the stomach with the hilts of her knives before bending and jabbing the inside of his thigh. As he dropped down to one knee she spun away and met Cayan.

"Oh. You didn't knock them out?" He glanced down at the woman on her knee. "That won't make me popular."

"How many did you have?" she asked, stepping away from the two she'd taken down with an imaginary kill.

"Just the one. I saw you with the man but figured you had it."

"We expected to amuse you." The woman stood and wiped at her neck.

"Amuse us?" Shanti asked in confusion.

"Ambush, she means." The man stood too, coming

forward until he stood in a patch of glowing moonlight. He glanced up at the sky and then in the direction Cayan came from. A foot was sticking out of a shadow, toe pointed at the sky.

"Shall we go back to your fire? We can see each other better and Patross can wake up. I don't want to have to carry him back." The man gestured Shanti toward her shelter.

"I guess." She stepped to the side, wary that her attackers now wanted to have a chat and pretend they were friends. Cayan stepped between her and the man, obviously thinking the same thing. It was impossible to say when the trials began and ended. They could easily be getting her to let down her guard so they could try something else.

When they got back to the shelter, Shanti stoked the fire with Cayan standing over her. His body was relaxed, but his readiness for an attack was evident with the way his hand stayed on his sword and his weight on the balls of his feet.

"The fight is done," the man said, sitting down on the wet ground before the fire. The woman joined him, sitting cross-legged and staring across at Shanti.

As the flame leapt, eating the new fuel, light began to dance across the features of those sitting in front of her. The man was slight of frame, lending to his quickness and agility, with light brown hair and sharp cheekbones. The woman had dirty blonde hair and calculating eyes. Neither seemed to mind that their butt was wet and would soon be cold.

"You are violet-eyed girl?" the woman asked, her gaze spearing Shanti's.

"Yes. A large release of power at five years old burned my irises." Shanti sat on her tarp. Cayan sat beside her.

The woman's sharp gaze drifted to Cayan. "And you are mate?"

"No," Shanti said, a little too quickly. "He's the Captain and leader of the Westwood Lands. His men are currently housed in your city."

"Power mate, I mean," the woman clarified.

Thankfully the darkness hid Shanti's blush. "Yes. He's my power's mate, yes."

That gaze moved back to Shanti, watching in silence for a moment as the man said, "Excuse us—where are our manners? I am Baos, and this is Jessta. We often lead trainings for stalking others unseen. Tell me: how were you able to spot us?"

"She has run from Graygual from west to east, Baos. Use your head," Jessta said, eyes back on Cayan. "How you find this man? Why he pledge to you?"

"She is our best hope of defeating the Graygual," Cayan said easily. "When I recognized that, I joined her cause."

"But you lead army?" Jessta pushed.

"It is his army and he leads it," Shanti answered, shifting to try and ease off her wounds. The scabs pulled at her skin, ripped in some places and oozed into the bandage.

"You have big army? Many friend-army?" Jessta asked.

"Is this an interview to see what you can gain from merging with us, or a means to decide if killing us will increase the threat to your lands?" Cayan asked. His voice was even and diplomatic, but an edge sharpened his words.

Baos must've heard it, because he grimaced. "Please bear with Jessta—she is very direct. And yes, this is an interview of sorts, as well as part of your trial. We've never actually given it before. No one has made it past our attack in the darkness, so an exchange of words has never been necessary—we knocked them out instead of sitting by their fire."

"So someone has made it this far?" Shanti inquired.

A smile ghosted Baos' lips. "Not in the way you have. We have not killed them, but they have not succeeded through the trials. It sounds monstrous, letting hopefuls keep their hope alive while they continue through the trials, but they are always good practice. And since they seek something from us, we feel justified in getting something from them."

"No argument there," Shanti said, adding a log to the climbing flames.

"I have a small army compared to the Graygual—easily overrun," Cayan answered. "I have many allies, each with their own armies. Together we are a decent force, but we don't have any mind-workers. Without Shanti, and you, we would be easily taken down. I have a lot of power, but I don't know its use, and I wouldn't be nearly enough."

"Your men well-trained. Very loyal." Jessta shifted her gaze to Shanti. "You need him for army, he need you for *Therma*. But he not here for us, he here for you. Why you here for us when you have his army already?"

"Because this is my duty. Following your rules, making it through the trials, and merging my people with our distant kin has been put on my shoulders since a very young age. It's why I survived the last Graygual battle. My duty was to run like a coward—to escape death. To let all my people die so I could live. Here I am, doing what I'm supposed to do."

"To run is no coward. To stay and die is coward," Jessta said, her gaze boring into Shanti as the light danced up her severe face. "Die is easier. Hurt less. You live in fires of underworld now, yes? You in pain, you hurt—" Jessta balled her fists up near her chest to accent her words. "But you no dead yet. To live with that pain—" she shook her head and blew out a noisy breath.

"That hard. Too hard for many. Might break me. But here you are. Is necessary, your journey. You can survive us. You have him," she nodded to Cayan, "We should brought more tonight, to make harder, but rules say three." She shrugged. "We bring three."

"Did you hear us?" Baos asked.

"Felt you, more like," Shanti said, thinking back. "When you're hunted, as Jessta alluded to, you learn a sixth sense. Usually it's my *Gift* that picks it up, but my body is in tune with what's out there even when my *Gift* isn't available."

They heard footsteps through the trees. Jessta looked behind her as their third member trudged into the ring of light from the fire with his hand on his temple. A dribble of blood made a track down his neck. Jessta turned to Baos with a smile. "I glad I choose girl."

Baos laughed and stood, prompting Jessta to stand with him. He looked down on Cayan, "Your men have saved a few of ours. They are clear what side they are on, look after each other, and are loyal to you. This is inspiring. It shows good leadership, and proof of good leadership was a requirement. I was hesitant about the two of you working together in this—it smacked of favoritism, allowing it. But one of the trials has been met by you, Cayan. Solely by you. Some have been met solely by Shanti. And many you are beating together. We always wondered what kind of person could possibly fulfill all the requirements... and now we know. *Joining* made you one entity—bonded you in *Therma*. Now we know."

"A hidie-ho might have been nice," Jessta said, shaking her head. "All the old parchment, and the rules, and all this. Nothing ever mention two candidates. We not plan for two. Bad joke."

Baos turned toward the man still holding his head. "Let's go and let them get back to sleep. They have another day tomorrow."

"We all have another day tomorrow," the third man said, glancing at Cayan and then Shanti. "Watch yourself in here. The Graygual army has grown. And you are not immune."

"It is you that are not immune. From me." Shanti folded her hands in her lap. "I have always been the target. And so has everyone in my wake."

"The entire land is target, violet-eyed girl. You are the hope that we do not succumb." Jessta nodded and walked out of the firelight. Baos winked before following. The third man wasn't far behind.

"Well. Another one down." Cayan pushed back into the shelter. "We'd best get an early start. I heard panic in their words. The Graygual are getting ready to make their move."

A thrill went through Shanti. "They'll move all their people in place, and then they'll strike. The Shadow seem to be preparing to resist their rule, which is good for us."

"Yes. But that might not matter, depending on the numbers."

"Killjoy." Shanti pushed back and lay down, snuggling into Cayan's body. His arm came around her and pulled her in tight.

He said, "How are your wounds now?"

"I'll need to change the bandages tomorrow, but I'm used to the ache."

Shivers let her mind drift, thinking about what would come. The Shadow had tried to sneak up on her twice, once in daylight, once at night. They'd tried a beast, they'd spoken to her, and they'd forced her to live in the wild. Now they would most likely hit her with a few battles, and a few things involving her *Gift*. All that she could survive. Those were things she excelled at.

Her worries consisted of the trials she couldn't see—like the leadership, or whatever else they were looking for. For those she had to trust to the Elder's guidance, and hope it was enough. That, and that her body would last before infection found its way into her wounds.

CHAPTER II

PORTOLMOUS WALKED THROUGH THE SQUARE on the way
to the Shadow Lord's office to discuss various events
taking place in the city. With the Graygual gathering at
alarming rates, the city needed to make some serious
decisions and prepare for the inevitable.

As he walked, preoccupied, he noticed someone col-
laspe in a group of black-clad men.

A Graygual tripped and skidded to his knees. Rather
than getting right up, though, he stayed down for a
moment. His hand drifted to his stomach and he let out
a loud moan. Another Graygual kicked the downed
man with a boot, asking a harsh question. The man on
the ground shook his head and tried to climb to his feet,
but staggered again. Another loud moan carried across
the square.

"Another," one of the guards said, standing at the
end of the trader stalls lining the large declaration
platform at the head of the square.

Portolmous turned to his man, a younger guard
new to the post—one of the many taken from training

to police the growing restlessness within the city. "What was that?"

"We've seen this all over the city today. Graygual and Inkna are faltering like that. It looks like a malady of some kind, but so far it's only affecting those two groups and two nobles. Nasty nobles, at that. But then, the Graygual really only keep to themselves, so someone probably brought something over and they are now spreading it around."

"Is it serious?" Portolmous asked as the man on the ground vomited. His army gathered around, none of them reaching down to help.

"Yes. I've not heard of anyone surviving it."

Portolmous looked at his guard in surprise. "Surviving? You mean this is killing them?"

"Yes, sir. Dropping them just like this."

"Poison, then."

The guard crinkled his eyebrows. "Could be, but those affected are spread out all over. They don't really keep the same company. I mean… they do, but I've heard mutterings that only a few have even been in the same room lately. The rest are on different schedules."

It was Portolmous' turn to crinkle his eyebrows as he moved on. He thought of the known poison-workers in the city, all of them sneaky, all looking for monetary gain. The Graygual had been reported as the biggest employers, aiming their assault at the contingent from the Westwood Lands.

So far, all had failed. The young woman with them had saved at least three so far, one of them from the brink of death. She appeared to be a healer, which had surprised many. When they'd first come, many of the Shadow people had thought the Westwood Isles men had brought a pretty, young woman to share. If that wasn't bad enough, they segregated her from the group when in public, making her stand to one side when the rest of the men sat and ate or drank.

As Portolmous left the square, he understood exactly what was going on. The Captain had come prepared, and had chosen someone no one would suspect to do the secretive, dirty work. Those men trusted her with their lives. They'd given her freedom to come and go where she would, while the rest were given commands as usual. It spoke highly of their unity and organization, especially since many in the mainland didn't allow females into their military units.

The Westwood Isles men continued to surprise him. The young woman was thinning the enemy's herd, and not a moment too soon.

CHAPTER 12

CAYAN AND SHANTI SET OUT early the next day once Shanti had changed her bandages and applied more salve. They headed north, aiming towards the city, hoping to get this leg of their journey over with. As the sun peered through the clouds now and again, Shanti turned up her face to catch the warmth.

"I missed this," she said with a smile, holding onto Cayan's sleeve so she could close her eyes while still moving. "It rains so often in this place, it's no wonder everyone is so pale."

"Your home had more sun?"

"Oh yes. Lots of fog, especially during the sum-mer—it rolled in off the ocean—but the spring and fall were beautiful."

"Yet you always complain about the heat in my city."

Shanti could hear the smile in Cayan's voice. She opened her eyes and enjoyed the lush green of their surroundings. "We had sun, but it wasn't the blistering kind."

"Ah."

They stepped through two trees close together. Their *Gifts* unfurled like a tongue from a serpent. It blossomed and flowed, plucking out and offering up small animal minds as it *searched.*

Shanti stopped dead as it rolled over a host of human minds, laying in wait.

Cayan dove behind the trees, dragging her with him, as a blast of power rocked into her mind. She slammed down her shields at the same time Cayan did, but not before she felt activity as the enemy rose up to attack.

"Shadow?" Cayan asked, jumping to a crouch and ripping out his sword.

"No!" Shanti snatched two knives, left her pack, and dodged to the other side of the tree, throwing her knife. It stuck into a Graygual neck, off-center. Despite the error, the man fell, clutching at the handle. Shanti ducked back at the sound of a bowstring being loosed. An arrow flew past.

"Let your power loose, Cayan!" she yelled, opening up and immediately fighting the barrage of power that battered her mind.

Cayan stepped around the tree, threw a knife and ducked back in as two arrows whizzed by. He gave Shanti a glance before his shields dropped. Shock waves of intense power boomed from him, heading toward the horde of Graygual and Inkna. The counterattack stopped the Inkna assault, having them ducking behind their mental shields quickly. Shrieks and grunts sounded, men now unprotected as the Inkna focused solely on protecting themselves.

Shanti sprinted toward the three nearest Graygual, hunkered on the ground holding their chests or heads. Another blast of power surged from Cayan. Shanti slashed through a neck, stooped to grab her knife from the neck of the Graygual, and stabbed another in the eye.

She felt the build of power as more than twenty Inkna merged together. A man in white stood upright before a single shot of fire pierced through Cayan's attack. Shanti's power was freed up with the merge she and Cayan had created, and more powerful for it. With her mind she worked within that tight weave, unraveling and redirecting, freeing Cayan up from defense.

His next blast of power pushed out as he ran into the clearing, sword swinging, movements so fast they almost blurred. Shanti stabbed her knife through a cranium as she dodged between the cringing men. She targeted the mind of the head Inkna and *blasted* into it, shaking his merge. As Cayan's powerful blasts fell she worked within them, *slashing* and *stabbing*, then *wrestling* with the other minds as she did the same with her knives.

Voices screamed around her. She dodged the feeble swing of a sword as the merged mind slashed at her. She shielded for a moment so she could smash her foot into a Graygual's face, breaking his nose. She tossed her knife up, grabbed it by the tip of the blade, and threw, hitting a Graygual in the back as he advanced on Cayan.

"Stop your power and take some of the men down, Cayan," she yelled, stabbing a Graygual chest before bending to grab another's head and wrench. His neck snapped. She scooped up his sword, hefted it twice, getting the feel for the weight, as Cayan's power fell away.

With a burst of single-minded focus, he whirled into the enemy, blocking and cutting people down as if they were tied together and unable to move. They were just too slow and less skilled than him. It showed.

The Inkna mind was back, hammering at her shield. She blocked a Graygual sword strike before turning to combat another thrust. She *stabbed* out with her mind, pushing back the mental assault while she physically stabbed the Graygual through the belly. As he fell she summoned all the power at her disposal, a huge undercurrent of her and Cayan's combined strength, and *thrust* at the head Inkna mind in the merge.

Horrified, terrorized screams erupted as the Inkna minds fractured. The white-shirted Master Executioner crumpled to the ground, his brain turned to pulp. The others withered in agony and confusion, barely alive. Shanti summoned another surge of power, gathered it up, and *TORE* through the minds that still remained. Her power *raked*, *clawed* and *chewed* through the intellects. The screams rose in pitch before one by one they fell silent as the Inkna died.

Wasting no time, Shanti whirled between two Graygual, slashing the chest of one, feinting, and stabbing the thigh of the other. The second man yelled and clutched at his leg. Shanti hacked down on his neck before ducking an attacker from her left.

Another man ran towards her, but didn't make it. As Shanti took out the man to her left, gathering her power to take out Graygual with both mind and body, the running man arched his back with a blood-curdling scream. He reached for his shoulders as he sank down to his knees.

Cayan stood behind him, huge and bloodied, blue eyes wild. He glanced at the man falling to her left before turning his gaze to the side, looking for more.

Trying to catch her breath, Shanti stepped backwards out of the tangled limbs of those on the ground and looked around. Blood ran freely from Graygual bodies, pooling in the mud and shining crimson in the wet grass. Cayan had taken down more than half as he'd worked his way through them. Lifeless Inkna lay on the ground, their faces still screwed up in pain.

She glanced down at the throbbing ache in her leg. Blood splotched her pants, both from the spray from killing and the seeping from bleeding. She pushed down her pants and stepped out. Her bandages were soaked through, the scabs torn open and bleeding freely.

"Blood is good—blood cleans the wound," Cayan said, catching his breath with his hands on his hips. "I tend to get a lot of practice with these Graygual." He smiled through his heavy breathing, his dimples masked by the shadow of his unshaven face.

"You took down more than me," she said in faux-irritation.

He laughed, a great booming sound. His gaze scanned the back line of Inkna. "Not if you count all of them."

"True." She searched the littered men for an officer. The highest ranked had four slashes, a few had three. These weren't the worst Xandre had to offer, but they weren't the best, either. He was testing her by sacrificing those he was most able to lose.

"He'll have learned a lot about the strength of our power and our fighting ability from this," Shanti said, finding a clean undershirt and stripping the Graygual.

"Without a verbal report?"

"He sent in this many, of this fighting caliber, and none will come back. It's a pretty clear message."

"At least he didn't kill or take us," Cayan answered,

rifling through a pack he'd taken off of a Graygual. "A map. They've mapped this whole place, it looks like. Whoever's in charge has been at this a while—he's done his homework. And this is a copy."

"Xandre always does his homework. At least this isn't my fault—this started before I got here."

"None of this is your fault, *mesasha.*"

Shanti suspected that Cayan was trying to soften his tone for that name, but with adrenaline running through his body, it came out more like a growl.

She kind of liked that better.

A disturbance fluttered the edges of her severely weakened power. More minds came, slow and focused. She knew it would be the Shadow people, readying their attack.

"More," she said, bowing with the strain.

Another flutter at their back, then their side. They were being boxed in. The attack was completely synchronized.

"*Flak,*" she breathed, plotting the minds in her head and factoring in her speed given her throbbing leg. "If we run, we may be able to get through on the northeast."

"You won't make it. There are only ten of them, though."

Shanti breathed deeply, trying to catch her breath before she willed her body back into battle-mode.

"Those ten all have the *Gift,* and will be well trained. They'll give us just as much trouble as these thirty."

"Forty. Almost."

"Forty. Right." Shanti looked around with wide eyes, not bothering to count. "No wonder Xandre wants me; but he's got better."

"And now he'll know he has to use them."

Cayan walked to her, his eyes lingering on her wound. "You should probably put your pants back on. We don't have much time."

Shanti shrugged. "What's the difference? Blood comes off skin easier than it does fabric, and they're the only pair that fit me. If they were armored, then we'd have something to talk about."

A grin quirked Cayan's lips. "I guess now we know there are benefits to not caring about nudity."

"Not caring in general, I think."

Shanti took a last deep breath before retrieving her knives. She took a few of the Inkna's, too. Then she faced the mind that seemed the strongest, coming from the north.

Cayan put himself at her back, facing away from her. He didn't ask why she hadn't picked another battle area. He was no novice. The new enemy would have to climb over all the bodies to get to them, and that would slow them down. Hopefully it would slow them down enough.

"I'm glad I'm used to beating on you or I might have a real problem hitting these women I feel sneaking in." Cayan's voice was hard, ready for what might be coming.

She felt them, but didn't hear them. They were right beyond the trees; excellent stalkers, one and all. They'd obviously had a lot of practice at it from the previous hopefuls, and more: they must've trained religiously.

Shanti saw a flash of movement to the right.

"One coming left," Cayan said.

Shock and outrage flared in the minds as someone called, "*Stop!*" in the Shadow's tongue. "*Wait until I assess.*"

"What did he say?" Cayan asked in a low hum.

Minds flashed with approval, some with validation, and one with traces of fear. The man in the north—the mind she had turned to face—stepped out of the trees. Bright orange flared as the sun caught his hair. His gaze was on hers before it swept the ground around her. Anger seethed from his mind as he stopped at the man with the white shirt. When he looked back up, he stared at her for a moment before he said, "You have no pants."

Shanti couldn't help the huffed laugh, expecting something completely different. "My leg hurts," she admitted. "Soon I'll be without shirt, too, because my side must be bleeding through by now."

"Yes." He shook his head and yelled to his people, "*Stand away. Come out. They have already fought enough for the day.*"

"He's calling off their attack," Shanti translated for Cayan.

"Can we trust them? Is what I feel from them correct?" he responded, not dropping his guard.

"Yes." She dropped her knife onto her pants. Her stolen sword followed a moment later. "I am very glad to hear you say that," she called to the orange-haired man. "I wasn't overly excited about fighting you."

"If there wasn't the ban on killing, the sentiment would be duplicated." The orange-haired man walked toward them before stopping at the edge of the bodies. His fighters stepped out of the trees, sheathing their swords or knives.

"Not everyone uses swords?" Shanti asked as she bent to an officer to retrieve cloth for bandages.

"Don't take that—" the man said, threading through the bodies. His eyes were focused on her wounds. "We brought bandages. And yes, we all use swords, but it was thought that this many against just two would be largely unfair, so we intended to even the stakes. Judging by what lays before you, I think my assessment was that of whoever sent these Graygual."

Shanti straightened as the man peeled away her bandages. The wound was a mess of scabs and oozing red. The light green salve began to drip down her leg as the pus and blood overwhelmed the gashes. "Are the other wounds this bad?" he asked in a soft voice.

"Yes. That beast wasn't very nice." Shanti winced as he pressed the swollen, red flesh around the wound.

"This is in danger of becoming infected. And you almost killed him—he would probably say the same about you, if he could speak."

"He is a pet?" Cayan asked with a flat voice. Shock radiated from his mind, however, something everyone in that clearing probably felt because he wasn't holding his emotions in check. But, with all she'd had to teach him, there had been little time to spend on that lesson.

"Yes. And will probably not be fond of you after this." The orange-haired man straightened. "I am Sonson." He offered a slight bow.

"Do the Graygual know about him?" Shanti asked as someone else threaded his way through the Graygual bodies. The others were picking pockets and analyzing weapons, no doubt trying to learn more of the enemy encroaching upon their lands.

"He killed one of theirs, but it wasn't a hopeful-Chosen," Sonson said. "There are Graygual slipping into the trials. I'm not sure what they are trying to assess…"

"They've made a map, for a start." Shanti handed over the Graygual pack. "And Xandre makes it his business to know everything about a nation he plans to rule."

"If you weren't so deadpan, I would think you were trying to scare me." Sonson smiled and stepped aside as a man dropped to one knee to assess her wound.

"Can we do this somewhere else?" Cayan asked, picking up Shanti's items.

"Not quite yet," Sonson said, looking over his shoulder, and then out to the side. He then glanced up at the fog drifting in to cover the sky. "I want to use her as bait to see if more are coming. They must know they've lost their Inkna by now."

"No more are coming," Shanti said in assurance. "I don't know if they were part of a test, but their not returning alone will answer certain questions. The next group will not fail."

Sonson squinted into Shanti's face. "You know him well, this tyrant. Or at least you think you do."

"I think I do, yes. Who knows how he has changed over the year since I've been running for my life, but I know his *way*."

Sonson's mouth turned into a thinking duckbill as he nodded. "Sounds reasonable. Okay, let's get you to shelter where we can play medicine." He winked.

TWO HOURS LATER, SHANTI WAS lying on her stomach on

a bed of soft animal fur the Shadow people brought. A vile-smelling salve covered her wounds and a fire roared by her side. Cayan sat a few paces away with Sonson, giving her space. Shadow people cleaned and skinned animals they'd recently brought back for a large supper.

"I can't imagine you treat all your guests like this?" Shanti asked as she rested her chin on her hands.

"We would, if any made it this far. I have your next instructions." Sonson looked to one of the people skinning. The woman rose, wiping her hands down her pants before pulling a piece of parchment from her back pocket. She approached Shanti, hesitating as her gaze scanned the wounds, and then handed it to Cayan instead.

Cayan glanced at the document. "You're showing us the way to the end?"

"Yes." Sonson folded his hands in his lap. "You'll need to cross some perilous land to get there. If we don't direct you, you might accidentally wander around that area and miss the trial entirely. The animals in that strip of land are not pets."

"Have your people been through it?" Cayan asked, setting the parchment to the side.

"Some. To become a leader of one of our factions, you need to make it through that land. If you do not aspire to be a leader, you will never be burdened. We've lost many teenagers trying to prove a point or show their worth. Bravery, they call it. Children are stupid, and young boys most of all. I have a feeling the hopeful-Chosen would have found her way down there…"

"It's a certainty." Shanti smiled. "I was more stupid than any boy, though I called it bravery. Rohnan, my brother, called it boredom."

Sonson glanced at Cayan in expectation. He raised his eyebrows in response.

"You're not going to rise to the bait?" Sonson asked, a smile tugging at his lips. "Not going to say she's still more stupid than any boy…?"

"He doesn't have a lot of humor when the people trying to kill him are hanging around," Shanti laughed, shifting her legs to get more comfortable.

"When do you advise we get moving?" Cayan asked, proving Shanti's point.

Sonson regained his seriousness. The sparkle of humor in his eyes turned into the gleam of viciousness. "Usually we allow the hopeful-Chosen to dictate his—or her—own pace. But we do not have that luxury in this case. You need to start tomorrow, early. You are being hunted, it seems, by someone besides us. Have no fear. That salve is created with a special blend of ingredients from this wood. It'll help you heal quickly, though you'll still be at a disadvantage. If you make it through, you'll have earned the right to lead our army."

"I don't want your army," Shanti said, the press of

her duty settling heavy on her shoulders. "I need your support. I need you with us. You and he need to lead your people, while working with me to lead…"

"The lost," a woman arranging a spit over the fire said, without looking up. "The lost, the weary, the distraught, and the voiceless. You'll lead more than any other battle commander, and you will help them triumph and restore justice for all."

The fire crackled loudly in the silence that followed. The woman glanced up and saw all eyes focused her way, turning her face red. "Forgive me. As well as trying to kill you, I am also on the committee to determine if you are the rightful Chosen. I've studied many of the doctrines. They rub off."

"She's the life of any party," Sonson said, laughing.

They spent the rest of the evening chatting quietly and eating, speaking little of the mainland and the strife going on there. Shanti told of her journey, making the group solemn and quiet as they learned what had been entailed in reaching them. Cayan shared a little about his city, laughing as Shanti filled them in about the extreme lack of taste in art.

When the sun left the sky and everyone sat around with full bellies, Sonson rose. He winked down at Shanti before shaking Cayan's hand. "I would have liked to have fought you. I think it would've been impressive entertainment. I would rather you live, of course, so be careful tomorrow. A few hours' hike will get you to the next trial, and then keep your eyes open. Nothing is as it seems, and strange forces on this island can confuse the brain. We'll be ready to fight you on the other side."

"Sir—" a man stepped forward holding Shanti's sword and a pack.

"Yes, of course." Sonson took them and placed them next to Shanti on the furs. "The trickery is mostly mental, but as I said, there are some aggressive animals in that area of this island. You'll need your sword and a few supplies."

"Thank you for your treatment," Shanti said in all seriousness. "I didn't expect this kindness in these trials. I thought I would find the Inkna-Chosen, kill him, then meet my death."

"You may meet that Inkna-Chosen yet," Sonson said with the vicious twinkle to his eyes again. "But I hope to find him first. He and his leader are making a mockery of my trials and it does not sit well." Sonson nodded at her, and then glanced at Cayan. "Good luck."

When they'd gone, drifting into the trees and fog like phantoms, Cayan moved to sit beside her. He brushed her hair back from her face as he stared at the fire. In a quiet voice, he said, "I can't help feeling nervous about what we'll face. It's different than facing an army. I know men—I know the way they think and the way they lead. But nature is unpredictable, at best, and… I don't need any help confusing my mind."

"If their leaders can make it through, we can make it through, Cayan," Shanti said, closing her eyes as his fingers wound through her hair. "*Men* are unpredictable at the best of times, led by emotions they often have no control over. Nature is brutal but beautiful—it gives more than it rips away. We have to read her motives, and steer clear of her cleansing. We'll be fine."

Shanti almost believed it.

CHAPTER 13

SHANTI STEPPED OVER A PATCH of weed with long, spiky thorns. Tree branches reached, just as before, and the rain drifted down from the sky in a soft caress, but land was quickly running out. Shanti took no more than ten paces and pushed back her hood, looking down a steep slide that ended in huge and jagged rocks at the bottom of a deep ravine.

"We need to find a way across," Cayan said from beside her. He glanced straight ahead and then off to the right.

Shanti did the same. The far side, crammed with trees huddled close together and strewn with hanging vines, was at least twenty-five paces away. The depth of the ravine was twice that. The winding, tree-choked edge appeared to go on forever before disappearing into the white mass of rolling, shifting fog.

Shanti wiped her face. They'd been walking at a pace that could almost have been called a jog since first light, pausing every now and then to consult the map. They'd believed Sonson when he said they were running out of time—his mind had been laced with anxiety. Cayan worried for his people. If the Graygual were sending people into the trials after her, they were certainly sending people into the city to eliminate any support she might have.

"Right or left?" Shanti asked, glancing at the parchment in Cayan's hands.

He handed her one side and traced his finger along a red line that marked the path they'd been following. The red line stopped where they were and met a blue line running along the edge. Cayan followed it to the left until it once again went north, and then glanced right, finally tapping the line on the right side. "This is the fastest way. Which also means it is probably the most deadly."

"Do we have time to play it safe?"

Cayan took the map and folded it. He tucked it into his makeshift pack and looked up at the sky, eyes fluttering in the drizzle. "On one hand, the Shadow people now know the kind of enemy they face. They'll expect an attack by the Graygual on my people. Within the city, they'll make sure they're there to stop any bloodshed. Sanders will run at an adversary without flinching at impossible odds, but he's no fool, and I trust he has control of those under him. He'll keep within sight of the Shadow so he can't be overwhelmed, and Daniels will make sure they aren't ambushed."

"And on the other hand?"

Cayan shifted before wiping his face. He turned to Shanti with troubled blue eyes. "On the other hand, Sonson didn't think we had much time. Not *we*, you and me. *We*—all of us. His body language was confident. He thought we'd make it through this. I bet he's counting on us to help fight what's coming. Which means it's coming rapidly. We're just two, but we have the power of six or more."

"Of eighteen or more Inkna."

Cayan's lips tweaked, but he didn't smile. Instead, he looked beyond her down the edge. "We've not shirked from a challenge so far…"

"I like challenges," she said in a dry voice. "I get suspicious when things are too easy."

"How are your wounds?"

"Amazingly not bothering me." Shanti slipped through the trees, pulling up her hood as the drops turned heavy. "They have excellent healers."

"As soon as we kill all the Graygual, we'll have to get Marc talking with them. Hopefully they have lots of patience."

"Or are willing to kick him in the head to make him pay attention."

"Or that… yes."

They walked in silence for a while, careful not to touch any hanging vines or stumble into any unidentified plants with needles. There was no telling what might be dangerous here. After half an hour, as the sun was approaching its zenith, Shanti caught sight of a long, narrow bridge leading across the large gap in the land. She stepped toward the ledge and exhaled out a "*Flak*."

Cayan stepped with her. He let out a breath too.

The bridge was nothing more than a large tree slit down the middle, laying from one side to the other. The top was flat, mostly; but shiny with wet, probably slippery, and half rotted in parts.

"How much more than Sonson would you say I weigh?" Cayan asked in a low voice.

"You're taller by a head, much more robust, and solid muscle—at least two stone. You outweigh him by a lot." Shanti started untying the rope from around her middle. "And now we know why he gave us very strong rope."

"Let's hope he also gave us very long rope."

"Yes." Shanti started forward again, heart starting to beat more rapidly. When they got to the edge of the log, once a great thing but now a brittle remnant of what it once was, Shanti hesitated.

The world fell away. Straight down on both sides of the edge, the ground below was so distant it was hard to see through the fog. Falling would mean certain death.

She leaned forward to touch the wood, turned deep

brown from years of being exposed to the elements. As she suspected, the top was slick. At the base it was twice as wide as her body, but as it neared the middle it slimmed down. A sudden gust of wind and she'd be falling. When she reached the end of the rope, she'd be yanked back toward the side and dashed across the rock face.

Shanti looked behind them, seeing the old and weathered stump that this log originally came from. The sides were cut. This bridge had been planned.

"There are big trees everywhere—why choose a place where falling would mean grave injury even with a rope?"

She rolled her eyes at her statement. This was a rite of passage and the Shadow were a hard people—failure to them meant death for themselves, or others.

"We'll be fine, *mesasha*." Cayan's fingers stroked the side of her face as he took the rope. "You're light on your feet and have excellent balance. You'll be across in no time."

"And then you will break the log halfway through."

"Yes, but that side has a little grass growing on it. Soft landing."

"The grass is growing out of the gaps in rock, Cayan…"

"Better than no grass. Come on, let's get ready."

With a tightness in her chest, Shanti tied the end of

the rope around her middle using a sturdy knot. Cayan took the other side and tied it to a tree. She edged out onto the log and jumped a little, seeing if it would hold her weight. The log didn't even wobble. *Good sign.*

"Wish me luck," she said, walking out a little ways.

"You don't need it. Get a move on."

Shanti smiled at Cayan's light tone, ignoring the anxiety bleeding through his emotions. She walked out further, feeling the breeze ruffle her hair. And then feeling the *other* breeze—the one ruffling the edges of her pants. She knew better than to look down. Looking down only made things much worse—

Death's playground, is there a bottom to that ravine?

Shanti yanked her gaze straight-ahead and steadied herself, stilling her suddenly wobbly stomach. Arms out to the side, she walked forward like she might with a sword in her hand. Balance was easy. Steady feet and a sure step were simple. Controlling her raging fear of falling to her death took a little concentration however.

One foot in front of the other, she made her way out to the middle. The log below her feet narrowed, crowding her steps. The wind kicked up a little, enough to gently push her body. The log wobbled.

"I have movement out here," Shanti said, passing the center of the now-swaying log.

"Just keep your focus," Cayan called out to her.

"That wasn't what I meant," she muttered, taking

another step. The wood creaked, bending under her weight. A small swirl of wind slapped at her side. Her balance teetered for just a moment. A thrill went through her, sending shooting shivers through her body. Her fingers tingled, thinking of the height. Thinking of falling.

"Steady," Shanti whispered, her gaze boring into the trunk of a large tree at the other side.

She placed another foot. The creak sounded again, followed by a groan. This log only had so much to give, and she was stressing it. *Best to get off before I use up all its goodwill.*

Shanti walked faster now, letting her mind go blank. Thinking of an enemy. Thinking of having a knife in her hand. Remembering her training. Her body steadied, ignoring another gust of wind slapping her. Salty air whipped by her face. The log whined as she sped up, stepping as light and balanced as possible. The creaks got louder. Something popped. The wood wobbled.

Her heart hammered in that way that meant danger was on her heels, but she kept going. She tasted salt, reminded of home. The smell of kelp drifted on the breeze—they must be near the sea. She clutched at the memory as her feet moved across the last of the log. She had reached the other side!

At the other end, she noticed the rope was barely dragging across the log. They'd given them just enough rope to cross this bridge. Either they knew she'd take this way, or the other way had something similar.

She untied the rope and fastened it to the nearest tree. On the other side of the bridge, Cayan had fastened his rope to his waist and was already walking out onto the log.

Shanti's heart started hammering again. Her chest felt tight and her toes tingled. She was terrified something would happen to him. That he would fall to his death and she would be left without him. She couldn't lose another one. She couldn't lose *this* one.

She cupped her hands around her mouth and yelled, "Maybe there's another way!"

Confidence welled up inside her, fed to her by Cayan from their merge. And then another emotion, one infinitely more tender. One that implied the term *mesasha.*

"Damn him," she breathed, heart thundering for a different reason—one that liked hearing that word on his lips.

She stepped near the edge as though she'd catch him if he fell.

He stepped out onto the log further and did a little jump as she had done. A soft few cracks whispered from the center of the wood. "Why do you have to be such a big bastard, Cayan?" she muttered, intent on his movement.

He stepped out a bit farther and tried again. More creaks, more ominous.

"Get on with it!" she yelled. She couldn't help herself. This is why she didn't want to care—it was very unpleasant when something bad was sure to happen.

Taking a deep breath, Shanti watched as Cayan started walking across the log as though sauntering through a park. Not slow, but not rushed, he strolled out along the groaning, creaking wood.

"Elders, please don't let him fall. Please don't take this man away from me," she begged, running back to the tree and shortening the rope as he moved across.

A loud pop shot out. Cayan took three more steps. He was now halfway. Another loud pop, followed by a crack.

"Hurry, Cayan!" she yelled, not realizing she used the language of her home.

He sped up, though. Cracks and pops sounded with each step, leading into a loud groan as he made it three-fourths of the way across. She tied off more rope as she yelled, "Almost there, baby! A little bit more!"

Wood squealed and strained. It was breaking. The whole thing was breaking. With a chorus of horror, the log splintered and tore, weightless for one moment before gravity took hold of it.

Cayan started to sprint. Shanti didn't have time to tie off more rope. She grabbed it in both hands and backpedaled as fast as she could. His hands pumped, muscles moving like a master fighter, until the log started to swing downward. Then he jumped.

Breath held, Shanti spun within the rope until it was wrapped around her, braced her feet against a big trunk, and then held on. Cayan's body disappeared from her sight as the rope yanked at her grip, burning away a layer of skin from her palms. The coil around her middle jerked taut. Rope squeezed the breath out of her, making lights dance in her vision. Pain blasted through her body. It felt like her intestines were trying to squish out of her. The rope tried to spin her around but she held on, digging in her heels, barely able to breathe.

Be okay, Cayan. Climb back up.

She held on as the pain dug into her. Giving him time to be okay. Giving him time to crawl up the rock face and make it over before she had to unwind the rope and see what lay at the end of it.

Seconds ticked by. Fog dusted her face. Worry brought moisture to her eyes. "Cayan?"

Please be okay... Please, Elders, don't make me responsible for another one. Please!

"Cayan?" she called again. More seconds of silence, dragging by into minutes. Still there was no movement.

A tear overflowed, but she did not yield. Not yet. The man could work miracles. He could do the unimaginable. He was created by the Elders for great things. It would take more than a battering against rock to take him out.

Another tear fell as the pain tore at her. As the rope continued to cut off her breath. Her hands throbbed in agony. Still she held on, now too afraid of what it might mean if she let go.

The rope jerked.

A half-breath, bordering on a sob, ripped from her throat.

The rope jerked again.

Oh thank the Elders!

"Are you okay?" she squeaked. She didn't have the breath to yell.

The rope tugged again, tearing a moan from her throat as the pain cinched around her waist. And then the weight was gone.

"Cayan?" she called, tears coming to her eyes again, this time in relief. Sanders was right—she did cry too much. She'd never noticed.

But as he appeared between the trees with a fantastic welt on the side of his head, and his left side all scraped, she couldn't help the flood of relief drowning her eyes. She dropped the rope, spun to get it off, and ran at him. He spread his arms right before she barreled into his body and yanked his head down for a deep kiss.

"Takes more than a rock face to kill me, *mesasha*," he said as he smiled down on her.

"You scared the shit out of me!" she said, afraid to let go of his body.

"Is this all I needed to get you to show you liked me? Almost die?"

She laughed and kissed him again until it curled her toes and spread warmth through her body. When she backed away, seriously considering fighting the pain so as to make love to him, he noticed her coat. His eyes traced the indents before his gaze hit hers again. Then he grabbed her hands, seeing the burn marks from the rope.

"I wondered how you held me," he said softly, glancing around. "We need to treat these hands."

"What about you? We should clean those wounds."

Cayan glanced at his skin through his ripped jacket. "Nah. I'm fine."

"Just like a man. C'mon. We'll play doctor naked and have some lunch before we move on."

LATER THAT EVENING THEY WERE walking again, checking the map every so often as they threaded through the thick undergrowth. While there was a narrow path, it was overgrown. People clearly didn't come this way often.

"So…" Cayan's voice seemed to drop dead in the trees around them. "Baby?"

Shanti was thankful she was in front—he couldn't see the redness creep into her face. "You heard that, huh?"

"Mhm. I didn't realize you were into pet names. What else are you into?"

Shanti's face burned. "Torture. You can be my first subject."

"Sounds fun."

"That wasn't sexual."

"Are you sure?"

A sparkle of light appeared to their right, thankfully distracting Shanti from the topic, then claiming all of her focus.

She slowed, captivated by the shifting colors of pinks and purples lighting up the darkening forest.

"What's that?" she asked. Her voice seemed to echo in the distance.

Her *Gift* sparked as the lights started to pulse play-fully. They called her closer with their light show. "So beautiful," she sighed, smiling as a delicious fizz crawled up her middle.

She stepped off the path, drunk with the sweet feel-ing created by those twinkling, pulsing lights. A soft melody sang to her. Everlasting joy filled her, making her laugh.

Her feet moved of their own accord, wanting to get closer. Wanting to follow those lights.

"What's going on?"

Cayan's words barely registered. A heavy grip circled her arm. She staggered backwards, pulled by something ugly and disgusting.

"Let go!" She struggled, twisting to try and escape the strong arms now wrapping around her chest, pinning her arms to her sides.

"Shanti, what's happening?"

Shanti couldn't seem to tear her eyes away from those colors, beckoning her closer. "Don't you see it? Don't you *feel* it? Let me go!"

"I feel you responding to something, but I don't see anything..."

The colors shifted and danced, twenty paces away through the trees. The singing grew louder, calling her. Begging her to come and play. Her *Gift* danced, knowing that following it was the right thing to do.

She tried to walk forward, confused as to why her body wouldn't obey. Her eyes stayed rooted to those beautiful, dancing colors.

Firm fingers wrapped around her chin and dragged her face away. She scowled as confused eyes swam before her. Her mind swirled in dizziness.

Suddenly, it all cleared. Reality came rushing back, and with it bile rising up from a swirling stomach.

"Let me go—I'm going to throw up," Shanti grunted, pulling to the side. Staggering a few paces in the opposite direction she'd been trying to go, she bent over and retched, heaving up the contents of her stomach. Spitting, she paused for a moment, making sure it was over. When her stomach evened out she wiped her mouth with the back of her hand and straightened up, breathing heavily.

"What's happening?" he asked with an edge to his voice.

Shanti glanced out into the woods. There was nothing there. Her *Gift* had stabilized. Dimmed light from the failing day sprinkled through the canopy overhead in places, but was mostly reduced to a greenish glow, turning the ground a dark, murky green.

"What was that? What were those lights?" she asked, remembering the sweet joy. Feeling the horror of realizing she was the only one seeing it. It had all been in her head.

"The wood playing tricks, I'd imagine," Cayan said in a calm voice, directing her along the path. "Best to keep going."

"I wonder what would've happened if I had followed."

"I don't know, but we have a disadvantage being foreigners. Having grown up here, people would've heard about the strangeness of the wood. About the pockets without access to your mental powers, the animals—and whatever else there might be. How would a traveler know to distrust the lights?"

"Maybe the spell wavers…"

"Maybe." Cayan's hand didn't leave her shoulder. "Or maybe you realize your error right after you step off a cliff. If they appear to me, and you can't get me to come around, punch me in the balls. That should work."

"As soon as I stopped looking at it, everything vanished," Shanti said, threading her way along the path. Vines hid amid the tall grasses, grabbing her feet.

"This time."

They continued as the wood pressed in on them, choked with high bushes and low vines between the trees. The air was moist and dank, with little air flowing through. A bird screeched before a flurry of wings and rustling leaves sounded.

Shanti's skin prickled with a presence and a warning shiver covered her body.

"Something's close," Cayan said in a whisper.

Shanti took out her sword. Her *Gift* spread out as far as she could push it, but she felt no life. She hadn't even felt that bird.

"Do you feel anything?" she asked in a quiet voice.

"No. But something is out there. We're being hunted."

CHAPTER 14

SANDERS FILED OUT OF HIS room and met the rest of his men and woman in the hall. All wore newly purchased garments made of treated leather that they had seen the Shadow people wear. Two dead men lay face down only a few paces away, both wearing black.

"Graygual or Inkna?" Sanders asked, not bothering to look harder.

"Graygual. Tried to get the jump on Marc as he came out of his room." Tobias clapped Marc on the back. "He reacted by shoving a knife in the guy's throat, then running away."

Sanders glanced at Marc, red-faced and looking at the ground. The youth said, "S'am always jumps out at us. If you don't strike first, you get punched really hard."

"And the running?" Sanders asked as he checked his weapons.

Marc shrugged. "I was always too slow to get her, so rather than getting thumped after I struck out, I ran."

"Ruisa got the other one." Tobias threw her a proud

wink. "Who says girls are only for cooking?"

"Not me. She's a terrible cook," Marc mumbled. Ruisa shoved him.

Etherlan was up and moving around, pissed off and ready to kill the first person he saw. He was still a little weak, but he would make a full recovery. The whole group was damn glad.

Rohnan stood beside Burson, as far from everyone else as he could get. He was probably trying to block out whatever people were feeling, which Sanders figured was probably a mixture of fear and panic. They all knew they'd have to fight their way out to the main square, where the Shadow people would protect them, but then slip out to perform an extremely dangerous task.

They were going to try and poison the Graygual's water supply.

Leilius had found a few places where the rainwater was captured for the Trespasser Village. From the large metal tank ran piping that fed a system of pumps in the Village.

Poison the inlet, poison the Graygual.

The plan seemed easy, but getting to that inlet meant sneaking through enemy occupation. If they succeeded, they would still only get about a third of the population—and that was if no one figured out where the sickness was coming from quickly.

Sanders had discussed the plan at length with Daniels, figured out a route and a way, and then talked it over with the more experienced of his men. It was risky, but with the overwhelming amount of Graygual on the island, they had to try and even the numbers somehow. The risk was worth it.

"Ready?" Sanders asked.

"Yes, sir," everyone chorused.

Sanders started off at a brisk walk, seeing a couple more dead men as he passed Tobias' quarters. A few more littered the hallway.

"The enemy has tried this before—they don't learn." Sanders took the stairs two at a time, hearing the thundering feet behind him.

"None are officers," Daniels commented. "They were either thinking for themselves, or aiming for cheap shots."

"Probably thinking for themselves. Succeeding, with even just one of us, would mean a step up onto the first rung of captaincy," Rohnan explained as they stopped next to the door leading into the alleyway. "The first rung is still considered garbage by anyone who matters, but these men wouldn't understand that. They are the worst society has to offer. Just a little power is enough to excite them."

"Not any more. Ready?" Sanders glanced at those close, and then those stationed up the stairs, waiting. All nodded.

Sanders pushed through the door with his sword in the air. Daniels and Tobias filed out to either side, bows at the ready. Rohnan was right after.

An empty alleyway greeted them. Sanders saw the shapes at the mouth at either end, four of them in all, standing guard.

Sanders drifted to the right until he was close enough to two of the guards to be heard. Tobias still had his bow at the ready. Daniels had remained in the doorway, covering the other side. Everyone else filed in the middle.

"What are you doing here?" Sanders asked the nearest guard.

The man's shoulders turned toward Sanders, but his features were lost to the night. "Keeping you alive. Our Battle Lord, Sonson, said it was necessary. He told me to let you know that your Captain and his mate, the hopeful-Chosen, are nearing the end of the trials. Stay alive until then."

Sanders snorted. "His mate, huh? This Sonson is a bit mixed up. Is this a city-wide mandate, or will you be wandering out of the city limits?"

The guard glanced across the alleyway to the guard opposite, a woman by her stature, her face also lost to the shadows. She said, "I would not advise leaving the city."

"Neither would I, but it has to be done."

"Then we will go with you. I am Denessa." She didn't offer the names of the men with her.

"Sanders." He didn't offer any other names, either. There was no time for introductions.

He started forward, his men at his back. They stuck to the shadows and side streets, moving quietly. Graygual loitered around the city, some watching crowds with alert eyes, some staggering from drink, others playing dice against the walls.

"With you here, are we forbidden to kill Graygual within city walls?" Sanders asked in a low voice as he edged around a spill of light from a window. Ahead a group of Graygual were crouched down and playing their games. A woman was among them, breasts mostly hanging out of her top, a dopey smile on her face but with a sharpness in her eyes. She was playing a part, and she'd make off with all their money before the end of the night, Sanders was sure of it. The foreign women in this city that chose to be here were smart and cunning. They knew their game, and they knew what they could get away with.

Sanders applauded them for their business sense. There was more than one dirty job in the land, and he'd slogged through his fair share of shit to know better than to judge.

"There are many women of the night," the Shadow woman in charge said quietly as they approached.

"They've been arriving in large quantities over the last few days. We have reason to believe many enemy have died by their hand. I want these women left alive."

"No argument there." Sanders took out his knife and was surprised when the Shadow woman did the same. "Since when do you people pick sides?" he asked.

"Since they broke the laws of our land. They will all die, it is just a matter of when."

Sanders felt a shiver from her impassive voice. She showed no anger toward the Graygual. Instead, her people had been wronged, and she would right that wrong with cold calculation. He couldn't say it wasn't justified, but her even tone gave him the creeps. He had a feeling these Shadow could be a very brutal people when pushed, and the Graygual were certainly pushing.

They approached the group of jeering men at a fast walk, sticking to the shadows. Someone yelled in an unfamiliar language and scooped up money off the ground. Jeering, he picked up the dice to throw. Sanders ducked in, slapped his hand over the man's mouth, and stabbed him under the arm. He then struck out to the side, stabbing the neighbor in the side of the neck before sliding his knife across the throat of the man now struggling in his grasp.

The whore didn't scream once, but she took off at a jog. She knew better than to stick around.

Denessa dispatched two other Graygual in the same

amount of time as Sanders, knife work quick and precise. Rohnan hooked a man with his staff, ripping his neck as Tobias took out the last with his sword. The dying men gave a scream or groan before sinking down to the ground. Silence filtered into the scene while everyone caught their breath.

"Take the money," the Shadow woman said, wiping her blade on one of the Graygual uniforms. "Spend it on one of the poorest merchants in the square."

Sanders was refusing as she finished her statement. He paused before he nodded, grabbing what lay on the ground and passing it off to Burson. The older man pocketed it and said, "Our window is closing. We must hurry."

Sanders started off at a jog, taking the route Leilius had planned with the least amount of eyes or Graygual. When they neared the front, crowds of Graygual loitered around the gate, watched by Shadow. There would no doubt also be a few Inkna within the crowd.

"The crowd has grown way bigger," Leilius called up in an apologetic voice.

Sanders slowed to a walk, analyzing. There really was nothing they could do. All the exits would be guarded. He half-turned to tell his men to spread out when Denessa put a hand on his shoulder to stop him. "Side gate," she said.

Without delay, Sanders let her lead. They backtracked before jogging to a small wooden building set against the city walls, with stairs leading up to a ledge where an archer would stand during a siege. The woman flicked up a piece of wood at waist height and reached into the hole created. The area where the wood met the stone wall popped. A crack formed along the wall, and then across the top. When the woman pried it open, Sanders saw that it was actually an extremely well hidden door.

She stood to the side, opening the door as she did so. "Through here."

"This exit would've been handy a few times," Sanders growled as he stepped through.

"Be glad you can use it now," Denessa answered, following him in.

She directed him for the first few steps through the pitch black with a hand on his shoulder. He stopped when she did, before feeling her brush past him. Even though she was probably nearly touching him, he couldn't even see her outline.

Somewhere close by, stone squealed. Something crunched. Then another squeal before the soft moonlight fell into a small chamber.

"We do not use this door often," she said. "Only for occasional training. The outside is masked with moss and scrapes in the stone. There are a few of these, just in case. We hoped they'd never have to be used."

"Keep hoping. War hasn't broken out yet." Sanders jogged through. His men came out after him, silent and serious apart from Marc, who looked terrified.

Denessa left the door open no more than a crack since there were no handles on the outside.

Sanders waited, glancing around the wood. He had no idea where they were in relation to where they were headed.

"Where to?" Denessa asked, rejoining him.

"The nearest water intake for the Trespasser Village," Rohnan replied softly.

The soft moonlight fell over Denessa's straight face, as impassive as her voice had been as she regarded Rohnan. She turned to Sanders. "There are innocents in the Trespasser Village. I cannot allow—"

"Not anymore," Leilius piped up. "Most left in a boat this morning—"

"Ship, idiot," Rachie muttered.

"—and the rest were murdered earlier this evening to make more room for the Graygual that arrived today. Why you guys are allowing more of those Graygual into—"

"Thank you, Leilius," Tobias said, putting his hand on the boy's shoulder.

"How do you know this?" Denessa asked Leilius.

He withered down to a hunch within her gaze, whether out of fear that she might kill him, or because she was beautiful and had breasts. Sanders reckoned it could've been either.

The boy stuttered, "I sn-sneak around. That's my job, Miss. They stomped on me pretty g-good, but Marc fixed me. Just a crack in the back, Miss. Right as rain. I just stay away from that area, now. They'll kill me if they see me again. And they'd see me, they would. I don't think—"

Tobias put his hand on Leilius' shoulder again to stop the blathering.

"See? Clear conscience. C'mon, we gotta go," Sanders said urgently, noticing Burson's gaze going skyward with tight eyes. Sanders had learned that a smile to the sky was a good sign, and this was not. They were running out of time.

Sanders took up a fast jog. He heard the soft footfall of a couple of the boys, still not great at stealth, and the hard breath of Burson, the oldest among them and not as able to keep up. They couldn't slow, though. Burson, more than anyone, knew that, since he was the one advocating haste.

They weaved in and out of trees, Denessa taking the lead and going a different route than Leilius had originally identified. Only a fool would argue with a woman, let alone this woman—she'd win the argument and then kill the man for her troubles.

The canopy of leaves overhead closed out the sky,

blocking out most of the moonlight. Without breaking her stride, Denessa veered right. Sanders was about to tell her to slow down as his men didn't know this land as well as she did, but then his feet hit smooth, packed dirt. She'd led them to a road through a deep cluster of trees. Smart.

They picked up speed as more moonlight broke through the canopy, splattering the road. Men started panting, but the woman was still breathing easily. She had to be in great shape.

They rounded a bend before she slowed.

Up ahead, lighting the road in flickering orange, was the light of a fire. Shadows danced along the ground, thrown by the light. Hushed voices with an occasional burst of laughter hit Sanders. The dull clinking of dinnerware permeated the night.

Sanders motioned behind him for everyone to stay put. He quickly and silently crept closer, realizing belatedly that Denessa was still behind him. Clearly his command didn't apply to her.

As he neared the flickering light, Sanders braced his hand on the rough bark of a large tree and waited for Denessa to take her place by the tree next to him. He peered around.

Three men sat at a small fire about ten paces beyond a large, metal circle. Nearly as tall as Sanders, the sides of the circle flared toward the top, creating a larger area to catch rain. Trees, overhang and all debris had been cleared away, leaving only open sky between the heavens and the water collector. Still, it was open. Bird poop, bugs, dead things—things could still get in. An open water source had the potential to cause sickness.

"That doesn't exactly look safe—anything could get in that water…" Sanders said quietly.

"It is mostly clean, but those in the Trespasser Village all know to boil the water to clean it," she whispered.

Sanders' heart sank. Why hadn't someone told him this before they'd trekked all the way out here? Boiling the water would kill any poison they used.

Sanders backed away carefully. Once back on the road with his men, he stared at Leilius. "They boil the water."

"So?" Ruisa said, stepping forward. She held a large vial filled with clear liquid.

"So, that'll make the poison useless…"

Ruisa shook her head in impatience. "You're thinking of bacteria. Boiling water gets rid of most bacteria. This poison was made from boiling various elements, it'll survive just fine."

"But they don't boil it," Leilius said quickly and a little too loud. He looked back and forth between Ruisa and Sanders.

"*Shhhh,*" Xavier said, elbowing him.

"They don't," Leilius repeated in a breathy whisper. "I've been around the Village, and I've been around the water place a lot, and I've been around the camp—I've only seen people boil stew. But to drink, they just drink out of their canisters, which they fill from the water bucket. I've seen them drink directly from the tap, too. I've never seen anyone boil water without food stuff in it."

"It is mostly clean," Denessa nodded. "With so many humans here, and their stink, the animals probably find elsewhere to get water."

Ruisa looked at Sanders. "Moot point, anyway. The next question is, how do we get the poison into the water supply? If we kill those guys, someone's going to make the connection as to why. At least, with the first death they will. They'll suspect the water right away."

"You've accounted for the rain?" another Shadow person said, a man with dark, fuzzy hair. "It rains a lot. It will dilute your formula."

"Oh, good, everyone's an expert at underhand killing," Sanders said under his breath. Marc shifted, hunched and nodded all at the same time—clearly he was thinking along the same lines.

"I did, yes," Ruisa answered the man, her gaze lingering on his a little too long. Sanders was about to say something when she shifted her gaze to look at her feet. Apparently she had no plans to lose her head over a pretty face, unlike the boys. Sanders was liking her more and more every day.

"It's made to take effect immediately, and kill within half a day," Ruisa continued, looking everywhere but at the man. "I didn't know how long we had. I could've made the kill immediate, but Leilius said that they often hang around the tap and drink while there, so a bunch of dead Graygual around the water supply…"

"Good thinking," the man said, still staring at her.

She shrugged, not meeting his gaze.

"We need a distraction," Sanders said. "What's our timing like, Burson?"

Burson stared toward the flame. "We can wait, and we will get a helping hand. That will lead to death for the Graygual as a whole, which will help us in the days to come. That is the best option for the future, but the worst option for this night."

"What happens tonight if we wait?" Sanders pushed, shifting in impatience.

"We will need to fight our way back. There are three possible outcomes, and two of those will mean a loss. One will mean a narrow escape. I cannot tell what decisions will lead to which. It is all muddled."

"I'm sorry I asked," Sanders growled, staring at the flickering light up ahead, and the shadows dancing around it. Thinking.

If they didn't reduce the Graygual this way, they'd

probably lose a lot more than one in whatever was coming. They might lose everyone. The journey could be at an end here, on this wet, miserable island.

Making the decision to stay meant he was cutting off someone's head. It meant he would be sacrificing one of his own. The greater good didn't matter. What *might be* made no difference. He was sending someone to the chopping block if he chose to stay.

Sanders shook his head and stared at the ground, purposely not looking at anyone else. This was his decision, and the consequences would rest on his shoulders, no matter what happened.

He sighed, refocusing on that flickering light. He felt a hollowness inside of him, a sickening twisting of his gut, as he said quietly, "We should wait."

Shuffling feet interrupted the silence that followed, but he couldn't look back at his men. He couldn't see their faces without wondering which one he was throwing into the fires. Even if he tried to sacrifice himself, there was no guarantee that's how it would play out.

And so they waited, the sickening weight hanging on Sanders' shoulders. No one spoke. No one condemned him out loud.

The Shadow people stood still and quiet, waiting with them. For all Sanders knew, it could be one of them that would meet their end. They were in just as much danger as his own men. Yet, they stayed.

After half an hour or so, a grueling, guilt-filled half hour, Marc said in a harried whisper, "Someone's coming!"

Sanders turned around then, noticing two figures walking up the road. Their outlines suggested females with a heftiness in the bust and through the hip. As though suddenly realizing they were the subject of scrutiny, both woman slunk down as they walked, swaying their hips from side to side as if walking on the deck of a boat deck in the middle of a raging storm.

"Women of the night," Denessa muttered. "It is a strange place for them to be."

The women walked up to Sanders' men and glanced around. The moonlight sprinkled the first, showing a heart-shaped face and a lot of cleavage. The other remained mostly in shadow, but Sanders could see her sleek smile and half-closed, bedroom eyes.

Xavier stepped away. He'd learned his lesson.

The first woman opened her mouth to speak, but Marc reached over Tobias to slap his palm on her mouth. "*Shhh!*" he said, using his other hand to press air repeatedly toward the ground. "Quietly. Eh?"

Marc yanked his hand away and wiped it on his jeans. "She *licked* me."

"Do you boys need a little entertainment?" she said in a quiet purr filled with sex. All the boys but Xavier and Marc stood up straighter. A lazy smile drifted up Rachie's face.

Her eyes told a different story. From what Sanders could see in the dim moonlight, those eyes had a dangerous gleam. A deadly gleam. And suddenly, he remembered where he had seen a whole bunch of eyes like that.

Tomous reached out and put a hand on the woman's shoulder. "We've come to kill the Graygual. We could use your help."

The woman's gaze slid from Tomous' hand, up his arm, and finally rested on his face. The other woman looked over, eyeing him too. Their gazes drifted around the group, noticing the Shadow people, hesitating on Ruisa and then sticking to Rohnan.

"You are with the violet-eyed girl?" the woman with the heart-shaped face asked quietly.

"Yes. You are suspicious, but I do not know how to prove it to you," Rohnan responded.

"Who are you, then?" the woman pushed.

Sanders' brow furrowed. She obviously knew who he was—or at least, she'd guessed he was with Shanti. What more could he say?

"The Ghost," came Rohnan's reply.

The second woman elbowed the first and pointed at Burson, who was smiling at them. He nodded to their scrutiny, "I am the Guide to the Wanderer, and was freed from the Hunter by her hand. She is claiming her right as Chosen, and we need your help."

"I've heard about you. The Ghost and the Madman," the woman with the heart-shaped face said, straightening up. The sex act melted from her demeanor. In its place stood a curvy woman with a scowl and determined, scarred eyes. "You are the reason we are here. Helping you means we help the violet-eyed girl. She is in grave peril here. The old gypsy woman said women like us, like Rosy and me, needed to help. So here we came."

"And you marched into a camp infested with Graygual, into danger, because a gypsy told you to?" Sanders asked with disbelief.

"They are speaking the truth," Rohnan said. "And you are in time. We need those three men distracted. We need to get at the water supply."

A merciless smile drifted up both girls' faces. "Then we are your girls. I hope whatever you have planned makes them shit blood like the last little surprise you left."

"Word's out. They know it's you," Marc muttered to Ruisa.

"It was ingenious work. Of course it had to have come from a woman." The woman with the heart-shaped face laughed as she sauntered forward, hips and breasts all over the place. Even Sanders was mesmerized for a moment; watching that flesh sway made a man feel young again.

As they passed, he motioned Ruisa forward. "Do you need to dump it in, or can anyone do it?"

"There's nothing special. Just upend the bottle," she answered in a hush.

"No stirring or anything?" he clarified.

"No. Just upend and go."

Sanders nodded and took the formula. The fuzzy-haired Shadow said something to Denessa in their language, but she shook her head. Her gaze rested on Sanders. "I will be your backup. I can confuse their mind with my mental power if need be. It is my special gift."

"Great." Sanders couldn't help the sarcasm. It had been so simple when the rule was that dangerous people had a sword, and peaceful people did not. Now there was sneaky poison that didn't kill for three days, mental killing, and reading thoughts. Sanders didn't like this new set of rules. It was too hard to know what was coming at any given time.

He took the poison and waited to give the two women a little time to work on the Graygual. Then he snuck up in time to see one of the women drape herself onto a Graygual lap. She traced her finger down his cheek before outlining his lips. "How about me and you, friend, have some fun?"

"Disguising her knowledge of the language—smart. They will think she's not educated," the Shadow woman said quietly, watching with interest.

"We don't have any money to spend on you gals, honey doll," one of the Graygual said, tracing his hands down her sizable chest.

"I give sample," she countered, gyrating across his lap.

"I'll take a sample of that," another of the men said, a sexual fire in his eyes.

The other woman had her top down and was pulling the third man's head toward her nipple. "You like?" she asked the second man.

That man got up as though in a daze. He was already undoing his pants.

"We go in darkness," the second woman said, looking all around. "You head man no like us around. But you like—we give sample. Maybe you like so much, you pay."

"Maybe…" the second man pulled her up by the hand. The other man rose, too. They drifted off into the trees, the men following with dazed, lust-filled eyes.

The other woman tried to stand and take her man with the others.

"No, no, we can just do it right here," the man said, digging between them and fiddling with his pants. "See, I'm ready."

"No, no!" The woman adopted a terrified voice, looking around. "I threatened. No! I supposed to stay away."

"It's okay, I'll protect you." He palmed her breast and tried to situate her.

"No, no! I scream! I bring your leader man."

The man tightened up at that. He glanced off through the trees, pausing for a moment in thought. It must've been hard, with his dick taking all the thinking power away from his brain. Finally, he pushed her up and then grabbed her hand. "All right, fine. Let's make it quick, though. If they find out I took off, they'll cut off my dick and put me on display."

After they cleared away, Denessa stepped forward with a sneer. "Those men are filth."

"You wouldn't let a handsome man lead you away if he offered roses and candy and all that crap women like?" Sanders accused. "I bet you would. He'd offer to clean your house so you could take a bath, and you'd club him over the head and drag him home. You women are no saints."

"I would have sex with a handsome man if he offered himself for free, sure, but those men will take the goods without paying a fair wage. It's a disgrace."

Sanders couldn't help a chuckle as he poured the liquid into the water. "Not the roses and chocolates type of girl, huh? A woman after my own heart."

They moved away quietly.

"I think I would take the chocolates, actually," she said. "And the clean house and bath, but I would give him something for his trouble if he didn't talk too much."

Sanders laughed quietly. "You and Shanti will get along fine. It makes me wonder what my wife giggles to her friends about, though…"

"The size of your penis, probably."

The humor drained from Sanders. He shot her a glower, squinting his eyes at her soft laughter. "On second thought, maybe I'll make sure you don't meet Shanti."

They made it back to the others. Sanders handed over the empty bottle as Burson stepped toward the city. "We must go. *Now!*"

"What is he?" Denessa asked.

"No time to explain," Sanders said, jogging down the road.

"Weapons out," Burson called.

Swords slid out of sheaths. A bow creaked.

"This way is faster," Denessa said, starting to run right.

"No!" Burson replied, slowing the group in confusion. "We take the secret passage. It minimizes the possible death-outcome."

Sanders didn't hesitate. They continued up the road

before they turned right and saw a group of twenty or so Graygual making camp in the trees. The group was organized and efficient, spreading out and hunkering down. Away to the right more noise caught Sanders' ear; the sound of other troops setting up a barrier in the night.

Denessa slowed with the rest of them, sword at the ready. A wicked gleam burned in her eyes. "They are trying to block escape through the wood to the dock we use for fishing. They are preparing for war."

"So are we." Sanders looked back, focusing on the boys. "Fight as a group, like Shanti taught you. Keep yourself alive, you hear me? I don't want to lose a single one of you."

"What about me, sir?" Tobias said with a grin. "You ready to lose me?"

"I was ready to dump you off at sea. You're hard to kill, just like the rest of us."

"Got that right," Tobias answered.

"All right, kill at will," Sanders said as he started jogging again.

Everyone fell in behind. The Shadow took the outside, swords low, running like predators. As Sanders neared the Graygual getting ready for the night, he put on a burst of speed and whirled through the crowd. His sword slashed down on a shoulder, cutting in through the neck. Someone hopped up, faster than the trash in the city would. Sanders stabbed him through the gut before turning to another man.

Denessa danced through, her blade flashing so fast he lost track of her strikes. She stabbed a man through the throat while someone at her back dropped his sword in confusion and then stared down at it dumbly. She whirled, hacking deep into his neck.

Her mind-power was causing them confusion.

Sanders slashed as someone rushed at him, dodged a strike, and then lunged, getting the man in the chest. A sword came up behind him. He spun and struck, taking his attacker down before moving a few short steps and stabbing in the back a man who was running at Etherlan.

Another Shadow ran through, clashing with a Graygual who moved with precision. It must've been a fairly high-ranking officer. The Shadow was no slouch, though. The officer feinted, then struck. The Shadow blocked effortlessly, countering quickly. Someone ran at his back, but Sanders charged forward and took the Graygual out while the Shadow still battled the officer.

A man went down grabbing his head and screeching. Sanders hacked at him, cutting off the scream. He stabbed through an enemy back who had an arrow aimed for Tomous. The arrow flew, high and wide, lost to the darkness.

Sanders turned, directly into the enemy, only to see

the arc of a blade slicing toward him. He had time to blink. That was it.

Wind washed his face, forcing out a sputter.

When he opened his eyes again, a dead man lay at his feet, and Denessa was working on another right beside him.

Sanders sprang into action, pushing away the fear of a close call. Fear got a man killed.

He ran at two Graygual advancing on Xavier. The youth used his blade like a veteran, turning one before blocking the other, and then advancing on the first. A veteran in skill, but apparently not in final execution. He was taking too long.

Sanders rushed in and stabbed one in the side. Xavier, freed up, downed the other. They turned as one to face three running their way.

"How many more?" Xavier panted, blocking a thrust, parrying, and then stabbing. He clipped the side of the enemy as Sanders blocked a sword strike and stabbed the Graygual in the eye.

"Don't know…"

Sanders downed the third, only to see ten more running their way.

"Attack hard and fast, boy. We're better," Sanders encouraged. "Charge on my word—surprise the fuckers."

Without warning, the Graygual staggered, clutching

at their bodies. Screams rose. Feet became tangled. More than a couple crumpled to the ground among tortuous noises of anguish.

Howls filled the air behind them, making Sanders look back toward the way he'd come. More Graygual, at least a dozen of them, sank to the ground.

Three men jogged from the direction of the front gate. All Shadow, and obviously strong in power, the men approached the Shadow woman who had accompanied Sanders. Panting and covered in blood she spoke in a language Sanders didn't understand.

Instead of standing around like a fool, he quickly worked around to his men. He sought out Marc first, knowing he'd be with the worst off and wasn't surprised when he found it was Etherlan, the weakest of them all.

Etherlan looked up as Sanders approached. He winced as Marc fastened a bandage to his arm. "Moved too slow. That officer was damned fast. Almost had me. Had to have a woman save me. Now I know how you feel, having one come to your aid."

Sanders huffed, seeing Ruisa on the ground holding a bloody cloth to her leg. "Get used to it—there are women with weapons all over the place now. It's terrifying."

"*We're* terrifying?" Denessa said as she walked over, face grim. "You are the one with two heads and only one brain."

"You gonna let her sass you, sir?" Etherlan asked with a weak smile.

"I figure if I nod and smile, she'll go away," Sanders growled, catching sight of Leilius standing up by the door with a knife shaking in his hand.

"My men are alive," Denessa said quietly. "I come to inquire about yours…"

Sanders gritted his teeth, seeing Tomous leaning against a tree, trying to catch his breath. Daniels spoke with Burson, both okay. Tepson, the lucky bastard, would live to win another game at dice, and—

Sanders' breath caught in his throat. Tobias lay on the ground, arms wide. His hand was open, his sword resting gently on his fingers. Blood covered half his body.

A Graygual lay next to him, huge and muscular. Easily as big as the Captain, if not bigger. His black uniform was covered in glistening liquid that would surely show red come dawn.

Sanders hurried over and knelt beside Tobias, a burning in his throat. Sanders was responsible for this. It was his decision that had caused this.

He clenched his jaw and fist, keeping emotion in check.

"Not gonna cry, are ya, sir?"

Sanders blinked a few times, leaning way over so he could look into Tobias' face. The man blinked one eye open, then closed it again. "That big fucker fell on me. Slow as hell, but I didn't get out of the way in time. Flattened me. Rolling that big bastard off added insult to injury."

Sanders gently touched Tobias' chest. "Anything broken?" he asked with a badly masked, shaking voice.

"Nah. Just tired. Damn tired. We've been doing nothing but battling against all odds. It really gets a man down when all that ends with a big fucker falling on you…"

Sanders huffed out a laugh. "Get up you lazy sack," he said, straightening.

"I'd ask if a pretty woman could be brought to my room, but all the ones in this city come with a warning label. I think I'll take my chances with my hand," Tobias mumbled, not bothering to move.

"You'll fall down and be asleep in minutes," Sanders responded.

"That would be good, too." Tobias rolled to his side and slowly got to his feet.

"All right, everyone—let's head in before any more arrive." Sanders made a circle in the air and headed up the small hill to the secret door.

"We were lucky they didn't set up camp a little higher," Denessa said as her men caught up to walk by her side.

"It was you who was predicted to die," Burson said,

catching up with Sanders.

Sanders groaned. "Saved by a woman again. This is getting to be a bad joke."

Behind them, Tobias started laughing.

"Next time, Burson, just spell that out." Sanders threw the older man a scowl. "I've been feeling guilty this whole time thinking it might've been someone else. That's a rotten thing to do to a man."

"Telling you might've changed the outcome of your narrow escape."

Sanders rolled his eyes. There was always something.

"They are organizing," Daniels said in his customary serious tone. "We need to strike now, before they are set."

"We wait for Chosen," one of the mental-workers said in a gruff voice. "Only win with Chosen. Big battle decide fate. Doctrines say."

"Does anyone know if she is close to the end?" Rohnan asked quietly.

"Last we heard, they'd reached the trial of the land," Denessa said. "If they make it through that they will be at the final trial, which is the battle. We've always thought we needed to stage the final battle, but… now the Thinkers aren't so sure."

"You won't need to stage a battle—the Graygual will do that for you," Daniels said in a solemn voice. "If the

Captain doesn't finish up soon, the battle will be over before he joins it. All that will be left to do for the Graygual is to grab the foreign woman and head for the mainland."

CHAPTER 15

SHANTI FELT HER WAY ALONG the path as night descended. The thick canopy above strangled the light, leaving her and Cayan in darkness. Vines still grabbed her feet, and more than once Cayan tripped, finally leaving his hand on her shoulder to stay close.

Another creature had joined the first on the hunt, stalking silently through the foliage. The only way she knew this was feeling that presence moving ever closer. Watching her. Ready to strike.

Thoughts of the boys flashed into her head. Their parents had said goodbye amid tears and proud smiles upon hearing that the Captain chose them, above all others, for such an important journey. They'd be battling for their lives as the Graygual gathered en masse on the island. She thought of people like Tomous, and Tauneya, who had had their lives ripped out from under them and looked for guidance to stand on their own again. She thought of the justice left unclaimed that would receive a huge setback if she and Cayan failed in these woods.

As if in perfect clarity, it finally hit her. After all this time, after all these years, and all her suffering, it finally made sense, She may not be the best one to lead people into battle, but she was the only one standing up and saying she'd do it at any cost. That alone meant it was her responsibility. Someone had to have the courage to step forward, to say that what was happening wasn't right, and to fight back. Someone had to push back regardless of the opposition. If not her, then who?

She would let herself be a beacon for others to gather around. She'd be the example of what it was to lose everything, yet not give up.

She'd be the one to put a knife through Xandre's eye.

"Let's stop here and wait for them. There's no use continuing in the dark." Shanti stopped and dropped her pack. She glanced up, seeing the glow of moonlight in the very tops of the trees. Like the light, no rain made it through to the ground level. They wouldn't need much of a shelter. "Let's make a fire."

"That'll cut down our visibility past the flames."

Shanti chuckled. "What visibility, Cayan? Our eyes are used to the darkness, and still we can't see. At least a fire will cut down one of the sides they can come at us."

Cayan's pack thumped to the ground. "Predators would've attacked by now," he said, feeling his way through the pack.

Shanti closed her eyes and felt the night, something she'd done so often when traveling the wilds, feeling for Graygual. Letting her natural sense pick up on various dangers. Humans had these capabilities, as much as animals, but they were far buried by reason. All it took was living in constant danger for those abilities to surface like a buoy in calm waters.

She felt them, out there. Close. Stationary in the trees, in two different areas, watching. Cayan was right. Normal predators hunting for food would've attacked by now.

"They are hidden from the *Gift,* they are absolutely silent. They can obviously see something, even in the dead of night…" Shanti crouched next to Cayan. "Maybe they're waiting for us to stop moving. Letting the night trap us here."

"We've been moving so slowly we might as well have been still." A click of rock announced the flash of spark. The next spark was lower, illuminating the small fire-starting fuel supply they'd carried with them and kept dry. A third strike had a tiny flame growing to life, flickering in silence.

"You're getting good at that," Shanti said quietly, facing toward one of the two presences. Facing the attack that would eventually come.

"I can be taught."

Shanti let a smile curl her lips as the glow from the

fire crept along the ground beneath her. It slowly reached out, burning away vegetation around it. Cayan added what fuel they had left and sat back on his haunches. "We need more wood. This won't last long."

"As I recall, by your standards, getting wood is the man's job. As is hunting. Off you go."

Cayan looked around them. He stood and took out his sword. In another moment, he stalked off to the right.

"Wait," Shanti said, jumping up and following him. "Don't be absurd! I was just—"

Cayan cut her off by picking up some dead wood at the bottom of a nearby tree. He turned around and held it up, the night mostly masking his smirk. "Done. Go gather, woman."

Shanti sighed, dropping her sword. Cayan laughed and bent to hack off some of the hollow, thin trees that grew in this wood.

A flash of movement in her peripheral vision caught Shanti's eye. A warning blared through her body as something lunged. A black body shot toward her. Great white teeth flashed in the firelight.

Shanti threw herself to the side. A claw scraped her shoulder, ripping through her coat to the skin underneath. She stabbed as the animal landed quietly and gracefully on padded feet beside her, ready to lunge again. Her blade sank into the flesh behind its shoulder.

The animal screamed, a sound chillingly like a baby's cry.

Before Shanti could stab it for a final kill, another flash of movement had her pulling back. Another body came at her, huge and robust, claws out wide in the leap. Cayan stepped in front of her, thrusting his sword forward. It pierced the animal's middle. Cayan's larger body barreled into it, knocking it out of the air. The black, furred animal tumbled into the dirt.

The one under Shanti tried to stand, but she didn't hesitate in sticking it again in the side. And again, until it lay down and died with that terrible scream.

In thirty seconds, it was all over.

Shanti stared down at the large black cat. Crimson caught in the firelight, coating its side, and started to pool under the body. Standing, it would have reached her middle. Muscular but sleek, this was a predator of the darkness.

"That's why we didn't see them," she said, placing a hand to her wildly beating heart. "Why does killing animals like this seem so much worse than killing Graygual?"

"This one is a female," Cayan said, out of breath. He knelt by the animal he'd killed. "She's had cubs... recently. There's milk."

He looked up. Firelight illuminated his eyes making the remorse plain in his features. A profound sorrow welled up out of nowhere, taking over his emotions, blasting out through his *Gift,* and overflowing into her.

A lump formed in her throat, reacting to his feelings. In a thick voice he said, "We had to kill her, but we can't kill her babies. That's just not right."

Shanti sighed as she looked down on the great beast. "What are we going to do, Cayan? It's pitch dark and these animals won't leave much in the way of tracks in wood this thick with live vegetation."

"It'll be light tomorrow. We have to at least try. We can't leave them to starve."

"Can we leave your men to be killed by the Graygual?" she countered. It was nature, after all, and nature was brutal. If some other animal, higher up on the food chain than these great cats, had fought back and won, they wouldn't go looking for the cubs. "And what are we going to do when we find the cubs? I'm not lactating."

Cayan stared at her for a moment, pain bleeding through his expression. That heart-wrenching pain was so strong it consumed them both through the merge. He nodded, turning away. "You're right."

Like a child that had been whipped, he hunched as he gathered more wood and built up the fire.

Why do I suddenly feel like a monster?

Shanti threw up her hands. This was not logical. It was nature, for goodness sake; this stuff happened. But his reaction was beyond anything she could have expected. An old pain haunted him to the point of distraction, and the trigger had been those cubs left defenseless.

Her heart squeezed, responding in a very illogical way. "Fine. We'll take a quick look. *Quick.* If it eats too much time, they'll just have to figure it out on their own."

"I'm not making any sense, I know," Cayan said in a soft voice, placing a piece of wood on the fire. "I was twelve or so when my mother died. I'd just returned from hunting and had gotten my first big kill. A wild boar—a sow. I'd almost been gored trying to kill it. They're vicious animals. So when I got home, I showed my dad what I had. The first thing he noticed was that it was female, and the second thing was that it was still nursing. Instead of the praise I was expecting, he chastised me. Said I was disrupting the food chain and killing off our food supply.

"My dad was always hard on me. I was the only son, I'd have to lead one day—nothing I did was ever good enough. So I figured this was another of those times. I tried to ignore him."

Cayan absently stoked the fire, his eyes distant. "My mother had been sick, she took a turn for the worse that night. Her fever came back strong, and her strength… evaporated. I sat with her all night, holding her hand. I remember her last words to me. 'Be good, Cayan. You have so many gifts. You must help those weaker than you. Stay true to your heart and watch out for those you love.' She gave me a small smile before coughs racked her body. I felt her grip getting weaker. I heard the fluid in her lungs—the awful wheezing."

Cayan shook his head. "She was always my biggest supporter. Always rooting for me. She was a sweet-natured woman, pliant and quick to smile, but when my dad took it too far she stepped in and showed her core of iron. When she was sticking up for a loved one, or something she cared about, the earth couldn't move her. She'd step in front of an army and lift her chin, defiant to the last."

Cayan broke off and swallowed, blinking quickly. He was trying not to cry. Men from his land could succumb to rage and fury, using their fists and killing at will, but they weren't supposed to allow the "softer" emotions. Only women cried they said, and by this reasoning, that made women weak. Lesser. All for a natural emotion they held inside, bottled up, and that eventually fueled their destructive nature, needing release in some way.

Asinine behavior. Why express one emotion and not another? Why push back on one's humanity? Shanti didn't understand that part of their culture, but now wasn't the time to question. Instead, she moved close to him and ran her hand up the center of his back, giving support.

"She died that night. Just smiled one last time, closed her eyes, and…" He shook his head again, willing strength. "Her death hit me really hard. Really, really hard. She was my favorite person in the world. And her last words stuck. I knew she'd be disappointed in me for killing a mother. Not angry, like my father, but disappointed. I'd left defenseless young animals to suffer. It wasn't right. By the time I got there to right that wrong, they were gone. Some other predator had gotten to them. What was left was blood and gore. She'd just died, and already I felt like I had failed her."

He blew out a breath, still willing control. Trying to force back the memories and emotion. He'd just lock them up, trapping them inside him. He needed to find release in order to heal.

So she initiated another outlet men reached for in times of vulnerability they didn't want to face. She crawled into his lap and kissed him softly. He responded by crushing her to him, deepening the kiss until emotion overcame him. He tore at her clothes, letting passion overcome his sorrow. Letting love fill in the pain. She accepted him into her body, holding him tightly. Kissing the stray tear that escaped and meeting his ardent passion with her own.

In the aftermath Cayan held her firmly against him,

near the fire. She rested her head on his shoulder and let him trail his fingertips up her back slowly, comforting her as a way to comfort himself.

"I've never told anyone that," Cayan said softly, stroking her hair now. "It's not really something you talk about. It's just…"

"I get it," Shanti said softly. "We'll look. I have no idea what we'll do if we find them, but we'll look."

"Thanks. I owe you an absurd request."

"I'm repaying you, I think," she scoffed. The man had pulled her from Death's grip more times than was healthy. The least she could do was let him look for some wild animals to cure an old, aching wound. *Nothing I do is ever normal it seems.*

After a moment of listening to the crackling fire, she ventured, "Would it be obtuse of me to cut up some meat now? We really shouldn't let the kills go to waste…"

"No. Let's eat what we can now. We'll need the protein."

"Let's hope there's nothing that hunts these things close by. Or scavengers. It's not exactly safe in the wild with food laying around."

"They are over there, we are over here. We'll take what we need, and hope any scavengers are happy with the easy meal and leave us alone."

Shanti pulled on her pants. "Should be a restful

night, then…"

DAWN CAME SLOWLY. THEY'D TAKEN turns keeping watch, and had the rare opportunity to see a wolf wandering into their camp to get at the leftover carcasses. It growled at her. She'd jumped up and yelled at it before adding wood to the fire. Cayan had bounded up a moment later, sword in hand.

The wolf, eyeing them with bared fangs, had stood its ground. It had friends hovering close by. Shanti and Cayan didn't. So they sat next to their fire, built high and burning brightly, and watched as dangerous animals ate just a few paces away.

Shanti hadn't slept much.

The next day, puffy-eyed and strung out, they trekked through the thick vegetation, trying to keep an eye on the map for their location as they sought out the creatures they had little hope of keeping alive. Their men could be fighting at that moment, but instead of rushing to join them Shanti and Cayan were looking for the product of nature's brutality.

The Elders are laughing right now. I can feel it.

But Shanti had said she'd help, and Cayan needed to get his head in the right place. He was living in the past, and it would severely disrupt his ability to fight until he worked it out. So this was what they had to do.

"Here," Cayan said, bending down to point at a deposit of scat. He then pointed at some fresh paw prints. So far, he'd only needed Shanti's minimal help. It was obvious that he was a master huntsman. He might not have survived in the wild much, but for day-hunting trips, he'd had more than a little experience.

They were closing in on a large predator's den.

"I can feel your crankiness," Cayan said with humor coloring his voice. "Think of the story you'll have to tell."

"I'm tired. I'm never happy when I'm tired."

"At least we're still going the right way."

Shanti grunted her assent to that statement. It was true. They were, in essence, cutting across the land at a diagonal to connect with another, wider path.

And it would only take an extra hour.

But still, it was a pain. Being tired wasn't helping.

They stepped into an open field and felt glorious sun for the first time since they'd entered the suffocating wood. The warmth beat down on them, rising Shanti's spirits. She took a deep breath and gave a small smile. "That helped."

"Look!" Cayan pointed to a small rock outcropping at the other end of the clearing. Trees sheltered it from above. At the base was a small black hole.

They moved toward it swiftly, seeing more scat and plentiful tracks. Once there, Cayan got on his hands and knees and looked into the hole while Shanti shook her head and kept an eye on the surrounding area.

Cats weren't normally pack animals, but this was a strange land. Anything was possible.

"Ow!"

Shanti snapped her attention back to Cayan as he pulled out a little fuzzy black ball. It was the size of a loaf of bread. Its eyes were opened, so not newborn, but not much older. He set it on the ground and reached back into the hole, pulling out another. And then one more. When he was done, he knelt by them and smiled down, resting his hands on his thighs in childlike delight.

Shanti blinked down at the fuzzy little things. They were definitely cute, but they'd grow up. The adult version was large, agile, and dangerous. "So... now what?"

He shrugged. "Take them to the Shadow people and see what can be done. They have monstrous beasts in their pens. I doubt these will be too much for them to handle."

Shanti sighed as she squinted into the light of the clearing. "Fine. How do we get them there without killing them and making you jump off something high?"

His smile burned brighter. The dimples made deep indents in his face. He was a handsome bastard, that was for sure. A lot of trouble though.

"We carry them in our packs, and feed them… mush or something. I don't know. We'll figure it out. This is good, though. This feels right."

Cayan scooped up one of the small animals and handed it to Shanti. She dropped her sword in surprise and cushioned the little thing against her chest, instantly responding to the warmth. It squirmed until it burrowed deeper into her jacket, curled up into a ball, and settled.

"That's not fair," she said in irritation, stroking the downy soft fur. "It's playing on my heartstrings now."

Cayan laughed and gently put two cubs into the middle of the extra garments in his pack before closing it up and slinging it over his back. He looked at her. "Ready?"

"Oh, *now* you're in a hurry," Shanti muttered, tucking her cub away. "*Now* we have places to be, with live cargo in our packs that will someday grow up and eat us."

CAYAN COULDN'T HELP THE LAUGHTER bubbling up as Shanti pet the cub one last time before closing up her pack. Her terrible mood was endearing in a way he couldn't explain. She couldn't be taken seriously when she was like this, and she seemed to know it. She thrived on it—it was probably why Rohnan laughed at her so often.

Feeling lighter for finding the cubs, feeling as if his mother was smiling down on him, he consulted the map and found their route. As they left the clearing, the trees once again crowded in, reaching overhead and blocking out the sun. Shanti grumbled behind him.

They cut through the undergrowth, excellent at navigating the catching vegetation now. In less than an hour they pushed through a wall of green, and ended up on a rocky path winding away through the trees.

That's when Cayan saw the lights. Blue and orange and sparkling, they sang to him in a way he could describe as heavenly. The sweet music filled his ears and drowned out his thoughts. His limbs became weightless. His power surged and rolled within him, spreading out, spiraling up, and joining with whatever power beckoned him closer.

It was so beautiful.

He followed in a daze. A smile plastering his face, his eyes hooded, he let his body lead. Something pulled at him, hindering his progress. He ripped away. He heard a voice next, but he couldn't focus. He couldn't quite hear it.

Pressure erupted in his side. He hardly felt it.

He continued to walk. Something brushed his face and his feet caught something every few strides His eyes remained focused on those glowing lights. On the hypnotic singing, so beautiful. A splash of violet infused the colors, singing in his heart.

Deep in his mind, something awoke with the thought of violet. Like a cancer the thought spread, eating away at that sound. Dripping through the euphoria like acid.

Shanti.

The name repeated in his mind. Slowly, like awaking from a sleep, he connected the name to the person. He connected the person to a deeper feeling, residing in the middle of him. With that feeling came reality. And the memory of her touch, so real. So heavenly.

This was wrong. These lights were wrong. This euphoria was not as pleasant as her soft body moving against him, or the delicate moans he could coax out of her.

The lights!

Warning blasted through him. He wrestled for control, understanding what was happening now and fighting it. He crawled out of his stupor to find himself pushing through a shrub to the top of a high precipice. A sheer rock face led down into a ravine far below.

He felt the tug before he toppled over backward and landed on Shanti.

"You are a God-damned strong bastard, you know that?" Shanti seethed, crawling out from under him.

Her intense presence left his mind in an instant. In its wake he felt strangely hollow. He realized that he'd connected with her through the lights because she was making her presence in his head stronger. She had used her *Gift* to try and knock him out of his daze.

"What did you plan to do?" he asked, breathing hard.

Shanti stared into his eyes for a moment, probably making sure he was lucid, before straightening up and wiping the hair and sweat from her face. "I tried pleasure, but that made it worse. I tried pain, but you didn't even recognize it. I kicked you in the kidney; nothing. I couldn't get to your balls because you were heading right for the cliff. I was about to suck all the energy out of you when you stopped."

Cayan dusted off his pants and got up. His knees felt weak and his side ached from where she'd kicked him. Straight ahead stood a few low bushes, and then nothing but sky. He had almost walked off a cliff to his death.

"And that is what those lights do."

"I took your pack off you," Shanti said as he reached around for it, "I figured if you survived, and killed the cubs in the process, I'd never hear the end of it."

"You're so charming when you're in this kind of mood," he said, willing his heart to stop pounding. He couldn't stop from looking out at that patch of sky.

Feeling the light rain drifting onto his face.

It had been close.

"C'mon, let's go," Shanti said, walking back the way they came. "I can't wait to see what else this place has in store for us."

CHAPTER 15

PORTOLMOUS STOOD IN THE SHADOW Lord's office, staring out the window overlooking the square with growing unease. Graygual had gathered in the square. Squads of them, standing in organized groups, monitoring the gate, looming over Portolmous' guards, and securing the area.

Portolmous turned at the heavy footsteps racing up the hall. His head guard Shom stepped in, an aging man with an eye for tactics. "Sir," Shom said, offering a slight bow. His chest heaved. "Sir, we've verified the rumors Denessa brought back last night. Those who hadn't already left the Trespasser Village have been killed and dumped into the Trial Bay. Every last man who couldn't fight."

"What about those who could fight?"

"They now wear black shirts."

"The Graygual," Portolmous spat, looking out the window again.

"The Graygual are arming and organizing. They surround the trials, blocking all entrances and exits, including the one they created. We've stopped all ships coming in, and we've evacuated all foreigners who have no part to play in the upcoming battle. Those who refused to leave know they will no longer be protected."

"The men and woman from the Westwood Isles— did they leave?"

"No sir. The leader, a Commander Sanders, laughed in my face when I told him he should go."

"The Graygual guard the entrances to the trials," Portolmous repeated, acid rising in his stomach.

"We have the entrances and exits into the trials covered from the inside," Sonson said as he strode in. He glanced around the office. "Where's mother?"

"She issued the evacuation of our people," Portolmous answered, eyes glued to the window. The groups were starting to spread out. A gathering of Inkna walked through the gate.

"She is overseeing their leaving before she returns. I am initiating the battle in her stead. For now. What of the hopeful-Chosen?" Portolmous faced his brother.

For the first time Portolmous could remember, Sonson's eyes were tight, his mouth a thin line. No humor permeated his thoughts. He felt the pressure, and he knew it was something they would be hard-pressed to beat.

"They are in the final trial. We have no visibility, but I estimate one more day and we should know."

Sonson glanced at the window, but did not walk closer. "It doesn't look like we have a day, brother."

Portolmous set his jaw. "She *has* to get through those trials. That is foretold. She *has* to, Sonson. It is non-negotiable."

"We need someone who knows the Graygual to lead this, Porto," Sonson persisted. "We've never faced an army this organized before. We are unprepared for this."

"That is why she *must* get through the trials. She must *earn* her right to take the lead, Sonson. She has to *earn* it."

"What of those accompanying her?" Sonson asked. "They're greatly outnumbered, and today they will die if we leave them isolated."

Portolmous clasped his hands behind his back. "It's not our way to invite foreigners into our fold…"

"We've already fought with them, Portolmous. Denessa said they are excellent in battle," Sonson growled. "Their Commander is a vicious but loyal warrior that can take three Graygual to his one. His men are all top notch, even the young ones. He's got a doctor who's not afraid to run into battle, and a man with Salange's capabilities who has turned his talent into a warrior's skill despite his affinity for peace and healing. The man knows what his attacker will do at the same time the attacker knows. We need them."

"I agree with that assessment," Shom said. "Their small force is extremely effective against the enemy. I would greatly like to meet their Captain…"

Portolmous pondered the ramifications of breaking one of the city's oldest laws when shouting echoed down the corridor. Sonson brandished his sword and stepped out into the hall quickly, before returning a moment later with a knowing gleam to his eye. A harried guard rushed in after him. "I didn't think I should kill them, but I couldn't—"

The commander from the Westwood Isles barged into the room with an air of violent impatience. He glanced around before settling his eyes on Portolmous.

"You in charge?" The man spoke in his native language, somehow knowing Portolmous knew it.

A tall but thinner man with shoulder-length, white-blond hair followed the commander in. He could've been Portolmous' twin for how alike they were, even though this man was a little younger. An older man with a mad grin came in next, along with an elegant man who reminded Portolmous of his mother. The rest took up position near the doorway but did not enter.

"I am in charge at present, yes," Portolmous said in an even tone.

"You got yourself a shit-show going on out there. We need to combine forces to hold them until the Captain and Shanti get out of those damn trials with whatever title they need to get you to heel."

Portolmous stiffened. "And what makes you think we need your help?"

Sonson's lips pursed, no doubt frustrated with Portolmous' question. But he couldn't let foreigners walk into his world and start trying to dictate. Loss of control created confusion, and confusion created death.

If the commander was fazed, he gave no sign. "I'll tell you why you need our help. You have no idea what these bastards are capable of. We were hunted by one of their best, and he was no picnic. I've battled some of the best warriors in my time, but their high ranking officers are made to fight. Not trained, *made*. I cut a man's hand off, and he still kept at me. Didn't even scream out. Now, you move like a good fighter. And that orange-headed man over there could definitely give me a run for my money, but you need Daniels." The man pointed at the elegant, graying man behind him. "He's been studying these Graygual, and he's made a map of their movements around the island. Not only that though, you need this man, as painful as it is to admit it."

"And why do I need him?" Portolmous asked uncertainly as he looked at the man's slightly protruding belly, lack of warrior's movement, and strange look to his eye. He didn't seem entirely sound of mind.

"Well, you have that mind-power, don't you?" The commander stared at Portolmous with an expectant look. Suddenly, the man's mind disappeared. All their minds disappeared! As if they were unconscious, every Westwood Isle mind blinked out of existence.

"How…?" Portolmous let the word drift away.

In a perfect accent no foreigner had ever displayed, including the violet-eyed woman, the man said in Portolmous' tongue, *"It is my own power that is the only remaining, isolated* Therma, *is it not? Everyone has found a mate but me."*

"You can prevent the use of Therma?" Sonson asked with hungry eyes. *"You can isolate it—just pick out those you want to prevent from using it?"*

"It's rude, speaking in a language no one else understands," the commander said with hard eyes.

"Yes, I can cut out the Inkna faction," the older man said in the Mountain Region's tongue. "They are not great warriors—without their mind, they are useless."

"What is your range?" Portolmous asked.

Before he could answer, the Shadow Lord walked into the room wearing battle leathers. A sword rested at her hip, throwing knives in her custom-made harness around her middle, and a bow at her back. An aging woman with refined taste and grace, she was known for her vicious and cunning fighting prowess. She still trained to keep fit, and because she loved the physicality of it, but it had been a long time since she'd fought in a real battle.

Portolmous cleared the way so she could take her seat at the large desk. "We must get ready," she said, sitting down and focusing on the commander. "I hear you would like to offer your aid. We accept."

The commander nodded, spread his legs in a solid stance, and clasped his arms behind his back. "It took a woman to talk sense. What has my world come to…?"

Sonson laughed and the Shadow Lord smiled gracefully. Portolmous glanced back out the window. "We don't have long."

"No." The Shadow Lord held out her hand for Daniels' map. "They are ahead of us, and their main focus is the hopeful-Chosen."

"How do you know?" the Commander asked.

The Shadow Lord gave the Commander an assessing stare. "And your name is?"

"Sanders, ma'am. Commander Sanders."

"I know because they are blocking all exits out of the trials, with most of their focus on the landing point. When the hopeful-Chosen comes down off the hill to collect their title, they will have two armies waiting for them. One will be ours, and the other will be the Graygual."

"Their title?" the blond man asked.

Portolmous' mother's assessing stare landed on him next. "Ah. Salange must be pleased to find another. Remarkable—you could almost be a second son. You are?"

"My name is Rohnan Fu Hoi," he said diplomatically. "I am Chance to the *Chulan,* also known as Shanti Cu Hoi and leader of the Shumas. "

"Yes, the *Chulan.* A language out of legend and a name to accompany it. Half of me is excited to see the doctrines come to life, while the other half wishes this was after my time. However." She looked over the map. Daniels stepped up with a straight back and an air of importance. He didn't speak, just waited for questions. "Their title, yes," the Shadow Lord said, tapping a place on the map. She glanced up at Rohnan. "The hopeful-Chosen is two individuals who have been *Joined* into one with their *Therma.* The Captain of these men, and your... sister, is that correct?"

"Sister in name, not in blood," Rohnan answered.

"Same thing, I think. At least to you." The Shadow Lord looked at Daniels. "This map is well-drawn. Sonson—"

Sonson stepped up, looking down on the parchment spreading across the desk. He traced an area that resembled the outskirts of the trials before pointing to the Red-Zone water supply. "Have they started dying yet?"

"Yes, it seems so. Started early this morning, and killed a fourth of the camp, including a few high officers, before they honed in on the water supply.

Smart thinking, Commander." Her sharp stare hit
Sanders.

"It was our poison-master, actually. I'm just along
for the ride," Sanders answered. A vein pulsed in his
neck. It didn't take a friend to know he was eager to get
out of the office and get into position.

"Well, it certainly helped. Still, we are outnumbered.
If the hopeful-Chosen doesn't come down off that hill
with an offering of which we've never seen the like, we'll
be crushed."

"Whether they have an offering or not, they will
help," Sonson said with gravity. "I've seen what they can
do together. I've felt their power and there is nothing
like it. The doctrines cannot possibly prepare you to feel
what rolls off them in waves even when they are idle.
They are a force of nature, and the Graygual will not
expect it."

"Yes, they will," Rohnan said in his smooth voice.
"From what I have heard, whoever runs these Graygual
sent in a force. That force did not return. Their leader
will use that knowledge. He already knows Shanti's
ability, and guessing the Captain's is not hard. He will
be ready."

"Their leader is on this island. Have none of your
people thought to go looking for him?" Sanders asked
with a growl.

"We have," Sonson replied, a fierce gleam in his

eyes. "Everyone that went looking, even our stealthiest, did not return. We know the area where he resides, but we'd have to send in a force to make it in and then drag him back out again—assuming we can figure out who it is. By the time that could be arranged they had too many, and all were high officers. He's shielded himself. He is highly intelligent, well-trained in tactics, and he is about to challenge us in the open."

"Who is he?" Sanders pushed.

"Either one of their highest Captains, or Xandre himself," Rohnan answered with a hollow voice. "It can be no one else. Not with the Chosen right here, in a place with no escape. We are in a battle for her life."

"For our lives," someone muttered at the door.

"For our lives, correct," the Shadow Lord returned. She stood and looked at Sonson. "Time to get everyone in action. We are the last, is that right?"

"By now, yes." Sonson took two steps toward the door. "I have a team waiting to clear that courtyard, with your help. We have horses ready to take us to the field."

"Have you ever found a mate for your *Gift*?" Rohnan asked quietly.

The Shadow Lord glanced up. Her steel grey eyes lingered on Rohnan before she motioned for Daniels to take the map, then moved around the desk. "Yes. He gave me two headstrong boys, but he died young. I took over his mantle. We could never *Join*, though. He was my power's mate, but he was not my power's perfect partner."

"And have you produced any others on this island with a full dose of power?" Rohnan asked as the Shadow Lord walked toward the door.

"No, but I knew one was coming. I knew my *Therma* was rare, but not unheard of. I never, in my wildest dreams, expected three with a full dose of power to show up. And now we must battle one of them."

"It won't be much of a battle with that Inkna. His kind don't fight like warriors, even with their minds," the older man said, smiling at the sky.

"What are our chances?" Sanders asked the older man as everyone filed out of the room and marched down the hall.

"If Shanti and Cayan join the battle," the older man answered, "We will have heavy losses, but we will still have a future. If not, we will all die or be taken."

"Sorry I asked," Sanders snarled.

Sonson huffed a laugh despite the situation. Portolmous felt a weight settle in his gut. Their whole way of life depended on the hopeful-Chosen. Getting down off the hill would be easy for them if they withstood the lure of the lights, but they needed that offering. The question was: what could they find that could possibly fulfill the criteria?

CHAPTER 17

SHANTI GLANCED UP AT THE sun. It was midday and dry. There were plenty of clouds coming, though. Thick, heavy clouds promising rain rolled in from the horizon.

"I just want to get to a place with a roof, a hot bath and a warm blanket," Shanti said, following behind Cayan as they emerged from the dense wood. "And a massage. I could really use a massage. My legs are tight, my wounds itch, and I ache all over."

Cayan said nothing. There was an urgency in his step that gave her a nervous tingle. Like when she felt presences in the wood, he seemed to feel the need to get back as fast as possible. She agreed, and used just as much haste. She'd walked into the snake pit often in her life—she refused to let fear rule her. Not before the worst presented itself, anyway.

They'd each seen those lights once more, and had used the other as a lifeline to pull themselves out. This last trial hadn't been easy by any stretch, but it also hadn't been the nightmare she'd expected.

"The Shadow people probably test themselves with

those lights," Shanti mused, noticing the trees thinning as they walked down a gradual incline. "It took great strength of will to resist that temptation."

The heavy fall of Cayan's feet mingled with the chirping of the birds in the trees. He didn't respond.

"The terrain too, I imagine. Even getting across that bridge took a lot of courage. And being stalked in the night by something you couldn't see or feel—yeah, I can see how a prospective leader would go through that trial."

An insect jumped out of their path, and flew away. The cub moved around in her pack before settling again.

"Cayan, talk to me," she tried.

"I just feel like something is coming, Shanti. I feel like we can't go fast enough. I can't explain why, or how I could possibly know, but my gut says this is it. The Graygual will make a grab for you, and the Shadow and my people will be the only thing preventing your capture. I'm worried about losing you."

The nervous tingle exploded from her stomach and raced down her arms to her fingertips. She itched to grab her sword and felt the press of the knives against her leg. She smelled the crisp air of the day, welcoming her to yet another battle.

This time, she was not afraid. This time she would not run—she would fight Xandre's minions to the death. Theirs or hers.

She took a deep breath and let the adrenaline seep out of her body. It was too soon to get ready. It was too early to hear the call of battle. She'd be worn out before she'd begun.

She'd enjoy these last moments of freedom.

SANDERS STEPPED OFF THE STAIRS with Burson and allowed Portolmous and Sonson to walk forward, toward the door. A team of men and women wearing reddish-orange cured leather from head to toe were waiting for them. A sword hilt peeked out behind the shoulders of some while others wore bows. All had knives strapped somewhere on their bodies. Two wore silver whistles around their neck.

"Shadow Lord," many said, offering her a slight bow.

"Merge together," the Shadow Lord said, stepping in amongst them in her black. Sonson peeled off a loose layer of cloth to reveal a blue leather suit. Portolmous did the same.

"Awfully colorful for battle," Sanders muttered.

The hairs on Sanders arms and neck stood on end as the eyes of the Shadow people glowed. They were using mind-power. Sanders nodded in approval; they needed as many mind-workers as possible.

"We do not need to kill—save whatever energy you can," the Shadow Lord said as everyone prepared to leave the building. "We need to keep them down and prevent them from joining the battle. Reduce them to their knees, and cut them while they are down. Then, we join the others to secure our land."

"Yes, Shadow Lord," many said while others stood in silence, tall and straight, with fierce eyes and confident bearings.

The doors burst open and the Shadow went out, organized and graceful. Sanders rushed forward, joined immediately by his men. They couldn't use their minds, but they could use their swords just fine.

Sanders felt the cobblestone of the city greet his foot as he heard the first scream, followed by a chorus of many more. Jogging, sword in hand, he sped up as the Shadow in front of him started to run. Long, even strides took them around the building and into the square.

A wall of black greeted them. The Graygual stood in front with crinkled uniforms and dirty faces, all clearly lower ranks. They had been sent to die—to slow the Shadow down while the Inkna in the back engaged.

But the Shadow had Burson.

Howling erupted from the crowd of black uniforms, many grabbing their heads and dropping to the ground.

Sanders barreled into the line of Graygual, knocking

three down and cleaving them where they lay. He worked through the agony-ridden men, sticking and hacking, not worried about killing as much as keeping them from joining a larger conflict. He jabbed his sword through a chest, hacked at a neck, and waded through even as the Shadow worked ahead of him, using both their minds and swords. Even the Shadow Lord was using her weapon, brutal in her strikes and confident in her ability.

"If it wasn't Graygual, this would feel wrong," Xavier said as he brought his sword down on a man cowering on the ground.

"They outnumber us five to one," Sanders said in a string of grunts. "And they planned to do to us what we are now doing to them. This is the way the game is played, boy. New rules."

"Wait… until—" Leilius stabbed someone in the eye, gagged, and slit someone's throat. "—S'am and the Captain come through." He stabbed again, grimaced, jabbed, gagged, and kept moving forward.

The gagging didn't appear to slow him down.

"There're no officers," Rohnan yelled as they worked to the back of the crowd, leaving a large pile of writhing bodies in their wake. "This is just to thin the Shadow numbers."

"Didn't work," Sanders grunted as he stabbed down before stepped over the last body. Ahead of him lay

Inkna, many on the ground with their backs to the sky, having tried to run when Burson cut off their power. They didn't make it far. A stronger power came calling.

"Do we have enough horses?" the Shadow Lord said as they jogged around the side of the building.

"Yes, with a couple to spare. I thought the Graygual might try to get into the city stables and take down our mounts," Sonson answered, turning left at the back of the building.

"Yes, I wonder why they did not…" The Shadow Lord glanced back the way she'd come, her eyes distant.

"The officers must have organized this group, and left them to it. Their chief concern was not the city," Rohnan ventured.

Ten minutes saw them all mounted and ready, riding fierce-eyed animals of decent breeding. Sanders' horse pranced until given the command to trot forward, doing so with vigor.

They rode out of the city, ignoring the bodies littering the ground or dragging themselves along the cobblestone. Once in the wood, they branched off into three groups, riding fast along well-used roads and trails wide enough for two horses to ride abreast through the trees. They wound around north, climbing in elevation. The salty air whipped by their faces as the sound of hooves thundered along the path.

At the top of a hill, the trees started to clear. As they

did, Sanders saw other men on horseback alongside others on foot. Some wore reds, some purple, and only Sonson and Portolmous were dressed in blue. Their colors denoted their rank with their leathers providing some protection.

It'd be nice if it also kept them alive.

There were at least a couple of hundred people gathered, but the only sounds were animals. No murmur of voices rose to meet them. No jittery laughter or harsh growls. They stood and waited for their leaders to take them to battle.

"Oh… shit…" Rachie said as they crested the top of the hill on the outskirts of the gathered Shadow.

Sanders' men weren't so disciplined but when Sanders learned the reason for the outburst, he didn't blame the kid.

In the valley below them, nestled between the trees, were many specks of black. Like ants around a leftover picnic, the Graygual gathered en masse.

"They know where the Chosen will emerge, and they are in prime position to take her," Rohnan said in a flat voice.

Sonson walked his horse alongside Sanders. He pointed to the east where the blue of the sea glittered in the distance. "They have ships stationed over there. They took a fishing harbor last night. By the time we suspected what their plans were, we were too late. They plan to grab her and ferret her off to the ships."

"Are these all the men we have?" Sanders asked, glancing back at the Shadow who would not be nearly enough.

Thankfully, Sonson shook his head. "These are all those with *Therma*. I believe we might at least match the Inkna. And then, with the older man—Burson?"

Sanders nodded in confirmation.

"He will tip things in our favor. The rest of our people with non-fighting *Therma*, or no *Therma* at all, are stationed in those trees to the west of their force. We are about two hundred strong there. We are outnumbered."

"Why did you let them bring in so many men?" Sanders asked with a mystified voice.

"In the beginning, most arrived as tourists. With all the talk of this Inkna-Chosen, that made sense and we did not suspect foul play. We've always been neutral to all as long as our rules were upheld. By the time we realized…"

"They were always ahead of you," Daniels said from behind, plotting on his map. "They have been ahead of us too. Their leader lured Shanti here. He thought he held the upper hand. And he would have, if not for the Captain's power. Surely he will not expect their… *Joining*, or whatever you call it. It is too late for him to make drastic alterations to his plans now. The Captain has tipped our hand."

"What do you suggest?" the Shadow Lord asked Daniels.

"There are not many options, but the only problem will be their escape. We will apply pressure from this side and your other forces must come in from the west. We should be engaged in battle by the time the Captain and Shanti descend from that hill. We need their people engaged. *Thoroughly* engaged. Otherwise, they can simply put up a barrier for us, grab their prize, and head to their ship."

"My thought was to wait for the larger power to join us, but that is sound planning," Portolmous said, glancing at the valley below.

"We are sure the hopeful-Chosen has the power of legends?" the Shadow Lord asked. "If not, we waste lives on a battle that is not our concern."

"It is our concern, mother," Sonson said with steel in his voice. "They came to our home, flouted our laws, killed our people. This is our fight, with or without a Chosen."

"You are right. Forgive me. But without additional help, we will not succeed," the Shadow Lord responded.

"The man alone has enough *Therma*," Portolmous said. "If they *Joined*…"

"Let's get this show on the road," Sanders said. "The day is wasting, and I want to be in bed by dark." He twisted in his saddle and glanced back at his men. They were ready.

"I sure hope that leader presents himself—I wouldn't mind being the one to kill him. Think of all the girls I'll get!" Gracas blurted.

Sanders just shook his head. There was nothing to say.

"Alert the others," the Shadow Lord commanded. "Merge!"

Burson glanced behind them, "I have never seen so many with power merge."

Rohnan shook his head. "Not even my people attempted a merge this large. After twenty, it isn't needed."

"We have a special way of linking which builds the power higher," the Shadow Lord said, voice grim. "You do not have the type of power to see that. Your sister will tell you, if we ever meet her."

"You will, and she'll wreak havoc," Sanders growled, feeling the anticipation. Feeling the build of adrenaline. Feeling the sword in his hand. "Let me know when, ma'am. I'm ready to unleash Hell."

"Good luck to you all," the Shadow Lord said in a loud voice. "May you defend your home with steadfastness. With heart. May you find glory on the battlefield!"

A loud "*Huah*," went up. Swords raised. "*Huah!*" Weapons pulsed in the air. "*Huah!*"

Expectation rose. Sanders' heart thumped in his

chest. His horse stamped and pulled in expectation.

And the Shadow Lord's sword fell. "*Huah!*" she yelled.

Sanders kicked his animal and raced down the hill. The others were right beside him. Hooves thundered on the ground. The first sprinkle of rain whipped in Sanders' face. Thunder boomed overhead.

From the west horses launched from the trees, running at the Graygual full speed. Sanders urged his horse faster, mad grin on his face from the speed, the first line of Graygual crystalizing in his vision as he neared them.

He raised his sword, ready. Rohnan's staff whirled beside him. Fifty strides now, and the standing Graygual started to shift from side to side.

Thirty. Men began to scramble, but there was nowhere to run.

Fifteen. Graygual eyes rounded. Jaws fell slack. Badly cared-for steel rose.

Sanders' horse slammed into the front row of the enemy, trampling ten men before the horse started to wade through. Sanders hacked down, using the height to his advantage.

"Strike the mind-workers, not the Graygual," the Shadow Lord yelled above the clanking of steel, the *thrum* of bows and the screaming of men. "Take down the Inkna!"

CHAPTER 18

SHANTI HEARD THE ROAR AS she came down the hill. Like a wave of energy blasting her, she recognized the distinct sounds of a large battle in progress. Her adrenaline spiked, kept at bay for the last couple of hours, and now unleashed.

"We need to store these packs," she said to Cayan, tension rising in her voice.

Cayan started to jog.

"Cayan!"

"I know, I'm looking for a sheltered place along the way," he said.

Their *Gift,* fueled with anxiety, and answering the call of their combined distress, rose like a beast from the depths. Surges of power spiraled outwards, whipping around her and flowing through her body. Bliss and pleasure, as well as aching joy, pumped out of nowhere, filling her and heightening her mind. Their power spread, pushed to heights neither were expecting, flowing down the hill and reaching toward the battlefield.

"I feel great," came Cayan's startled surprise.

The spicy feeling singed up Shanti's limbs, bringing the comfort and mix of *Gifts* from her and Cayan. A shot of pure courage rose under it, making her feel invincible. Making her want to take on five armies.

"Careful with this feeling, Cayan," Shanti warned as they jogged. "It's the effect of what we did a few days ago. Our *Gift* has changed, but we can't hide within these feelings. We have to stay cautious."

"I know, Shanti. I know."

His voice sounded wary, almost fearful. They were dealing with a lot of power, a deceptive power to his relatively untrained mind. But she could help control his power as she worked with hers. Whatever they had done, it had been the best possible outcome for the amount of power they were dealing with.

"There!" Cayan pointed, but didn't slow as he veered toward a large tree with an extensive root system, some of which was above ground. He knelt by the trunk and carefully slid his pack into a large hole protected by the roots. He peeled back the top, revealing the awakening cubs. One yawned before nosing the other.

Shanti knelt beside him, the call of battle pulling at her. She slid her pack in beside his, also peeling back the cover. Her little cub gave a tiny roar, and made her smile. "I always seem to attract the ornery bastards."

"Fitting." With hurried movements, Cayan took out the bit of meaty gruel they'd made with a varmint kill along the way. It wasn't milk, but it would keep them alive for now.

If they were able to come back to fetch them.

"Okay." Shanti stood in a rush of adrenaline. Her heart was beating faster, anxious to get down to that battle. Cayan's men and the boys would be stuck in the thick of it.

Flashbacks flickered through her head. Her own people rushing toward the enemy, hopeless but determined. Blood and screaming filled her ears; her people defending their home.

"We must go," she nearly yelled, jogging away from the tree and beckoning Cayan on.

Together they took up a fast jog, the roar growing. Filling their ears. Drowning out their thought.

"We stick together," Cayan shouted above the sound. "We are stronger together."

"Don't weaken yourself by trying to protect me, Cayan," Shanti said.

"Don't get into a tight spot."

All there would be was tight spots, but Shanti didn't say anything. The battle came in sight.

Her mouth dried up. Her steps faltered for one brief moment.

A sea of black spread out before them, immersed in the speckles of green trees. From the north and west descended a variety of colors crashing through the black. Even from this distance, Shanti could see they out-fought their opponent. But they were few, and the Graygual were many.

A few horses charged away from the mayhem, running scared.

On their side there was only black extending out as far as the sea. They'd still left themselves an "out" for a few to make their escape, or to ferret away their prize.

"They mean to capture me," Shanti said in a distant voice. Rage welled up, overtaking any fear. "And they'll die trying."

"See how they are shifting?" Cayan said, pointing to those at the bottom of the hill. As a whole they were pushing forward, knowing the fighting was coming their way and anxious to meet it. Or afraid and wanting to get it over with. It was hard to tell. "They aren't watching for us. Most of them aren't, anyway."

"We'll get close before we hit them with power. Remember," Shanti turned to Cayan and leveled him with a serious stare. "In terms of using the power, this is a long jog, not a short sprint. We have to make our power last—have to use our energy sparingly. We can't go down and kill all at once, and then pass out from fatigue. That loses battles."

"I'll follow your lead with the power," Cayan answered, just as seriously.

She nodded and turned toward the battle. "Let's unleash Death upon this day."

CHAPTER 19

SANDERS GRUNTED AS A KNIFE swipe dug into his thigh. The horse reared as an enemy slashed its flank. Sanders slid off the rump, jarring when he landed. He shoved the enemy away and plunged his sword through soft flesh. With his shoulder, he battered two men, creating room, before blocking a sword, getting in a quick lunge, and blocking again. He turned his body and slashed with his knife, opening up a gash. When the Graygual flinched, Sanders finished him off with his sword.

A Shadow woman in red ran by, taking on two with the skill and mastery Sanders had only seen in Shanti and Rohnan, and few of the Captain's men. Unlike the Captain's men though, their movements were lithe and agile, seamless and efficient. Like a butcher with a razor-sharp knife, the Shadow sliced through the meat of their opponent in a way that made Sanders envious.

Three more Graygual pushed toward the Shadow. They faltered in their step due to whatever mind-power the Shadow employed, but they kept coming.

Sanders rushed to the defense, slashing through one

and punching the other before knocking him down and stabbing him. The Shadow took out her man and had time enough for a quick grunt before she moved on.

Sanders did the same.

FEAR OVERWHELMING HIM AT EVERY step, blood splattered all over his chest, Marc worked his knife and sword both, trying to cut through the black shirts. He was on the periphery, fighting the dirty, stinky enemy and leaving the clean, crisp ones for someone else. Marc wasn't good at this, so he figured killing those who were equally inadequate was a smart idea.

He gave a squeak as a sword came swinging at his head. He dodged out of reflex and stabbed upward with his knife. Blade went in body. Marc spun, clipped by a body running by.

Xavier barreled into two Graygual, taking one quickly before feinting and stabbing to get the other. Gracas appeared behind him, only using one knife, and more deadly for it. He moved with precision as he dodged a sword, then stepped in with punches and stabs. The Graygual fell while Gracas moved on to the next, face determined, eyes focused and sharp, movements lethal.

Ruisa jogged towards them, blood splattered across her face and her hair. She blocked a sword with a flash of teeth, roared, twisted, and dove her blade into the man's face. She turned to the next, angry and vengeful, killing like Sanders might.

Rachie was limping and holding a staff. It whirled in his hands, cracking out, breaking limbs and overcoming with a larger reach. He'd found a new weapon he liked, it seemed.

"Get to work!" Xavier shouted as he flipped a man over his shoulder before turning to stab him in the chest.

"Why are you here?" Marc asked as someone came at him with a terrifying expression. Marc's breath caught as he dodged a strike, battered the sword farther away, and stuck his blade into the man.

He took a breath as the next came.

"Work together. Fight as a team. Stay alive longer." Xavier said just as S'am always did.

Marc stepped forward into the reach of the next attacker, taking him by surprise. He jabbed and rent with his blade before stepping back out again. They'd been at this for two hours. Marc's limbs ached but he had no choice other than to keep going. He didn't know how much longer he could keep it up.

Sanders pushed through three Graygual to meet the back of Sonson and two other high-leveled Shadow with mind-power. They worked as one, spinning and dipping like dancers, leaving blood and limbs in their wake.

Sanders ran on, cutting through another Graygual to get to that far hill. But there were too many. They were too dense. Not as good, but as Sanders pushed on they got better, harder to kill. Requiring more energy.

Sanders didn't have much energy left.

He slashed and struck, growling at the weakness in his limbs to keep going. Begging his body not to give out on him.

A low-level blast came from the south and a crack of lightning illuminated the dark grey sky above. A huge boom shook the ground before another blast echoed out, riding the thunder. Sanders' middle shook and his legs quivered.

He slowed, not sure what was happening. Two Graygual in front of him had stopped, and turned. Sanders stabbed one in the back, saw that the other didn't turn despite the scream of the first, and stabbed him too. As they fell, he saw that everyone, including the Shadow, had slowed. Everyone was turning.

Another low-level blast shook Sanders to the core. Vibrated his body and made him want to curl up and die.

"They've come!" Sonson yelled. "They've come!

"I DON'T FEEL S'AM," MARC yelled with his heart in his throat. "I don't feel S'am!"

"You won't feel her," Leilius said, jogging out of nowhere with dripping knives. "You'll just see people die."

Another blast rumbled through Marc's core as an earth-shaking boom rolled overhead. Lightning cracked, striking a tree in the distance before the rain poured down in a torrent.

Water splashed his face and dripped in his eyes, momentarily confusing him. Another blast of thunder rolled through, but Marc couldn't tell if it was the Captain or God's hand above them.

Either of them would be just as destructive.

"DIRECT IT THERE, CAYAN!" SHANTI yelled, pointing to the thickest cluster of Graygual. "We are too spread out for Burson to shield."

Cayan hit the line of stunned Graygual like a falling star. Sword moving so fast it blurred, he cut through the enemy as if they were nothing.

Shanti joined him a moment later, whipping her power out around her, reaching into the middle of the crowd and picking out the Inkna. There weren't many left, and each was already under attack by the Shadow. Shanti slashed and cut those in front of her, working with Cayan in perfect harmony, feeling their *Gift* move and bend like a living thing around them.

Thunder rolled overhead. Lightning cracked. The energy in the air swirled and pulsed, beating into Shanti and Cayan, infusing their bodies like the lights in the trials. Beating more power into them. Sparking a hotter fire.

Shanti *struck* five minds to the east, watchful and intent. They winked out. She didn't hear the screams.

A blade came at her head. Cayan lunged forward and dispensed the Graygual before pushing into the fray. "We need to connect with the Shadow! We can't keep this up on our own," Cayan called, another blast of his subsonic power rolling out before him.

They hurried forward, tearing down the enemy while the blast of power confused them. The Graygual may have trained with Inkna, but they'd never trained with a power like this. No one had.

Another blast of power rolled forward, pushed higher and harder with an answering roar from the skies above. Another flash of lightning cracked. Shanti's power surged with the electric energy in the air, crackling with life, looking for prey. She found five more, widened to ten, and *tore* into soft brain matter. Then five more. Ten.

"There are too many. We're sieged!" Cayan rumbled, slashing through men.

This time Shanti sought out the familiar mind of Sonson, finding him not far away. She licked at his conscious with *need*, hoping he understood the appeal for aid.

Swords swung and fell, steel flashing. Rain pelted her face. She nudged Cayan and worked right, towards Sonson. Trying to unite with friendlies. Trying to slog through the endless sea of black.

"I FEEL HER—THEM," PORTOLMOUS SAID through gritted teeth, feeling the strain of his exertion.

"She needs help," Sonson said in a series of grunts, fighting back a Graygual with five stripes across his breast. "We don't have much more time, brother. The enemy is getting better."

Sonson was right. The further they worked into the mass of black, the better the class of soldier they met and the more tired Portolmous and his men became. The Battle Lord of these Grayguals was no novice and he had no concern for preserving his forces.

"Work toward her—them," Portolmous yelled. "Unleash Yari!"

"You got a read on the Captain?" came the gruff commander's voice as he ran through like a rabid dog. He jumped at a crowd of men, breaking them up with his body before getting to work on ruthlessly hacking and cutting through them. Despite his brutal style, he was exceptional in a way Portolmous had never witnessed. His energy, viciousness, and relentless forward motion confused the enemy. His grimace shot fear into their hearts and he killed in perfect economy.

"Yes, head right," Portolmous yelled above the din as he felt Sonson send the mental call to their brothers-in-arms.

A huge roar rent the battlefield, then another.

"What the hell was that?" Sanders growled as he dodged to the side in seeming chaos and took down two more Graygual. His men surged in behind him, helping him cut a path to the hopeful-Chosen.

"Help," Sonson answered, rallying his team, combining forces with Sanders. "Hurry—the hopeful-Chosen is losing traction!"

AN EAR-SPLITTING ROAR SHOOK SHANTI'S bones. She knew that sound. She knew the giant animal that made it and the destructive force it was capable of.

"They're using the beasts," she said to Cayan, words getting lost in the next roar.

She felt an officer's mind gush fear before it winked out. The beast was coming down from the north-east, closer to the ocean.

A push of Graygual came from the left. The tide of

black eddied toward them as people backed away from something. Xavier burst through, covered in blood and moving like a man twice his experience level. His sword rose and fell. Gracas was right beside him, his hands moving so fast the enemy couldn't keep up.

The people in front of her started to fall. Backing away from the Honor Guard, and then shoved north by her and Cayan, they finally sank to the ground or flew out of the way as a wall of reddish-orange leather came through, led by two in shiny blue. A growl and a screaming Graygual announced Sanders' arrival.

Like the wind parting the clouds, a clearing opened up through the Graygual as they all joined. Shanti couldn't help a smile of relief as her eyes met Sonson's. "Good to have you."

He matched her smile. "You made it."

The Graygual pressed in on them once again, allowing them no time to rest.

CHAPTER 20

THEY PUSHED THROUGH THE GRAYGUAL, aiming for whoever had begun this assault. Cayan's *Gift* rolled out in waves, dropping those close, making those further away falter. Shanti continued to work at the minds of only the sharpest on that field, taking them down quickly and efficiently.

Under their combined force, Graygual dropped like rain. The lesser tried to run, not getting far before being cut down by Sonson's extended force. Those with better skill provided opposition before succumbing to their fate.

Then Shanti saw him. Up on a small hilltop out of her range, standing beside a tree with his Inner Circle gathered tightly around him—Xandre.

"He's here!" Shanti yelled as a torrid of emotions assaulted her. Fear, shock, surprise, rage, and finally, *Wrath.*

Like a conduit of energy, she pulled the lightning out of the sky. She stirred Cayan, making him snatch up the thunder. Electrical current fired through her body and pushed her *Gift* to new heights. All she could focus on was that balding man. On his death.

"Get me to that hill!" she yelled. Her voice whipped from her mouth and carried. A beast roared in the distance. Lightning flashed.

Shadow surged forward, answering her call. Responding to her power. She felt Rohnan fall in behind her, his single-minded focus adding to hers. His rage increasing the velocity.

The man on the hill turned, facing directly at her, at the sphere of death opening up around her and at the unyielding fall of the Graygual as she and her army ran through the battlefield.

"Cayan, let's unleash our full power," Shanti said as a calm descended on her. As the rage blistered so hot, it stabilized into sharp intent. "Clear the way."

The subsonic blast of power turned into a massive flood unlike anything anyone had ever seen. It grew and boiled to colossal heights before rolling forward. Screams; terrified, agony-filled screams, drowned out the battlefield. Like a tidal wave, the power rolled before them. Graygual fell. Bodies sank, writhing. Limbs twisted, faces screwed up in pain, as they died.

The power washed toward the hill with the Shadow and Cayan's men racing the death to get to Xandre.

And there he stood. She just *knew* he was focused solely on her. He watched her advancing—his prize.

The one thing he'd wanted since she'd beaten him when she had been so young. More powerful now than anything out of history.

More out of reach.

He took one step toward her, and she thought he would engage in the battle. She almost thought he would run down to meet her advance.

But then he turned toward the sea. And started running.

"No!" Shanti screamed. "He's trying to escape!"

Her pace picked up. Her sword swung faster than it ever had before. She cut through unresisting people as if they were already dead and just needed to be knocked down. Cayan could barely keep up with her. No one could, except one.

Rohnan took Cayan's place at the front, his urgency matching her own. Together they acted like fire to brush, clearing a path to the sea. Following that disgusting tyrant who had ruined their lives.

The Graygual turned and ran. Some ran away, some ran east to follow their leader. They were retreating, taking Xandre with them in a tide of fear.

"Catch him!" Shanti cried desperately, sprinting. She stabbed a Graygual in the back and ripped him to the side. "Don't let him get away!"

A huge animal burst through from the left. Its jaws tore through a neck. It shook its furry head before seeing the movement, then it joined the fray, chasing the Graygual to the sea.

Cayan's *Gift* boomed out, knocking people down. But there were too many blocking the way between Shanti and her vengeance.

"Please," she begged the Elders.

"*We must go faster!*" Rohnan yelled frantically, his staff whirling.

Shanti and Rohnan cut down men and tore through, running for all they were worth. Running for their people.

A hole opened up. Shanti barreled through it, landing on the soft mud of the shore, looking around with wild eyes.

A sob escaped her as she looked out across the water.

Xandre stood on the back of a sleek ship. The sails streamed down. The crisp fabric sounded a *crack* as they immediately filled with wind. The ship was already on the move.

Away from her.

"No!" She looked around frantically, but all she saw were enemy ships. There was no way to follow him, because even if she ran across the island to the nearest port, she'd have to fight her way there. By then he would be out of reach.

She would never catch him, and even if she could

reach him with her *Gift,* as strained as it was after the battle, he'd have Inkna protecting him. There was no way.

"No," she sighed, deflated.

She stumbled into the water, right beside Rohnan, staring at that man.

He stared back.

A soft smile spread across his face. His hand rose, offering her a slow wave as the ship gained speed and took him away from the island.

Fighting still raged around her, but she was almost blind to it. She didn't care. She watched with a sinking heart as her one true enemy stood at the back of the ship, surrounded by his Inner Circle, smiling at her like an old friend as he drifted out into the ocean.

A tear fell before she felt Cayan's arms wrap around her and carry her away to safety.

CHAPTER 21

IN THE AFTERMATH, AFTER ALL the remaining Graygual had been cut down, Shanti sat on a small berm with Rohnan. Tears still swam in her eyes and dribbled down her cheeks. She'd been so close. She'd *seen* him. And he'd gotten away.

"There was no way you could have got to him, *me-sasha*," Cayan said, taking a seat by her side. He was covered in blood, with enough gashes to match her own. If he was like her, though, he wouldn't feel any of them. "He planned this all perfectly. He confronted his worst case scenario, I am sure, and knew exactly when the battle was lost."

"He was right *there*, Cayan!" Shanti clutched at the air with bloody hands. "We could've ended this whole war if I could've just reached him."

"He's too smart for that, Chosen," Rohnan said, tears in his voice to match his eyes. "But we did get close. Next time, we will finish the job."

Shanti sighed and bowed, letting her head hang between her knees. "What about the battle? Who is accounted for?"

Cayan stiffened. In an even voice that said he was suppressing emotion, he said, "Etherlan didn't make it. Neither did Tepson. Tomous took a bad wound—Marc is looking after him now. Ruisa and Gracas both have broken bones, but Marc assures me that he knows how to set them, and thinks they'll both be fine. The rest are exhausted and battered, but alive. Thankfully alive."

"All the boys?" Shanti asked with a tight throat.

"All the boys. And the girl. They all made it."

Shanti felt a moment of relief before the sorrow of losing Etherlan and Tepson consumed her. She didn't know them that well, but they had been part of their team. An important part.

"More to add to the butcher's bill," she said in a shaking voice.

Cayan didn't answer. She felt his sorrow well up, and then the guilt.

Blinking away the tears, Shanti stood. She met Cayan's gaze. "Let's not lose the cubs."

Rohnan rose with them, aching sorrow drifting from him, feeling the loss of their friends and family all over again.

They climbed the hill slowly, each lost to their own thoughts, before they found the tree. Shanti sat down and took out one of the cubs. She held it tight, feeling the warm little body against her heart. She dug her face into the squirming little thing and cried. She cried for the lost, she cried for her people, and she cried in gratitude for being alive.

A COUPLE OF HOURS LATER, after the pain and loss had subsided a little, and the three of them descended the hill again, Sonson, an aging woman with a regal stance and a full dose of power, and a man who looked uncommonly like Rohnan, waited for them. Their eyes were hollow, and sorrow radiated out of them, but they did not show her their emotion. Their faces were grim and set.

The woman stepped forward. "I am Emery, the Shadow Lord. I lead these people."

Shanti couldn't summon up the surprise she might've felt on a different day. "A woman."

Emery nodded. "A woman like you, forced to step into the role of leader."

"Yes, though you have done a better job of protecting your people."

Emery looked at her for a moment, her gray eyes soft, before turning to the men in blue beside her. "These are my sons. You've met Sonson."

"Yes," Shanti said in a flat voice. She was emotionally spent and hoped they understood.

"And this is Portolmous." The man who looked like

Rohnan stepped forward with an outstretched hand. She shook it before he stepped back.

Emery looked at Cayan and Rohnan in turn. She said, "I have met Rohnan."

"Right, sorry," Shanti said as fatigue tugged at her. She put her hand on Cayan's arm. "This is Cayan. He was with me in the trials."

"Yes. You two have *Joined*. I can feel it." Emery's gaze dipped to Cayan's neck. "Such a rare thing to find someone who is your power's perfect mate. There is only one, after all. The fates are at work here." She turned back to Shanti. "You have the ring that goes back generations, linking our people."

Shanti touched her throat. "Yes. It was given to me by my father, who received it from his father. I am the first woman to wear it."

"Which is why it hangs heavy around your neck. Fitting. I am the first woman to solely lead my people. I do not have a ring, but the same weight hangs heavy around me." Emery nodded toward Cayan. "And he has another remnant of days past…"

Cayan's brow crinkled as he looked at Shanti. Shanti said, "The necklace, you mean?"

"Yes." Emery smiled. It didn't reach her eyes. "He wears a piece of our distant kin, as do you. That is fitting, since the Chosen is said to wear something from our common ancestors. Now. Tell me. Do you have anything else?"

Shanti sighed as the last of her adrenaline trickled away. She shook her head. "No. I have people to look after. If you plan to kill us, can you do it tomorrow? I've had enough for the day."

Disappointment drooped Emery's expression. Emery nodded. "We will meet tomorrow."

Shanti should've been scared. Or worried. Or any number of things. Instead, she was just tired.

She shouldered her pack as Marc walked up on shaky legs and with uneasy steps. "S'am, I need to get Tomous back to the city, but I thought I would check on you first."

Shanti hugged him. He didn't bother to put his arms up to her. He just leaned against her. When she backed away, he blinked. "I'm tired, S'am," he said, his mouth turning down at the corners and wobbling. Emotion worked into his expression. He wasn't as good at hiding it as the older men. He hadn't had the practice.

"I know," she said, reaching up to cup his cheek. "We're done now, though."

He nodded and glanced at Cayan. His gaze took in Cayan's gashes, but seeing they weren't serious, he shrugged and slouched off.

Shanti watched him go before appealing to Sonson. "You have that beast, so I... well Cayan, thought you might be able to help us with these."

Shanti put her pack on the ground carefully and extracted the cub. It growled before wiggling into her hands and trying to snuggle in closer. Cayan extracted his, holding one in each hand.

Shanti didn't hold it out—she craved the warmth and innocence of its little body. Instead, she nodded at it. "We killed the parents. Cayan didn't want to leave them to die, but we don't have any milk for them."

A smile creased Sonson's face as he stepped forward to pet the little black fur ball. "This counts. This absolutely counts."

From five paces away, Burson laughed and clapped his dirty, battle-stained hands. "Our future has stretched years. Wonderful!"

"Welcome to the Shadow Lands, Chosen," Emery said. "You have passed all the trials."

FOUR GRUELING HOURS LATER, AS night fell to cover the loss and destruction caused by the biggest battle the Shadow had ever seen, Shanti followed Sonson down a wide corridor in the building where guests of the city were housed. This was a different area than that used for visitors and traders with enough money to house themselves. They were not visiting; they were family coming home for a stay.

It was a small building. It seemed the Shadow didn't invite many into their fold.

Cayan and Rohnan followed directly behind Shanti, close to exhaustion but still standing tall. Everyone had fought hard that day, and everyone had lost friends and loved ones—details that needed to be looked after before rest. It was what was right.

"Chosen…zzz." Sonson summoned up a small smile below his ragged face and dull eyes. Blood had been scrubbed away, but the memory would linger for the rest of his life, Shanti had no doubt. "Chosens." He opened a door leading into a wide living area. "These are your quarters."

Shanti glanced back at Cayan. Her middle tingled, but wariness encroached. She was too tired to think of how things would change between them. So she shuffled out of the way and mimicked Sonson's gesture. "Go ahead, Cayan. I'll just stay with Rohnan."

"Are you not…?" Sonson let the words drift away, but the confusion showed in his furrowed eyebrows.

"Yes we are, but she hasn't admitted it yet it seems," Cayan said. Humor and determination danced in his words and sparked in his mind.

Shanti ignored both.

"Ah." Sonson waited for Cayan to enter the room, and walked down the hall. He stopped at the next door and glanced at Rohnan. "The Chosen…zzz—I need to get used to having two. The Chosens have earned their status as family. You, however, are kin, however remote. Even without rings and golden charms, you look just like my brother. Obviously your people were as selective in breeding as mine. The origins stayed pure." Sonson laughed and opened the door. "You are welcome here, anytime."

Rohnan offered a bow. *"I am honored,"* Rohnan said in the native dialect. *"It's been a long road. You have no idea what it means to finally reach this place and have the door opened to us."* Rohnan shook his head. His eyes glossed over and he entered the room, saying no more.

"He's sensitive," Shanti said, trying to conjure a smile but not quite able. *"He'll probably be a puddle of tears in a minute."*

Sonson nodded. *"I can't imagine what you two have been through. But I have a feeling I will soon. We will follow you to the mainland, and then into Death's playground—I do like that expression. We have a score to settle, just like you."*

"It won't be easy, I'll tell you that much. I was so close!" A memory of Xandre's wave as he drifted away materialized in her mind. *"So close."*

"He is scared. He must be. He outnumbered us in both mental-workers and warriors... and he ran. He is scared, and we will ram that fear down his throat when next we meet."

A hard edge had crept into Sonson's eyes and voice. *"Until then, we will assemble, we will prepare, and we will follow you to battle. We have much to do yet, but we will all do it together, and we will succeed."*

Shanti watched him walk away, his mind as full of fire as the sweep of hair around his head. He was a worthy ally.

Shanti trudged into Rohnan's quarters. He sat on the couch with his head leaned back and his eyes closed. When she closed the door he asked, "Will he get you your own residence?"

Shanti shrugged, even though he couldn't see it with his eyes closed. "He didn't say. Doesn't matter, though. You have plenty of space. You'll share and you'll like it."

A grin drifted up Rohnan's face. "Yes. I've never been worried about having family close. What of the animals?"

Shanti thought of the small cats. She wished she could've brought them to these quarters with her, but they were dehydrated, tired, and no doubt feeling lost. "The Shadow have animal keepers—not just for horses. They have a plethora of exotic creatures it seems. The cats are being looked after."

"They won't be put back into the wild?"

Shanti took a plush chair made of fabric and soft stuffing. It wasn't even remotely as comfortable as Cayan's leather couches. Unexpectedly, her heart pinched. She felt his expectant relaxation from down the hall. The distance between them was nothing. Their *Gift* still mingled and mixed, sharing their bodies as though they were one.

Distracting herself, she crossed an ankle over her knee and thought about a bath. She desperately needed one.

Remembering Rohnan's question, she answered, "No. They'd be killed by other predators, and they don't have a mother to teach them. Killing the mother killed whatever chance the cubs had."

"So what will be done with them?"

Shanti grimaced. "Coming with us, I guess. It'll take a few months to get the first group of Shadow mobile. We'll head back to Cayan's land then and await the rest. But in a few months they should be able to travel with us. The beasts will be coming, too—though how the Shadow plan to get those huge monsters across the sea is beyond me. And what we'll do with them in Cayan's city…"

"You are excited about going back."

Shanti felt the swirl of expectation at the thought of heading back to Cayan's city, with the calm certainty that it was home; the only place she'd felt comfortable since she left her birth place. She longed for just that tiny bit of stability.

But Rohnan didn't need to know that, the nosy bastard.

"I've asked the Shadow Lord to send a message," Shanti said, then watched as Rohnan's eyes opened gradually. His head tipped forward. His gaze came to rest on hers, blazing with hope. "The message will instruct our survivors to get to Cayan's city without raising any eyebrows. It is time for our people to come out of hiding."

Rohnan's eyes filled with tears again. Shanti rolled her eyes and pushed herself off the chair. "Compared to you, I hardly ever cry at all."

Shanti wandered through the spacious interior of the living space and into one of the two bedrooms. Beside them was a room with a large tub, empty of water. Sonson had assured them someone would be there soon with hot water for a bath.

Shanti took the smaller of the two rooms since these weren't her quarters, and stared at the empty bed, still big enough for two. She thought of trekking through the wild. Of sharing small spaces with the large body of Cayan behind her, his big arm wrapped around her protectively. She'd become used to it. In a few short days, she'd grown accustomed to his presence being just that bit closer. Going from being on the other side of the fire, as he had been through the journey, to being next to her, then to sleeping beside her. The gradual closeness had become the norm, and now she felt lonely without it.

She wandered back into the living room.

"There is one thing that bothers me," Rohnan said softly, his head leaned back and eyes closed again.

"What's that?" Shanti asked, wandering toward the walls to examine the art. She felt unsettled, like she couldn't relax.

"The Hunter wouldn't have given up, but he wasn't there today. You would've felt him, or I would've. We recognize his mind now. So... where was he?"

Shanti stopped and turned to Rohnan, thinking. He wasn't dead—she'd seen him struggling to get up after their battle, and Rohnan was right. She was sure he hadn't been on the island.

"Maybe he knows he'll be punished for his failure and ran?" Shanti tried.

"Likely. But where would he go? He's been trained to the point that he has no free thoughts."

Shanti shifted, putting her weight on one hip. "You think he'll try to complete his mission..."

"What else would he do? If he secured you and Burson, he'd be forgiven."

"So you think he's lying in wait somewhere?"

Uncertainty and wariness drifted from Rohnan's mind. "If I had to guess... yes."

Shanti shook her head and turned to look at some art decorating the wall. "It changes nothing. On our way back to Cayan's city, we'll face a great many dangers lying in wait. He's no different."

Shanti felt the spark of uncertainty. That statement had only been partially true. The Hunter was the next largest threat to her life besides Xandre. Xandre would be licking his wounds and planning his next step, but the Hunter was mostly exiled at the moment. His determination would not only double, an edge of desperation would creep in. He'd be twice as deadly.

A knock sounded at the door. Shanti's heart gave a violent lurch. With butterflies, she opened the door. A tall man with a bronze bucket of steaming water waited, a line of water bearers behind him.

She smiled, sighing through the strange nervousness, and stepped aside for him to enter. Then waited with the door open, looking down the empty corridor after they'd passed. Another group of water bearers entered the hall, stopping at Cayan's door, bringing back Shanti's butterflies.

"Go, Chosen," Rohnan said with fatigue in his voice. "I want to take a bath first anyway, and don't feel like fighting you for it. You and he can share."

Shanti scowled, but her gaze drifted back down the hall. As the water bearers passed again, headed to get more water, she followed, closing the door behind her. She knocked softly at Cayan's door, her heart in her throat.

"Come in," came his muffled voice through the door.

She entered with a sudden bout of embarrassment, not really sure what to say. He glanced up from the couch. His shirt was draped across the top of the chair, showing off his perfectly defined and cut chest. Dimples heightened the attractiveness of his face as he smiled knowingly. "I told them not to fill the tub as much, since there'll be two bodies in it. They have one more trip, they said, and it'll be ready for us."

Shanti flushed. "How'd you know?"

His smile burned brighter. "Your first impulse is to run. But I know that you'll eventually find your way back if I'm patient. The time it takes for you to return gets shorter and shorter, and soon you'll stop running."

Shanti felt a flash of anger, and then a rush of something else. Something infinitely deeper. Something terrifying that she'd have to deal with, because she was tied with him now. Together, uniting forces and power, they could beat Xandre. Together, they could claim justice.

She closed the door and started toward him. He was right: whatever came, they'd face it together.

THE END